Aberdeenshire Libraries
www.aberdeenshire.gov.uk/libraries
Renewals Hotline 01224 661511
Downloads available from
www.aberdeenshirelibraries.lib.overdrive.com
22 OCT 2013
22 NOV 2013
14 MAR 2014
-5 AUG 2014
14 DEC 2015
D0315005
ABERDEENSHIRE LIBRARIES
1937087

FT
Pbk

VAIR, by Stewart G. Dickson. ISBN 978-1-60264-875-3.

Published 2011 by Virtualbookworm.com Publishing Inc., P.O. Box 9949, College Station, TX 77842, US.

Printed in the United States of America.

SESTINA: ALTAFORTE

Ezra Pound

Damn it all! all this our South stinks peace.
You whoreson dog, Papiols, come! Let's to music!
I have no life save when the swords clash.
But ah! When I see the standards, gold, vair, purple, opposing
And the broad fields beneath them turn crimson,
Then howl I my heart nigh mad with rejoicing.

VAIR—one of the three ornamental furs allowed in heraldry. Once associated with royalty and dynastic power, any pretender caught wearing them could be put to death.

Historical Note

In 1536, the English King Henry VIII suffered a near fatal fall while jousting near London. For over three hours he lay unconscious, near death. Some historians believe that traumatic injury marked the emergence of the bloodthirsty tyrant remembered today.

CHAPTER 1
GREENWICH PALACE,
January 24, 1536

A beam of light cut through the gray, lowering sky and splashed the armor with silver.

For the first time since his troubled youth he felt uneasy; not in control of those around him, his wits scattering like the ragged clouds above.

He had run this violent course many times, but this cold day he felt no thrill or excitement. Today was different. The 350-foot, wooden tilting rail looked alien. The heavy, Italian destrier he was to ride had become a testy stranger shying from him.

He hefted the 12-foot lance in his right hand and grooved it into a metal couch by the side of his armored waist. He led the iron-tipped coronel at a 30-degree angle over the left ear of the stallion's arching head and raked its flanks with his spurs.

The war horse, schooled in the peculiar gliding run which stabilized man and lance, powered down the six-foot high canvas-covered divider. The rider, almost standing in the long stirrups, saw flecks of ice and frost twinkle from the soapstone surface of the tilt alley.

He thought of starry nights, jewels on a pretty maid's dress, betrayal. His mind kept drifting. Three seconds into the run, the black, antlered helmet of his crouching opponent filled his jarring vision. They collided at a shocking combined speed.

The impact slammed him against the high wooden back of his saddle sending stirrup and armored boot into the animal's chest. The reins snagged and caught in the metal crinet protecting the horse's neck. The white of its bulging eyes flashed as its head was twisted violently. The 1,500-pound Neapolitan courser, carrying almost 400 pounds of man and armor, lurched into a grotesque stagger.

He felt the drunken reeling of the horse and the ground reach up as if to break him. A flare of brightness in his brain, then the plunge into darkness. He heard the whispers of the plotters, saw their backs slowly turn away from him as if he were dead. Then the journey began.

CHAPTER 2
BIRCHVILLE, ILLINOIS
(Date: The present)

The harness jingled as horse and rider pivoted and charged. The pony's sphincter tightened reflexively as it shouldered into its rival. The jarring, fleshy smack pitched the opposing rider headfirst into scattering spectators.

Without sparing the downed rider a glance, the man with the royal blue flash across his white polo shirt wheeled his trembling mount and kicked it toward a new target.

"Christ! Walesey's getting a tad wild," said a jaded onlooker.

Hours of stifling humidity and stale champagne were reflected in Major Ronald Annieson's testy reply.

"Nonsense! Show the Yanks what the bloody sport's about. Half their bloody team's made up of glorified shopkeepers and fucking hairdressers."

The "shopkeepers" and "hairdressers" the crusty, red-haired major referred to preferred to be known as the social and business elite who made up the Birchville Country Club and Polo Grounds just south of Chicago.

The visit of royalty and its attendant press coverage had insured that each tented pavilion was crowded. There had been furious in-fighting to secure invitations to the Royal tent, flagged with the scarlet, gold and blue of the Prince's personal standard.

Bitter feuds had developed only the night before over who got to sit nearest the Prince's table at a huge catered dinner held on the second floor of one of Chicago's legendary fashion stores.

To the Prince and his retinue, ostensibly helping promote British exports in the United States, it was amusing. For the elite of Chicago it was, in society terms, a matter of life and death.

The stakes and the security thicket had risen even higher that morning when U.S. Vice President John Neville had paid a flying visit to the Polo match. Neville was widely tipped to win the next Presidential election. He had met the Prince in Washington and liked him. He also appreciated the fund-raising opportunities not so subtly promised by the big-bucks social crowd behind the event.

Throughout the long late-summer afternoon, employees of the fabled Swiss watch company that was sponsoring the match plied the V.I.P. guests with champagnes and *amuse bouche*.

A few more hours and then the circus would move on to Palm Beach in Florida for the final stop on the Prince's U.S. tour. A photo opportunity in a Worth Avenue retailer selling British imports, then another game of polo.

It was a "support British exports " tour championed by his father years before, that always luckily coincided with a series of matches in the strategically selected polo circuit cities.

The Royal Pavilion—a large, white marquee—had tables lined up along the canvas walls for buffet food and a small bar in a corner. Rubber matting covered the moist floor. Draped from one of the walls was a large silk banner with the Prince's heraldic arms.

When the first chukka had begun, the tent was deserted. Only the occasional caterer or wait staff member entered, then quickly left.

Now, a horrified equerry rushed from the tent and ran 300 yards down a gravel path towards Annieson. The Major quickly signaled to the nearest security detachment.

Back in the marquee, a swath of crimson swept diagonally across the Royal coat of arms. Its base, still dripping shining blood, seemed to point to a large silver punch bowl on a table beneath it.

Rising from among the strawberries and the gallons of yellow mimosa, was a bloody hand, the hamate fingers reaching up out of the thick juice like claws.

Annieson's face paled. He could smell the blood and the sweetness of the mimosa intermingled. His stomach heaved and he controlled an urge to vomit.

He rounded on his deputy, a serving Royal Navy officer whose father had attended the Prince's father, and commanded: "For God's sake, intercept H.R.H. Get those damn State Department fuck-ups to clear the area. Keep the press away. Keep everyone the hell away. Seal the place off and see that the Prince's helicopter is ready to go—NOW!"

For the Secret Service and State Department agents, it was their worst nightmare come true. An embarrassment for the President, for America. More importantly, it would culminate in career-smashing purges. Adding to the shame was the presence of the Vice President. His pavilion was 100 yards away, but in terms of blame it might as well have been 8 inches from the Prince's marquee and the bloody dismembered hand.

As usual, one of their main security focuses had been photographers and the press, journalists who had been herded into roped-off areas to have their bags sniffed for explosives by some tired old Labrador. Meanwhile unsearched local dignitaries and the loosely credentialed public were waved through the club's gates.

For the Prince's own Royal Protection squad, Scotland Yard comers approved by the Palace, it was scramble time. How to get him out of Illinois and the United States—quickly. How to hide it from the British press covering the polo match from their New York bureaus. Luckily, the regular Royal Correspondents in London had not considered the trip worth covering.

With luck, drinks, dinner and swift casuistry by a popular British Embassy press secretary, the New York men could be led in another direction. For a few vital hours. With luck.

The tannoy sound system around the polo field crackled. The silky, English tones of the match announcer were heard:

"Unfortunately, due to approaching bad weather and a subsequent change of flight schedule, the Prince will have to miss the cup award ceremony. The Vice President is graciously escorting His Royal Highness to the airport. We thank them both for their wonderful visit with us."

At a far corner of the field, three Marine helicopters roared and took off. They circled, then speared northeast like olive green dragonflies.

Overhead in the altostratus, yellow, violet and purple arrows moved in from the West, heralding the approach of a cold front from the prairies. A wind picked up and the temperature fell.

Inside the marquee in the cooling air, the blood coagulated in the champagne and orange juice. The crimson and yellowed claw of fingers pointed vindictively—damning every security agent and policeman who entered.

CHAPTER 3

The day Lucy Samuels Sullivan was hacked to death began with her concern over a tiny spot of blood. Instant frustration, anger, had quickly turned into wry amusement when she spotted the faint stain on her nightgown.

Anticipation, and an aching sensual dream, had tempted her to linger in bed in a drowsy half sleep. It would be easy to surrender to the roiling estrus.

After a fastidious toiletry and a long search for the perfect silk panties, she saw the tell-tale spotting as she placed the gown in a laundry basket.

Not today. Please, please let it be tomorrow. The affair, exciting, illicit, her first could not be ruined. She didn't know him well enough. Would it turn him off? Would he take it in his stride? Some men even liked that signal offering.

It had begun as an adventure, a romantic break from the genteel drudgery of the Birchville social calendar. It was, more importantly, retaliation against an unfaithful husband.

They had met at the Polo club two weeks before. He was handsome, a graying bachelor with a devastating smile. His eyes seemed full of mischief, as if he could read her thoughts and desires.

Last night at the Polo club dinner they had silently drifted into the darkness of an adjacent floor of the famous department store. There among shadowy mannequins and displays of lingerie, they had held each other, kissing fiercely. Flushed and trembling, Lucy had forced herself to leave his embrace. They separately wandered back into the romantically lit dining area.

No one noticed them rejoin their tables. All eyes were on the Prince and his party.

This afternoon, while her husband ingratiated himself with the society crowd at the match, she would make love in the wood bordering the polo ground. It was going to be an exciting, wonderful day.

CHAPTER 4
WASHINGTON, D.C.

Taylor had noticed that the rats grew bolder each time he passed them on the crumbling, litter-strewn towpath.

The heat and humidity refused to retreat in the face of approaching autumn. All that was needed was another mild winter and the rats' biological clocks would refuse to wind down.

The plethora of student and tourist fast-service cafes masquerading as restaurants along one of Georgetown's busiest streets provided a constant food supply for the rodents, telling their reproductive organs to breed, breed, breed.

Some of the towpath rats held their ground, glaring at the intruder. Others scurried into the shadowy banks of the canal or into unseen cracks in the older buildings lining the path, their mocking retreat leading to God knows where.

Taylor found their ugly boldness at one with his depressed mood.

A refugee from the once bleak streets of New York, he had watched passively, then with growing revulsion, as the pavements of old friendly Georgetown surrendered to hordes of youthful wilders and insensitive tourists.

His punishing run along the towpath led eventually to the street and the Key Bridge over the Potomac.

At the bridge, a veiled sun filtered through the haze and scattered banks of river mist. The hotels and office skyscrapers of the business section of Rosslyn, Virginia, lost their softness and became garish.

As dawn retreated to a high, brassy sky, the first passenger jets concussed the heavy air as they snaked and hugged the curving contours of the Potomac glide-path to Ronald Reagan Washington National Airport.

Taylor stood and watched the dark river flow by. Today the dense waters looked foreboding. Perfectly attuned to his thoughts.

John Taylor had spent a lifetime not fitting in. His lonely path had begun in childhood.

A military brat, he had moved from base to base in Europe with his English mother, who had married a U.S. Air Force officer.

His father was seldom home — either flying or bending elbows with colleagues at Officer's Clubs. Taylor had followed his father from country to country. Alarmed at what she considered educational interruptions, his mother, a former teacher, insisted on extensively home schooling him, subtly imprinting her British speech and grammar patterns onto his sub-conscious.

The father's frequent absences in the air and in the bar provoked a simmering resentment in his mother who, unprepared for that lifestyle took out her frustration and anger on the nearest male target, Taylor.

A storm, a faulty computer gyroscope and the Italian Alps ended that particular misery and ushered in another.

A 14-year-old Taylor had returned home from baseball practice and opened the door upon a solemn tableau, which he would remember for the rest of his life.

As if frozen in time, their heads turned toward his noisy entrance, were a uniformed base chaplain and two female neighbors comforting his seated mother. Their strange stares, a mixture of surprise and pity, would haunt him for years.

Afterwards, he found it hard to understand why the woman who had dedicated so much of her time to angry words for her husband spent what was left of it grieving for him.

The widow and the boy were invited back to New York and the home of her in-laws. When Taylor was 17 she became ill, ordered him to stay in New York to get a college education and returned home to England. Seven months later she was dead.

His short-lived career in the New York Police Department had been marked by resentment from colleagues. He refused to join the drunken cronyism and tireless networking that was expected.

His acceptance by the FBI rescued him and he thrived on the training, then marveled at the mental acuity of some of his new colleagues. For

10 years, he had been devotedly happy, reveling in the sheer professionalism of the small group of friends he acquired.

Then once again, like an Arctic winter, the darkness of office politics and ambitious players fell on him.

It seemed his luck had finally changed when the Agency granted a leave of absence and his posting to study criminal science innovations at a City University for the year. It was described as a learning post—allowing him a grace period from the agency while occasionally lecturing students. That 12-month course was a technicality, the faculty unofficially assured him. He would almost certainly be offered a permanent lecturing position and freedom to resign from government bureaucracy. He could start his new life in academia. The present hierarchy at the Agency would shed no tears on his leaving.

After six months, Taylor was now facing an unpalatable truth. He had jumped from the pan into the fire. There was no sanctuary from the political bastards, no Ivory Tower.

Tenure and pecking order at the endowment trough were put ahead of the chore of teaching students. And of these students, Taylor found very few ever arrived prepared to learn.

What in God's name was he to do? He spat into the river, turned and headed back to Georgetown. He ran with an easy grace belying the turmoil inside him.

CHAPTER 5

One of the few aspects of his life John Taylor took comfort in these days was his apartment. He had discovered it in a most curious way, browsing through dusty prints and cartography in a cluttered shop between the old canal and a busy tourist packed street in Georgetown.

The two friendly owners of the two-story, 120-year-old building had smiled when Taylor told them he was looking to move into the area.

After gently pulling information on his background from him they had showed him what they called their jewel — a wooden floored, self-contained apartment above the shop. It would be ideal they said, if he wouldn't mind keeping a weather eye out for the growing numbers of housebreakers in the area.

The brick walls of the building, a former stable mews, backed onto the towpath of the canal. To the left, a narrow wrought iron bridge arched over the canal lock, leading down to the marina and the river.

The shop had not yet opened, and he let himself in through a side door next to the stairs. He pulled off a sweat-stained T-shirt as he headed for the bathroom and a shower.

The telephone rang harshly. He answered gruffly, then heard the deep tones of an old and valued friend. Dr. Daniel Samuels was calling from New York.

For once the easy-going doc seemed flustered, bereft of humor.

"I need a big, big favor, John. You're the only one I can think of who can help. Lucy has been murdered and the bastards won't tell me anything."

CHAPTER 6

The conversation with Dr. Samuels only seemed to deepen Taylor's angry depression. There was of course sympathy for the Doc's loss of his only child. Taylor had met Lucy only twice. She had appeared shallow and flighty to him, a spoiled child constantly testing the love of her parents.

Her marriage to an Irish-American commodities trader in Chicago had been as much an act of rebellion against her family as love for the twice-divorced speculator.

But Taylor knew the doctor loved her unconditionally. Since the death of his wife, Miriam, their daughter had become his whole life.

He knew how important Lucy was to his friend, so why had he spent 10 minutes arguing how impractical and unprofessional any intervention with the Illinois authorities would be.

He had hung up, promising the doctor that he "would think it over."

Now, in quiet reflection in his study, he felt ashamed. He was so caught up in escaping his own problems he was running away from a friend's. He felt like the hermit fearing the unwelcome visitor.

He picked up the telephone and dialed Dr. Samuels' office number. Laurie the receptionist quickly buzzed his call through.

"Look, Daniel," Taylor began, "I owe you a big apology. You caught me off balance when you called. I don't know what I was thinking about. Of course I'll help."

Dr. Samuels gently interrupted: "It's all right John. All right. I shouldn't have asked you to get involved. It wouldn't be professional for you."

"You couldn't stop me helping now, old buddy. It's a done deal. I'll visit you in New York tomorrow afternoon. That OK?"

"You're a good friend, John," the doctor said with emotion.

CHAPTER 7

Taylor awakened as the first light began to filter into the apartment. Gradually, the darkness slipped away and the comforting solidity of his bookcases appeared like sentinels guarding the walls.

The shop owners below, Lester and Gabriel, joked that just one more book would send Taylor crashing through the straining floorboards. But his books were his comfort, his passion, and sometimes his solace.

Naked, he padded over to the bow window and looked uncritically at the flotsam in the canal below. He thought about the trip to New York and the inevitably sad meeting with Dr. Samuels. But for one morning, at least, the apathy had gone. His mind and body felt engaged. He was on the move, and it was what he needed. His classes were not due to resume until later in the month and he had already noticed the storm signals from the University hierarchy. Doors that were needed for his FBI required analytical study were being firmly closed. His promised university lecture workload had been shifted to other lecturers and adjuncts. They were getting ready to phase him out for someone more politically correct. Good. That would suit him just fine.

He would see the doctor, and, if necessary, take a trip out to Chicago, a city he had visited twice and enjoyed. He packed a small luggage case with essentials.

Taylor loathed the air shuttle to New York and decided to indulge himself. He phoned Amtrak at Union Station and, using his Amex card, booked a seat on the first-class Acela Express just after noon.

At the station, he walked past the stylish shops and restaurants, showed I.D. to a ticket clerk and picked up his reservation. A Redcap quickly led him past a long line of economy passengers waiting for a Metroliner and opened an iron gate to the platform.

He was comfortably settled, half way through his first Molsen beer when the train silently pulled itself north.

After a lunch of lasagna and two more beers, Taylor took out his cell phone and called Dr. Samuels' office in Manhattan. He would be with the doctor before 4 p.m.

After stops at Baltimore, Philadelphia and Newark, the train tunneled under the Hudson River and emerged into the noise and claustrophobia of Pennsylvania Station in the heart of Manhattan.

CHAPTER 8
MANHATTAN, NEW YORK

Patients liked Dr. Daniel Samuels. He was always quick to smile, to gently reason and, if needed, patiently lecture them.

He was a handsome, graying man but years of battling the obstinacy of his patients had etched the faint overprint of the perpetually care-worn to his expression.

His offices were small, but bright and airy. From the back-room surgery, the roof of Bloomingdale's department store could be seen beyond the small backyard gardens of white-washed century-old apartments.

Today, grief furrowed the normally pleasant features — grief and a seminal anger, a drive for revenge that unsettled and even frightened him.

"Thanks for coming, John," he said, rising to firmly shake Taylor's hand. Taylor noticed his effort to push emotion away. He was all business.

As if cutting off any objections or misgivings Taylor might raise, he went on:

"Look, I know how you feel about outsiders interfering with police investigations. But I'm positive they are covering up something about her death. John, you're my only hope. Just indulge me and check it out, please."

Taylor still felt a stirring of resentment at the request, then quashed it. The Doc had been a generous and loyal friend to him.

"I can't promise anything, Doc, but I give you my word I'll check it out as far as I can. But when I say it's over — it's over. Period."

Samuels slumped back into his chair and nodded his agreement. "Thanks, John, I knew you would help. I'll pick up the travel expenses."

Taylor agreed, knowing the doc would insist. Why argue?

CHAPTER 9

After the inevitable 40-minute delay on the ground at La Guardia, the Boeing- heavy jet heaved itself into a slow, curving climb to the West. At 6,000 feet, the dark blanket of cloud cover ended abruptly. Stark, brutal beams of sunshine shot through the scratched windows as the plane banked, eye pupils contracted and a buzz of talk and pleasantries filled the cabin. For the nervous and thirsty there soon came the welcome rattle of the drinks cart being pushed down the aisle.

Taylor ordered a Bloody Mary and pulled out the notes he had written after meeting Doc Samuels the night before. There had not been much to transcribe. There were few facts and much speculation. As he had suspected, the Doc's daughter had been his great love after his late wife.

Now the doctor was haunted by their recent quarrels over her marriage, her stubborn defense of her husband and, unsaid between them, her avoidance of his invitations to visit in New York.

All he could tell Taylor was where she had been killed; the reluctance of authorities in Illinois to give details and his belief that some powerful, wealthy connections were protecting her husband, whom he had never trusted.

The doctor was too emotionally involved to supply any objective motives for the killing.

Taylor would have to detach himself from his own feelings for the doctor's family.

Treat the victim as a stranger. He would have to do some digging of his own. Call in a few favors from an old friend. Zuk in Chicago could provide some answers.

He had met Ira Zuk at a criminal justice course at New York's John Jay College, hard by the then-vacant, rotting piers on Manhattan's West Side.

The tall, lean Midwesterner had quietly impressed Taylor, sharing his uneasiness at rowdy drinking sessions held by the visiting cops. The men found themselves easing away from the clubby atmosphere, enjoying quiet moments, talking about ideal justice and bitching about their shared frustration over police bureaucracy.

Taylor had jumped to the Agency. Zuk had gone on to head a large Chicago security corporation. The fact that his business still recruited local and government law enforcement personnel for its highly paid positions gave him unusual clout with the main players in Illinois and Chicago law enforcement.

Seven miles above Ohio, a buffeting wind from the northeast pushed the jet onward to Chicago. As it descended, Taylor saw the glittering crescent shoreline of Lake Shore Drive.

The same following wind lifted them over the skyscrapers of Michigan Avenue and beyond the city. Air traffic led them 30 miles west of O'Hare Airport before banking back for the nerve-jangling snap of landing gear and the ground-traffic chaos of the airport below.

Taylor slung his carry-bag over his shoulder and spotted Zuk, still without a gray hair at 50, smiling by the gate.

With a gleam in his green eyes, Zuk greeted him. "You've sure picked a humdinger to get involved with. A real beaut, my boy."

CHAPTER 10
CHICAGO

Zuk had a company driver navigate them through the crowded expressway to downtown Chicago. He had secured Taylor a suite at the 90-year-old, but still elegant, Drake Hotel.

"It's not quite on the arm but the management has given us a great break on the room rate," he winked as they entered the high-ceilinged rooms of the suite.

The two men stretched out in plush, blue armchairs and popped open two lager beers from the room bar. Zuk produced a large-scale photo map of the Birchville polo grounds area and spread it on the clear glass coffee table.

"This is where the body was discovered."

He pointed to a stand of thick scrub and trees at the top left of the parkland of the Polo Club.

"It's heavily screened from view, remote," he said.

"Was she killed somewhere else and the body dumped there?" asked Taylor.

"No. She was attacked in that wood. The blood spatters at the crime scene show that clearly. She was literally hacked to death.

"The other corpse was found a mile and a half downstream in a river that bisects that northwest corner of the grounds."

"The other body? I didn't know about any other body," said a surprised Taylor.

"The corpse was discovered two days ago. Male, head injuries from an axe or a machete-like weapon. Stomach gutted like a deer kill."

"I.D.?"

"One Laurence Carson — local playboy, Polo Club member, ladies' man. It seems likely the two victims had made an assignation, which somehow blew up in their faces."

"Now comes the $64,000 question. Is the husband capable of that?" asked Taylor.

"Kevin Sullivan, commodities trader, 46 years old. He was accounted for by friends at the Polo Club throughout the afternoon," Zuk answered.

"As you can imagine, he's still a suspect. He could have paid someone to get rid of his wife and the lover got in the way. They had a rocky marriage. He played the field. He also had lost a lot of money in the markets recently, but he's been up and down before. Police are running a check on any insurance he might have had on her and what his full financial picture is."

Taylor frowned. "Any other strong suspects?"

Zuk, sipped his beer thoughtfully, then replied.

"This is what has me intrigued. I get a bad feeling. I smell a huge cover-up. Everyone concerned in this investigation is stone-walling on that, but the word I get is that there is nothing simple or clear cut about this case. It is not what it appears to be. There is a big flap on at the highest level. The fact that it happened while the Vice President and British Royalty were there would account for a lot of the hysteria. But the guys I know in the State Police say they are being cut out of the loop by some heavy government agencies. And the few who know anything are being told to shut their mouths or lose their careers and pensions."

Zuk fished in his black leather briefcase and pulled out a sheaf of crime scene photographs.

"These are not very pretty," he said. He moved over to the small room bar refrigerator and grabbed two more cans of beer. He tossed one to Taylor, opened his own and went over to a window.

He looked out at the view of Lake Michigan; the white sails of the yachts, the blue waters. He had deliberately turned his back on Taylor. He did not want to see these pictures again.

Despite years of grisly murder investigations and countless crime scene horrors, Taylor gasped: "God, the savagery!"

The Doc must never see this or know how cruelly Lucy died. He continued to look at the photographs. No weapon had been found but whatever had been used must have been heavy, an extremely sharp cutting instrument. It appeared that the second victim, Carson, had been slaughtered in another part of the woods, then dragged into the river and pulled or floated downstream. Taylor knew immediately that they were not dealing with a hit man hired by the husband or anyone else. These people had been killed by a monster.

Zuk tossed an empty beer can into a waste basket 20 feet away and turned toward Taylor. He saw the distraught expression on Taylor's face, the anger in the blue-gray eyes.

"Do you feel like going out there to dig around?"

"Do I?!" Taylor growled, reaching for his jacket.

On the ride out to Birchville, Zuk explained that the security firm at the Polo Club was affiliated to his corporation.

"They're not happy about getting involved, but they say they'll give me what they can. The authorities have threatened their asses if any information leaks."

"It's better than nothing," Taylor sighed resignedly.

At the gates to the club, two guards, their gray shirts and trousers piped in navy blue, stopped the limousine.

The senior man, whose nameplate announced him as Turner, pointed to a parking slot then beckoned them into an open-top recreation vehicle, painted the same blue and gray.

"You'll get a better feel for the place if I take you there," said Turner. It would also give him a chance to talk to Zuk out of earshot of his fellow guard, Taylor noted approvingly.

"It's much appreciated," said Zuk. "I won't forget your help, Mr. Turner."

The jeep swung up a curving drive, past the west end of the vast, emerald-green Polo Ground. Three quarters of a mile along the dusty graveled path, the foliage became heavier.

Bright-yellow crime-scene streamers sagged from the trees.

Turner stopped the jeep with a rasp of tires on the gravel. He said: "We'll take it on foot from here. The cops and the powers-that-be have made it clear they don't want anyone up here." We've been told to chase off anybody in this section of the grounds."

They walked into the wood with its dense canopy of late summer leaves. It was quiet and Taylor heard the faint sound of running water. He looked in the direction of the gurgling noise and arched his eyebrows quizzically to Turner.

"It's a fairly fast, broad stream — connects to the river a mile or so from here. That's where they found lover boy's corpse, wedged under a river bank. The little fishes, rats and insects had done a thorough job on him. They think he had been in the river for four days before he was found.

"The stream is lucky if it reaches four feet deep in the summer. But we had heavy rains recently and it flows pretty fast," the guard said.

Taylor slid and shimmied through the undergrowth until the ground started swiftly down from him. The stream seemed sluggish today, the sun casting shadowy pools through the overhanging tree branches. But it was deep, almost five feet.

Taylor didn't have to elaborate his thoughts to Zuk.

Whoever cut Lucy and Carson to pieces would have been awash in blood.

Running water; a way to cast off the damning murder evidence like a snake shedding skin, and a solitary way out of the club grounds. A hunter's dream.

From the stream's bank, 50 paces into the wood, the shrubbery cleared into a tiny dell.

"This is where she was found," said Turner.

A sharp smell of detergent and disinfectant raked their nostrils. Rich arterial blood had jetted all around the grassy hollow. As the victim had staggered back from the frenzied attack, her blood had spurted some 10 feet, painting the lower tree branches crimson.

They saw the remnants of multi-colored plastic markers in the soft, damp ground where body parts and some organ tissue had fallen. Streams of ants delved through the crushed undergrowth as if searching for miniscule traces of the corpse.

Soil samples had also been taken by crime scene scientists, leaving little patches of red-brown earth like abandoned mole hills.

"We won't learn much here," said Zuk. Taylor shared his unspoken but palpable unease. The bird songs and chirping had been silenced. The wood suddenly became oppressive, the brook's murmur resentful. A chilling feeling, like an unexpected cloud shadow on a sunny day. There was a heavy, indefinable sense of something evil.

The three men were fighting to control their growing uneasiness.

"Let's get out of here," said Taylor.

Turner controlled his relief at the suggestion and nodded his head. "OK. If you want. The spot where Carson was killed has been pretty much cleaned up. Nothing there. We can go there if you want?"

His bravado did not fool anybody. Taylor and Zuk declined. They were all anxious to leave the slaughter grounds.

The men headed east, left the woods and entered a large cleared area where the royal marquee had stood. The tent had given way to a rectangle of bare earth.

It was obvious the police had finished their work there. It seemed that all their trip had accomplished was a geography lesson but, like most veteran detectives, Taylor needed to have been there. To walk the killing ground, stand still and sense the victims' fear, the killer's adrenaline. See what they saw.

Taylor watched Turner absently toe soil into a depression at one corner of where the tent had stood.

Turner started when he saw Taylor looking at him, like a school kid caught daydreaming in class.

"That's where they found it," he said sheepishly.

"Found what?" asked Zuk.

"The arm," said Turner.

Spots of rain streaked the smoked glass of the limousine. Above them daggers of lightning and cascades of sparks flashed from the trains rumbling along the elevated railway. The flashes seared and illuminated the garish tenements next to the track.

Taylor wondered how the occupants handled the day and night bombardment of blinding light. He and Zuk were back in the heart of the city.

The driver sped through the rain slicked streets to what had once been the traditionally German section of town. The cavernous restaurant was low key and crowded with locals and German speakers.

On a small corner stage, a five-man band, dressed in worn lederhosen played. Their thick dialects baffled Taylor's schoolboy German.

Zuk was expecting additional company, an Illinois State Police Intelligence officer who wanted to keep his retirement options open.

Karl Schumacher valued Zuk's friendship and more importantly the chance to make some real money in the private sphere when he became pensionable in two years.

Zuk and Taylor ordered half-liter glasses of Krystal Weissbier. Schumacher arrived at the same time as the frothy beer.

All three ordered the day's special, Sauerbraten with pickled red cabbage.

Schumacher was a small, but powerfully built man with thin facial features and an engaging smile.

"Let me tell you right away you're trying to pick up a frigging red-hot potato," he counseled.

"Your story about the severed arm is true but no one's supposed to know. It was found in the Prince's tent poking out of a punch bowl. It really sent the shit flying, I can tell you.

"There was a shit-storm of a panic to get the Prince and the Vice Pres out of the area as fast as possible.

"They were shuttled by choppers to Midway airport. The Vice Pres went back to Washington; the Prince took his Royal Squadron transport jet back to London. They got out of the Country Club and Chicago like bats out of hell."

Schumacher continued: "It was only after the arm was found that they discovered the woman's body in the woods behind the tent.

"The state and local police have open case files on the murders but the real skinny is that it's out of our hands.

"Everything connected with the murder goes directly to the Secret Service, the Fibbies, Homeland Security and God-knows-who-else in Washington. We are effectively out of the loop."

Taylor scooped some pickled red cabbage from a dish onto his plate and asked: "Why the hell would THEY get so exercised over the murder of a lovelorn housewife.

"The police and lab boys in this area are as good as any."

"Difficult to say," said Schumacher, "Sure, the Vice President was there but he was half a mile from the murder scene, surrounded by club officials, Secret Service and Christ knows how many local cops."

Zuk asked: "Were there any death threats to the Prince or the Vice Pres received prior to the polo game?"

"Not even the usual cranks," said Schumacher. "The oddballs were all duly surveilled by the Secret Service days before the visit. None of them got near the country club."

The new information had given Taylor a lot to think about. He looked at Zuk and read the silent apprehension in Zuk's demeanor, unspoken but obvious. They finished the meal pausing only for small talk, German food, the Cubs and White Sox, the State Police. Schumacher was obviously a regular at the restaurant and they were treated to complimentary desserts and a round of drinks on the house.

As they left the restaurant, Zuk's concerned expression returned.

"Your best bet is to stay away from this, John. Just step away."

He saw the set of Taylor's mouth and sighed.

"But of course you won't, you stubborn sonofabitch."

"It's for a friend," said Taylor somewhat lamely.

"Let's have a brandy back at the hotel," he proposed. "Then it's back to Washington to get some answers.

CHAPTER 11
WASHINGTON, D.C.

Security at the British Embassy on Massachusetts Avenue had imperceptibly relaxed. They would deny it, of course, but the edge had dulled.

Throughout the country Homeland Security forces and a new public awareness flourished.

Ironically, as the public and state and city police forces became more alert, there was a tendency in the embassies to relax slightly. There was a feeling that at last they were no longer alone.

As dusk fell, a steady rain began to fall, darkening the sky above the tree-lined avenue known locally as Embassy Row. Scores of ambassadors and their staffs lived and worked in huge mansions by the sides of the hilly, winding road which stretched from Dupont Circle to the National Cathedral.

As the gloom descended, lights were slowly switched on throughout the Embassy Residence, a private area equipped like a small but luxurious hotel.

In a ground-level drawing room — a favorite of visiting Royals — Jules Pettifer carefully carried an armload of logs across the deep pile of carpet to a pink marble fireplace. As he stacked them, he was mindful of checking for any damp or green wood. A former under-gardener had achieved notoriety when a senior Royal Princess had taken her usual afternoon tea in the elegantly furnished room.

As the Princess, a chain smoker, day-dreamed in a chair in front of the fireplace, clouds of smoke from damp and immature logs filled the room. Alerted by her angry cries, staff rushed into the drawing room to find the apoplectic Princess streaked with soot, still puffing away at her cigarette.

The humor of the situation had been lost on the Royal personage and the gardener had been in disgrace for months.

Since then, the dry wood rule was written in stone: Double check every stick and twig of kindling that was destined for the fireplace.

On the south side of the room, large glass-and-wood framed French doors could be opened, giving direct access to the gardens.

Through the windows, Pettifer, a slightly built man in his mid-30s, saw the heavy figure of Bill Snow, a member of the Residence Security team. He was making a routine patrol of the gardens.

Snow had been immediately friendly to the timid Pettifer who had joined the staff just seven weeks before. Both men waved and Snow pointed to the downpour above him and made a face. Pettifer laughed.

As he layered the logs in a tight triangle, he heard a piercing scream, then a shout for help. Snow's voice, wounded and urgent.

Pettifer didn't stop to think. The litany of security rules and protocol he had been asked to learn went out of his mind. He rushed across the blue-and-gold carpets, unbolted and unlocked the doors and rushed into the now dim garden.

There, below a cluster of large rhododendron bushes, he saw the inert body of Snow. One leg, cut off below the knee lay at an angle to the torso. The skull had been cleaved and blood and a gray-bluish fluid leaked out. He felt his stomach start to heave, then the first slashing blow cut his right knee almost in half. The pain made him weep and he fell.

As he lay on the wet grass, he sensed more than saw the descending bloody edge of the weapon. He heard the grunt of his attacker. A meaty "thunking" sound as the blade sliced through his neck and through his collarbone, clear to his ribs. The blade continued to fall but, mercifully, shock and death had already claimed Pettifer.

CHAPTER 12

The savage double murders hit the headlines two days later. By then, a draconian investigation under a Detective Chief Superintendent flown in from Britain had the embassy in its thrall. The superintendent had been given powers to enlist the help of all of Britain's security experts, even the most covert.

The Secretary of State had offered similar help from Homeland Security, FBI and state agencies. In short, life at the Embassy was now hell. The reaction from London was pre-ordained. The hapless head of Embassy security abruptly resigned and took early retirement.

A massive overhaul was promised. The garden's motion sensors, continuously triggered by squirrels, birds and heavy storms, would be immediately replaced by state-of-the-art equipment. Television security cameras would be properly vectored to cover every foot of ground.

A few miles from the Embassy, Taylor sat by the window of his apartment, sipped a French Roast coffee and skimmed through the final edition of the Washington Post.

At first, the item "Embassy Slayings Revealed; Political Terrorism Denied" merely intrigued him. But as he read on, his interest intensified.

An "insider" at the Embassy had leaked to the Post that the killings were caused by a deranged man who was enraged at his rejection by a female employee.

A D.C. police source "confirmed" the story. The two Britons killed had the misfortune to get in the way of this love-crazed man.

In the London press, the two victims had become true heroes. An intensive hunt was on for the fugitive, believed to be heading for the Caribbean.

For Taylor, the newspaper version reeked of cover-up.

Police in Illinois were looking for a violent predator who attacked lovers, couples and women. Here in Washington, the same sort of butchery had been employed, but against two men. There was a common link — the Prince. The Prince had been scheduled to stay over at the Embassy between engagements the week of the killings. That had been promptly aborted when he had flown directly back to London instead. Was it someone close to the Prince who was the target?

Taylor knew his suspicion was pure speculation, but worth developing further.

He made note to get more details of the Embassy killings.

He was going to need help and decided to turn to the closest friend he had. He picked up the telephone and called the direct office number of Eugene Liddell at FBI headquarters. Taylor left a message.

Eugene Liddell was Taylor's best friend. In an age where personal loyalty had become unfashionable, he was a welcome anachronism. The tall, heavyset Liddell had looked after Taylor out in the field as well as in the minefields of agency politics.

But even Liddell, with his Machiavellian skills, had not been able to save Taylor's clashing with their immediate superior, a nakedly ambitious Arkansan called Gardiner.

Millard Gardiner did not like individualism, nor people who weren't "team players." He did not like John Taylor.

It was Gardiner's persistent interference and criticism that had led Taylor on his path away from the agency. It was Liddell's endless reasoning and gentle reassurance that had talked Taylor out of angrily quitting. He had told Taylor: "Take time away from the job. Don't burn any bridges yet. Things can change, you'll see."

Perhaps together Taylor and Liddell could make sense of Lucy's murder, come up with a rational explanation. Cold comfort for Doc but at least they might answer his questions on the total blackout of facts concerning her violent death.

Below the window, on the canal, two seagulls bickered over a scrap of bread. The crust dropped into the green and brown water and was instantly pounced on by a catfish. The birds cried angrily then wheeled away on their endless search for food.

Taylor went back to his notebook and reviewed the Embassy killings once more. Yes, he decided. There could be more than a coincidence here. All the victims presumably surprised, all hacked to death furiously and quickly. They had been cut to pieces by a bladed weapon capable of slicing flesh, sinew and bone.

Liddell would be in a position to gain insight into the official investigations and to contact FBI weapons experts. It might be a start at least. From a wall shelf by the side of his wooden desk, Taylor drew a fresh legal pad and a buff-colored folder. He did not trust depositing notes and thoughts onto the hard drive of a computer. He knew only too well what the tech geniuses could pull from seemingly cleansed drives. He began to write down all that he knew so far. He then compiled lists of questions that had to be answered. That list ran on for pages.

Then he looked through his yellowing contacts file book. He drew up a list of law enforcement friends and acquaintances. Any source who might be able to answer some of these questions.

A breeze blew in from a half opened window and broke his concentration. He decided to go for a run along the old towpath. The day was still cloudy and damp, but the temperature hovered in the 80s. The oppressive humidity of summer in Washington would soon be an unpleasant memory. When Liddell returned his call he would arrange a meeting. Then he would relax at home and try to develop a plan.

CHAPTER 13

At first he had resented the intruder's growing presence. It had started as a voice, gently whispering, trying to bewitch and manipulate him. A voice from the past, mocking him. Then it became more strident, more willful and demanding.

Soon its tentacles wormed and rooted themselves throughout his brain. He felt like the fly caught in a silk web as the advancing spider blotted out the light.

Now he was a mere vessel. A modern machine programmed to function in this technological age. A navigator through the alien-ness of this new century, a submissive adjunct to a terrible force.

Now, God help him, they were one. At one with vengeance and killing.

He had first heard the voice as he gazed down at the darkness of the courtyard below his study window. A full moon sharpened the ice-coated college spires but he was drawn to the shadows.

"Come to us," the voice had whispered. It had started softly, seductively, but then became impatient, demanding, like the scolding of a lover.

Now he detected an undertone of menace in the insistent whispers.

He had fled back into his rooms and the sanctuary of his books. But then ice on the frosted mullion windows cracked like a slingshot and tinkled to the yard 18 feet below.

He reached out to pull the windows closed but, ineluctably, was drawn to the shadows again.

A wind moaned through the tree branches and then the voice came again. "Come to us. Now."

The voice was near, almost below him. He peered farther out of the low-silled window to try to see the unseeable. He felt himself falling, and the now happy voice was welcoming him, louder and more triumphant as his body gained velocity.

CHAPTER 14

The Croft Elizabethan Theatre and Library occupied a two-story building in a more seedy area in the shadows of the Capitol.

But inside the wrought-iron railings on the library grounds, the grass was neatly barbered. In a large garden area, Shakespeare's favorite Welsh Tenby daffodils blazed against the purple of the crocus in springtime.

In the summer, marigolds and roses bloomed. Green beds of English Ivy corralled rows of lavender, rosemary, chamomile and saffron.

An Elizabethan transported to this fragrant bower would recognize each plant. Inside the colonnaded gray stone building, a library held thousands of historic folios and manuscripts. Shakespearian scholars visited from all over the world to research the treasure.

In the galleried library, they hunched over the centuries-old literary trove. They sat at a great oak table. High above, light shone from large chandeliers hanging from the wooden cross beams of the triangular oak roof. All was silent save for the periodic click and whir of the climate-control air-conditioners.

On the ground floor below the library, a long gray marble passage was lined with glass-topped exhibition cases. They held thematically organized collections of books. At the end of the public passage and to the right was the curtained entrance to the theatre.

Ann Powell walked quickly past the buzz of tourists peering into the cases and tried for the sixth time that morning to recall her lines. The meter and nuance of Shakespearean English could be testing at times.

Ann was above-average height with a firm athletic body she sometimes thought too heavy but one that men seemed to appreciate. She took pride in her carriage and straight back, a legacy from a long-dead mother.

Despite her blonde good looks, she dated rarely. She was determined to prove to her grandfather that she could make a career on her own, even if it was "acting." Only this morning he had asked in his genteel southern voice if she was "really sure" she wanted to continue chasing a stage career. The message had been implicit. Time to grow up, Young Lady. Make something of yourself. But he genuinely cared and was happy in any way to help her chase her dreams.

On the death of her father, a family trust fund had freed her from any financial insecurity. By any standards, she was wealthy.

Like many of those of inherited wealth, Ann often went on economy drives; watching her pennies, shopping for bargains. But she was honest enough to recognize she would never suffer the financial worries that haunted others.

It was the uncertainty of her personal life that worried her.

Just after midday, the theatre was dark. Through the gloom, she saw the welcome shape of Gerry, perhaps her closest friend. Slim, almost pretty, Gerry was her mentor when she tried to resolve the riddles of Elizabethan syntax and her supporter when she was racked with self-doubt. He and his companion, Roy, often had small suppers at her Watergate apartment after a show. They talked animatedly over cheap Chianti into the small hours, sometimes pompous, sometimes superficial, sometimes stumbling onto a great truth.

Today, Gerry's news was not good. The role of Helena in "All's Well" she had studied so hard to learn had gone to Lisa, a close friend of the stage director. Too close, thought Ann.

Gerry draped an arm around her and said archly: "Just once, couldn't we get a gay director. It's not as if there aren't any out there. My dear, you can't fight City Hall, or a horny director."

Ann laughed, but she was fighting tears of frustration. She would have to go through the farce of reading on-stage, knowing that, no matter how well she auditioned, she would not get the part — an important credit for her so far unremarkable resume.

She thought of just turning on her heel and storming out after a few angry words. No. That would only give them ammunition. Indicate she was not serious — that the rich kid was giving up yet again. One more dilettante episode in her life, like the equestrian competitions, the art studies, her language courses.

No. This time she would see it through. Damn them all. She had worked too hard to get this far.

Gerry fished into a backpack he had placed on one of the red plush theatre seats and produced a flask containing Tupelo honey and warm water. Sometimes it contained Southern Comfort.

"There, take this, control your feelings, Darling, and give them hell by doing a great reading. Go get 'em, Kid."

She smiled and hugged him. What a good friend he was, she thought.

CHAPTER 15

Gerry had sat in the shadows at the back of the theatre and watched Ann onstage. Her rich, warm voice, deep for a woman, projected well. It was a damn shame she wasn't being given an equal chance. He was proud of her. "That's my girl," he murmured to himself. "Show them what you're made of."

He had known adversity all his own life. His mother had left the family and Texas for a traveling lingerie salesman when Gerry was 10. His father, a pipe fitter at a refinery, had tried his best but even Gerry admitted he had been a difficult child — temperamental and emotional, deeply disturbed by the sexual conflicts he felt. He was too pretty for a boy, according to his father's workmates. Soon the snide jokes and his father's obvious unease seared the very heart of the boy. He knew he was different. He was certainly desperately unhappy. By the time he was 16, he took the Greyhound bus heading north from Galveston. As he passed through Oklahoma, he shed his old name Geraldo Cortez and emerged as Gerry Curtis.

For 20 years he had worked and kept himself going with dreams of an acting career. Every rotten waiting job, every failed romance, would be stoically accepted with a resigned "It just wasn't meant to be." He plunged into voice lessons, acting lessons, the wonderful escapism of the theatre. Now in his mid 30s, he found it had become more difficult to bounce back from life's aggregate of defeats, but he would keep trying. That was all he had going for him.

Now it was time to impart that resilience to Ann. Good, kind Ann, who had welcomed and returned his friendship. They would soldier on together.

There would be better days ahead for both of them, Gerry vowed.

The company broke at 5 p.m. for an early dinner break. They planned to return at 7 for the final selection of players.

As Ann walked back through the theatre, she asked Gerry: "Shall we go drown our sorrows somewhere?"

Gerry pointed his nose upward, peered over Ann's head and affected a Cary Grant accent. "No, my dear," he intoned. "Work to do. People to see. You just cut along. Carry on. Toodle-oo. See you later."

She smiled and made him promise to call her at home that evening.

Gerry was friendly with one of the gardeners and wandered out onto the grounds to a work station-storage shed. The man had set aside a posy of marigolds for him. The flowers and a second-hand pocket edition of the Sonnets Gerry had bought that morning might cheer up Ann. Let her know someone cared about her. He would surprise her and place them in the cramped cupboard the theatre laughingly called her dressing room.

A University I.D. and "introductory letter" from a recently dead historian had gained easy entrance to the library. As he pored over manuscripts, his eye caught a small glass display case at the side of a stairwell leading to a book-lined gallery. He frowned. He had found HIS book. He returned to one of the tables and loitered there for three hours, memorizing the plan of the entire building. He watched the comings and goings of the staff, where their offices were, the entrances and exits to the various rooms and passageways.

He left with a smile and a nod to the library staff. He walked swiftly out of the building and into the early evening shadows of the gardens. He would return quickly and search out his quarry. He flexed the muscles in his upper body and contracted his buttocks and quadriceps. He felt powerful, deadly.

CHAPTER 16

Taylor had called Dr. Samuels in New York and promised to visit him the next weekend. He hoped to have something concrete, anything, to tell his old friend about his daughter's death by then. What the hell that would be, he had no idea. He normally enjoyed brief trips back to Manhattan. This would not be one of them.

Liddell had called the night before and arranged to meet for lunch. His old friend had reacted strangely when Taylor mentioned the Chicago murders and his theory of a link to the British Embassy killings. Liddell had become surprisingly curt. A departure from his normal bonhomie.

The men chose an outdoor table at a popular chain restaurant on a tree-lined street off Dupont Circle.

Liddell was 6-foot-3, a muscular, wide-shouldered man, quick with a joke and a smile. The son of a Los Angeles doctor, it suited him to appear ingenuous with strangers, slow and deliberate in manner; a courteous, unthreatening, black man. A plodder.

But his phlegmatic demeanor masked a keen, analytic but imaginative mind. People saw in him what he wanted them to see.

Taylor sat outdoors at a table and ignored the car horns from a lunch-hour traffic jam. Soon the familiar, solid shape of Liddell loomed out of the crowd.

A red-haired young waitress in a straining white blouse took their orders of cheeseburgers and fries. On the pavement outside, a well-dressed man paused for a moment after glancing at Liddell, then walked on. It was almost imperceptible, but Taylor picked up on it.

He knew better than to ask who the stranger was or even acknowledge that something had happened. This was their world. The stranger could have been a suspect, an informer or another government agent. They all played by the same rules of secrecy.

After their initial hunger was satisfied, Liddell took a paper napkin and wiped off part of the tabletop. He then placed a Manila folder on the table and pushed it toward Taylor.

"This concerns your bit of business. It's as much as you need to know — at the moment," he said somewhat cryptically.

Taylor knew better than to appeal that decision just yet. He also knew without being told that Liddell would deny everything if the document's contents were somehow leaked.

Liddell wiped a crumb from his chin and leaned closer to Taylor. He wouldn't insult his friend with a warning of confidentiality.

"How's life treating you among the groves of academe?" Liddell asked.

"Getting by, getting by. Sitting on my ass. Goofing off," Taylor said.

"Bullshit!" Liddell barked.

Then his stern face relaxed into a smile. He added: "I might just have some good news for you, you lazy prick."

"Make my day," said Taylor.

"It seems Mr. Millard Gardiner, he who hates you, will be out of Washington within the week. He's being shunted up to head a New England district office."

Taylor couldn't stop a grin spreading onto his face.

"Who's replacing him?" he asked. "Not that shit Winslow."

"No," said Liddell. "Our friend Tommy."

"Tommy Grasso?"

"Yup. Tommy Grasso. He's been made a liaison with the Homeland Security bloodhounds and for some unfathomable reason he wants you back."

Grasso had just come back to Washington after a stint as a top field supervisor in New York. He had been a valued friend to both Taylor and Liddell over the years and had not forgotten them.

"I'll think about it," said Taylor. He knew damn well he would leap at the chance to get back to the Agency. Liddell rolled his eyes and started laughing. The two men shook hands and ordered beers.

"Now to business," said Liddell. "It so happens we have been officially drawn into this. The British Embassy invited us to help their investigation. We already had the reports on the Chicago murders from the State Department. With the Vice Pres and the Prince being there, our counterterrorism men were briefed by State.

"They in turn, briefed our esteemed leaders who have directed Grasso to set up a special investigative squad.

"We are sure the husband had nothing to do with it. The poor girl was just in the wrong place at the wrong time. So was the lover."

Liddell glanced at his wristwatch. "Look, I've got to go. Take this case synopsis file and have a look at home. I'll be talking to Grasso this afternoon. With luck you'll be back on board with us before the week's out. That's if you can be tempted away from University life."

A late afternoon squall darkened the apartment and Taylor turned on a wall lamp above a comfortable leather armchair. The cone of light fell on the round walnut table on which he had laid out the crime photographs.

There were three sets of prints. One set was similar to those he had seen in Chicago. They showed aerial views of the country club and the area surrounding it. Location points and compass headings of the bodies and terrain had been superimposed. There was a set of close-up prints of the crime scene, the blood-drenched dell where Lucy met her death. There was the riverbank and the body of her lover snagged on submerged tree roots. Then there were the gruesome pictures of the bodies — at the scene where each was found and on the autopsy table.

Transparencies had been made of the slashes and cuts to the bodies. If they ever retrieved a weapon, the blade would be matched to the transparencies for a possible fit.

For the first time he saw pictures of the bloody dismembered hand—hacked from the female victim — and dumped in the punch bowl.

He read the memorandum from Liddell. It was spare but detailed. He skimmed through it, highlighting several paragraphs. It had been printed via computer onto flimsy paper. The paper would burn without trace — another unspoken message from Liddell. Someone at the agency was taking this very seriously.

He read once more: "Local authorities at first concentrated their efforts on the husband and then the suspected lover after a romantic note was found in her pocketbook.

“It was four days until lover's body was found approx mile and a half downstream from grounds. It appears he was killed, then dragged to river's edge before female was murdered. Only slight traces of his and her blood led to river, probably from killer's shoes or weapons.

"The killer dismembered the female and placed her arm in the Prince's marquee. He then retraced his steps, left her where she lay and returned to the site of the first murder, the male lover. He dragged him to the river bank, then pushed or floated the corpse downstream."

Taylor read on. "Re the subsequent killings in the British Embassy in D.C., profilers were called in to check similarities of methodology and wounds. Reports not yet released but at this point they are being treated as separate incidents. Though the common denominator of the Prince's presence—he has an obvious link to the British Embassy—cannot be ignored.

The chair creaked as he dropped the folder and leaned back. He felt something rubbing against his calf, followed by a loud purring. The downstairs Gallery cat, Percy, was seeking companionship. Taylor lifted the red tabby to his chest and settled back in the chair. There was a lot of thinking to be done.

He stroked the cat's curling back and murmured as he began to doze: "Yes, Percy, a lot of thinking to be done."

He was happy and felt purpose coming back into his life. If Grasso gave him the OK to rejoin the agency, he would shoot off an e-mail tendering resignation to the University and the bastard who presided over it.

CHAPTER 17
WASHINGTON, D.C., THE CROFT THEATRE

The flies first appeared during stage blocking by the director and his assistant. When the lighting was tested, a swarm arose from the boards, unsettling the two men. Summer was ending but the notorious Washington humidity lingered.

Christ, not another drainage problem. The 80-year-old plumbing was temperamental.

The building superintendent found the corpse under the stage. He gagged, then crawled out of the wooden abbatoire and retched.

CHAPTER 18

He had enjoyed the irony, the exquisite death he had provided for the actor; the last sounds of his fellow players filtering through the boards to his captive ears. They had lain like lovers in the gloom of the under stage where he had dragged the man after the first stunning blow in a tiny dressing room.

There, in the darkness, he had watched over his terrified captive, breathing deeply the smell of blood, dust, wood, and his victim's fear.

By crouching, he had enough room to work his weapons but that could wait. He had tied his victim's limbs to four support posts. A cloth rag muffled any screams the man might make.

For hours he listened to the players above, then heard them exit the stage. Later, the solitary footfalls of a security guard echoed into the night.

He found wax candles in a spider webbed cardboard box, lit them and arranged them at the points of each limb. He began his work, slowly gutting and dressing the prey like the skilled hunter he was.

He had been moved deeply by the supplication and terror in the captive's eyes.

Timeless agony. Something to remember and ponder.

For minutes he had watched over the corpse. Then he forced himself to turn away. He had other things to do. Touchstones to gather.

CHAPTER 19

The mutilated corpse of Gerry Curtis was viewed as aberrational and even shocking to the crime weary D.C. detective squad who descended on the theatre.

According to the criminal behavior pathologies, the ferocity and savageness of the attack would indicate the killer to be close to, probably a lover, of the victim. Gerry's homosexuality played into this theory. His friends and fellow actors were all suspects.

The theft from the library upstairs could be a red herring. A desperate afterthought to suggest that a burglar had been surprised while breaking in, panicked and attacked the victim. Because of the nature of the attack, the D.C. Police Intelligence Office complied with a request to pass on all blade related murder to the FBI task force.

Just before 1 p.m. Liddell called Taylor, who had just returned from a Georgetown gym.

"Geez, I thought I'd missed you," Liddell rasped. "I've got good or bad news, depending on how you feel." Grasso wants you back and on this case. But it would help if this time you at least tried to toe the company line. He wants to see you late afternoon."

Liddell knew how welcome the news was to Taylor and he also knew not to expect any public show of emotion from the reserved agent.

Like the old friends they were, they didn't need displays of emotion to confirm their mutual understanding of each other's most sensitive feelings.

"When do we start?" Taylor said, trying to mask his excitement. For the first time in years he felt the adrenaline of the hunt surging through his body.

"We start in half an hour when I pick you up and we drive to the death scene."

"The British Embassy?" asked Taylor.

"No. The Croft Theatre and Library," said Liddell. "There's been another murder. They say it looks like a slaughter house. And there's been a very interesting theft."

Liddell parked on M Street, a main avenue of Georgetown, and waited for Taylor. Across the road, in a vacant lot next to a bank, a group of teenagers had been ordered to "assume the position" by police.

Their hands flattened against the red brick wall, their feet wide apart, they were quickly frisked for weapons or contraband. They smiled at each other and made a joke of their situation.

Taylor appeared at the passenger door and rapped on the window. He saw Liddell shake his head at the little street tableau.

"To think I used to envy your little palace in Georgetown," he told Taylor.

"Tell me about it," Taylor said sarcastically. "That's nothing around here these days."

Liddell was driving a top-of-the-line sports utility vehicle, government owned. It looked just like some affluent suburbanite's choice vehicle, a far cry from the dented family SUV parked at his home. As they drove in the afternoon traffic past bustling tourists, Taylor glanced back and saw the tell-tale signature of a working FBI agent.

A plain, silvered aluminum case that contained agents' tools of their trade: weapons, I.D. undercover documents. Most agents felt undressed without the small non-descript travel case.

They drove down past Union Station and turned right into a side street. Outside the Croft were a mass of police and unmarked government sedans. A large crime technician van had moved onto the lawn of the building. The street was closed to civilian road traffic.

On the way there, Liddell had explained that the corpse had lain hidden for nearly 48 hours under the stage.

"Some horrible things were done to the body. I just hope the poor sap wasn't alive when most of it happened.

"The murder was savage enough but another aspect that raised top priority flags with the task group was a theft during the same period."

"How does a theft come into this?" Taylor asked. "There were no thefts in the other two sets of murders."

"How do we know that?" Liddell said thoughtfully. "No one has been looking too hard for thefts. How do we know nothing was taken at the Chicago killings? Nobody thought too closely about that. If this murder is connected, we'll have to re-think the previous investigations."

Liddell showed his I.D. to a covey of Washington police officers and identified Taylor as a fellow special agent. It sounded good to Taylor's ears.

The two men entered the hallway of the Croft and walked past forensic technicians to the theatre entrance. Liddell consulted briefly with a D.C. police detective, then motioned Taylor to join them.

"It's not pretty in there," he said, pointing to a 6-foot-high area that supported the wooden stage. Sideboards from the space had been pulled off and stacked on the stage itself.

Strong, harsh lights hanging from supports flooded the death scene. Three white- over-alled crime techs patiently sifted among the dust and insects. Dark blood coated the concrete floor below the stage. At the back, anchor bolts for pulleys and ropes of cable for lighting snaked over floor and walls.

Liddell said: "The victim was one of the actors here, Gerry Curtis. He was 36, but everyone thought he was much younger. He was openly gay and very popular in the theatre company. Nobody can imagine him having any enemies but we're checking out possible boyfriend troubles."

"What's the big deal with the theft?" Taylor asked.

"Let's go upstairs to the library and see if we can find out," Liddell grunted.

In the large main room of the library, a team of staff members was scrupulously cross-checking manuscripts and books. Their greatest fear was that more than the one volume had been stolen.

A slim, agitated man seemed to be directing the others. Liddell introduced himself and Taylor. The thin man explained: "It's priceless, quite priceless. A child's illuminated prayer book that belonged to Henry VIII when he was a young prince.

"Of course there is no way you could sell it on the open market. If we don't find the thief, it will probably disappear into the art underworld for good. To think someone would murder just to get it. It defies explanation."

One of the librarians approached and submitted a large foolscap paper to the curator. "Yes, yes. Get it off immediately," he urged.

He explained: "It's an alert and a full description of the stolen book.

"It goes to a special art theft alert group set up by the leading insurance companies in the world. Within hours the description of the book will be in Europe and the rest of the globe alerting art dealers, police and insurance factors. It's a system that has been set up internationally just for this sort of event."

Liddell smiled sarcastically and handed the man an FBI card and number.

"They might just be able to help you too. It's the special FBI art recovery squad. They do tend to be quite efficient. They will give you their world wide recovery statistics if you ask."

Liddell left his own card with the librarian and promised to be in touch.

Taylor and Liddell had begun to descend the marble stairs to the theatre level when a woman's scream echoed up to them.

A young blonde woman was being comforted by two men and an older female. She began to sob deeply. Her body shook.

Taylor caught the look of pain and terror in her beautiful face and his heart went out to her. Someone must have told her who they were for she suddenly tore herself free and rounded on them.

"You're all the same," she sobbed. "You bastards are more concerned about a lousy book than Gerry."

She then turned and ran quickly back into the theatre. Liddell shook his head sadly. Taylor could faintly hear the woman's sobs from deep in the theatre.

As they left the building they pushed through a crowd of curious watchers. A dark figure in a black raincoat stood apart from the others. The man's eyes met his for a moment. Was it Taylor's imagination or did those dark eyes pierce through him. Taylor turned to draw Liddell's attention to the stranger. But when he looked back, the man was gone, instantly disappearing behind the crowd of gawkers. He dismissed his unease from his mind.

Liddell dropped him off at FBI headquarters for his meeting with Grasso. One hour later, a smiling Taylor walked out of the building past the lines of tour groups.

He was back where he belonged. He hailed a cab and set off for Georgetown.

As he opened his apartment door, the cat appeared from a shadow and rubbed against him. The telephone rang harshly.

"Mr. Taylor?" The voice, deep for a woman, was clear and attractive. "I think I owe you an apology.

"Please forgive me. I am beginning to realize you might be the only one to help. Can we meet? I'm the one who made that dreadful scene at the theatre."

Since her surprise call, he had found himself looking forward to their meeting. But first he had called Liddell and asked how she had got a contact number.

Liddell was re-assuring.

"I left names and numbers with the library and the theatre director. She called me but I thought you and your inimitable charm would get more out of her than me. I passed her on to you. It was no biggie. Let's meet her and hear what she has to say."

"Yeah, let's," Taylor said eagerly. "Tomorrow morning."

Liddell arrived at Taylor's apartment at 10 a.m. A crowd of German tourists were passing over the black wrought-iron canal bridge taking pictures of a brass plate describing the history of the canal.

He gulped the coffee handed to him by Taylor and pitched a Manila folder onto the coffee table.

"Here's what we got so far. We're still waiting on the full autopsy report, but it looks like the killer or killers might have spent the night slowly hacking Curtis to bits. How long he was alive while this was going on, we don't know yet. But one thing's clear — we have a real sick-o out there."

Taylor picked up the file. A look of disgust came over his face as he read. It looked like the killer had stunned and disabled the victim in one of the tiny dressing rooms.

He had not died until late evening or in the following a.m. He had been dragged under the stage and spread-eagled to wooden posts. Then he was slowly dismembered. A finger here, an ear there. Then a gradual, section by painful section.

Taylor gasped: "It's unbelievable. The killer must have been sitting under the stage beside the body all night.

"It's stranger than that." Liddell said. About five or six actors went over stage positions for over an hour that evening. He must have been sitting there under the stage, listening to them. We found a ring of spent candles round the body. What an unholy scene that must have been. "It looks as if sometime in the night he left his lair and broke into the library. God, he must have the nerve of the devil."

In the early afternoon, a fine rain turned the gasoline streaks in the road into rainbow slicks. Car headlights were switched on, adding to the colors. At 2 p.m. Ann Powell stepped out of a taxi at the walkway to Taylor's apartment.

Across the street, a man in a black raincoat admired the solid shapely body and clear-cut beauty of the woman. As she entered the building, he crossed the road and hailed her cab. He was driven to the Hay Adams. He asked the taxi driver to wait. A porter recognized him and brought out two suitcases.

They then continued to the Ronald Reagan airport, where the stranger raced to the gate for the shuttle to New York.

CHAPTER 20 — ROME—THE VATICAN CITY

Deep in the heart of the Court of the Belvedere, under the Tower of the Winds, the secrets of history lie.

There, many still waiting to be read and catalogued, are the most precious books, manuscripts and letters of the Secret Archives of the Roman Catholic Church.

Within their pages, are hidden the untold truths of the past — scandals and intrigues, plots and betrayals, murder, depravity and lust. They hold the most private observations of Caesars, the compromises and intrigues of kings and Popes.

Every 20 minutes, a machine whirs and the air in the library vaults is completely changed. The temperature is a constant 50 degrees Fahrenheit at an exact humidity of 55 percent.

The protection afforded the books is more than just climatic. Not even the world's most prestigious historians can gain entry to them without the permission of the Pope and their guardian the Prefect of the Secret Archives.

The archives and their secrets are owned solely by each succeeding Pope. The Pontiff has sole discretion on the use of the manuscripts and priceless volumes.

CHAPTER 21 — THE VATICAN CITY
(One year ago)

Brother Gino Valente would later say he could not explain what had drawn his fingers inexorably toward the stained packet of papers, held together by crumbling, pink ribbon.

This tattered bundle did not belong where he found it but that did not surprise him. There were many such mis-filings among the older documents in the Archives. In fact, so vast were the collections, it was not unusual to find virgin documents, papers unread for centuries.

The middle-aged Renaissance scholar had been combing through a pile of un-catalogued books and manuscripts among the 27 miles of shelves in the Archives. He had sighed as he noticed how many of the historic papers were purpling; the result of a microscopic, violet colored fungus which had withstood all efforts at eradication.

He had been curious about an old entry in an age-stained register, one of the thousands of huge, leather-bound books that took strong arms and shoulders to lift and handle. This index covered a stormy period in the history of England and a crucial one for the Holy Mother Church: the schism between Rome and Henry VIII.

Valente had been curious about an entry in the thick register. Sir Thomas Cromwell and his mentor Cardinal Wolsey had called it "The King's Great Matter," the attempt by Henry to bend the Roman Catholic Church to his implacable will and grant him a divorce from his Spanish wife, Catherine of Aragon.

When that attempt failed Henry appointed himself above church authority and split from Rome. Sir Thomas More and others' stubborn refusal to acknowledge Henry's new authority cost them their heads.

Now, perversely, it was one of the scheming architects of the historic split from Rome who was cause for Valente's excitement — the man who successfully counseled Henry to break the power of the Roman church, weaken the English nobility and destroy and plunder the monasteries to reap their riches.

Sir Thomas Cromwell was the *eminence gris* behind the English Terror which steered the new Anglican church toward Protestantism at the expense of thousands of Catholic martyrs. It was Cromwell who had contrived to force More and the King's former tutor Bishop John Fisher into choosing between Henry's position, that his marriage was nullified by Catherine of Aragon's earlier marriage to his brother, and the position of Rome that no divorce could be granted. Both men stood on their consciences and were soon kneeling before the executioner at the Tower.

The beginning and end of the 'terror' coincided with the rise and ebb of Cromwell's power and influence with Henry, before he too fell out of favor and faced the headsman's axe.

The fading pages, in front of Valente were all that survived from a letter written in 16th century Italian by Thomas Cromwell.

Like More, also the son of a London tradesman, he became a lawyer and rose to the most powerful heights in the English court.

He, like More, would stop at nothing to achieve his aims. More would torture Protestant "heretics" in the gatehouse of his Chelsea mansion, then happily go off to dine with his waiting family.

Unlike More, Cromwell would not die for a principle and, seeing his opportunity, happily saw More off to the Tower.

The fact that the letter was written in Italian did not surprise Valente as much as the contents and the letter's existence.

Quick with his fists on the streets of London as a youth, Cromwell had left hastily for Europe after getting into some sort of scrape with the authorities. At the age of 18 he found himself a soldier for the French side in their defeat in Italy at the battle of Garagliano.

Unbowed by his experience he stayed on, learned accountancy and trade, and set himself up as an agent between Florentine bankers and English and Venetian merchants. He traveled Europe on their behalf.

By necessity he had become fluent in Italian.

The pages Valente held in his hand had been written at the height of Cromwell's power. They spoke of the "King's Great Journey" from near death after a tournament fall in 1536 and his terrible wrath on his return. What Cromwell had witnessed in the privacy of the King's company had terrified even him.

Cromwell had chronicled "an ungodly and satanic journey" taken by Henry. He wrote fearfully: "He has boasted of it to me. Not content with his terrible vengeance on his enemies, he now claims to have been to the future and destroyed their progeny wherever he can find them. It appears to be madness but he is convinced. I fear we are all for the headman's axe. He is convinced that he has done this. If so, he has returned a Monster."

The find, exciting on its historic merits, had created an unusual and dramatic response from powerful figures within the Vatican curia—the inner cabinet of the Roman church.

Immediately a team of three *scrittori*, the archive's librarians, had been deputed to Brother Valente.

Resentment by the staff curators at this sudden elevation of the mild, studious friar was palpable until a visit to the Archives by Bishop Luca di Montevecchi, a man who moved in the top echelons of the Vatican power elite.

His presence and familiar greeting to Valente sent an unmistakable message. From that day they did every industrious task they could to help the taciturn friar.

For months the men worked tirelessly in the archives. Methodically, they investigated the documents relating to that troubled time.

They scoured the private papers of Pope Clement VII the leader of the church to whom, in 1528, Henry began his vain, six-year-long appeal for divorce from Catherine of Aragon. Clement, a de' Medici prince, patron of Raphael and Michelangelo, could not consent. They searched any documents written by the English Cardinal Thomas Wolsey, Cromwell's patron, who was tasked by Henry to obtain the divorce.

His failure led to his downfall and all his titles and estates confiscated by the furious king. He died of illness in an English monastery after being summoned to London and certain imprisonment in the tower. The papers of his successor Archbishop of Canterbury, Thomas Cranmer were scoured.

Every letter, document, and journal connected to Henry was searched.

Valente looked at the giant parchment with the personal seals of 75 English noblemen petitioning the Pope to grant Henry's divorce. On the enormous document each crimson colored seal was the size of a saucer. The *scrittori* noted the names of the noble supplicants and launched searches for any documents that had passed from their estates and contemporaries into the Archives. It became a massive hunt and more *scrittori* were added when needed.

Sir Thomas More's papers were examined. Those who had been his intimates were swept into the search.

The 17 letters from Henry to Anne Boleyn held in the Archives were read and parsed for any hidden clues.

The diaries of courtiers, diplomats and ambassadors of the Tudor period were meticulously researched.

Then, 11 months after the Cromwell documents discovery, a new, tantalizing shard of the puzzle had surfaced—by a man Henry had wanted to kill; a man who had fled his wrath and supported the Church's cause—his cousin Reginald Cardinal de la Pole.

Pole's papers and letters should not have been in the Secret Archives. They belonged with the vast document collections of all his brother princes of the church in the main Vatican Library.

But Pole's personal papers — letters, apparently to a long-forgotten mistress and mother of illegitimate children — had been uncovered in the Archives. Their contents perhaps explained why they had been "lost" for the centuries.

Like Cromwell, the Cardinal warned about what seemed to have been a para-normal event in the troubled king's life.

In a time when witches were burned at the stake and even the highly-educated King believed thunderstorms could occasionally rain down blood; superstition and belief in the unnatural were rife.

What made these claims so unusual were their sources: The intelligent, pragmatic man of the world Cromwell and the highly principled intellectual aristocrat Pole, a man with good reason to deeply fear Henry's wrath.

Valente had taken the papers and walked up the narrow, winding staircase to a room at the top of the Torre dei Venti, the Tower of the Winds, above the old archives. He wanted to be alone, with no distraction, as he read the letters. He saw the late afternoon sun wash the Belvedere courtyard and heard the cooing of doves in the eaves. He carefully spread the papers out. And adjusted his reading glasses.

Pole's cryptic and fragmentary message from the past was chilling.

Echoing down the ages came yet another warning to add to that of Cromwell.

Pole had written "There is a horror abroad in the unholy shape of my Cousin, the King. He has gone beyond even his heresy toward the Holy Mother Church. He has enlisted the devil to travel with great disregard to Time itself. He has thinned his thick blood and come back angry and full of deadly action.

"You must flee take everyone and ……."

Frustratingly, the letter, still missing vital pages, abruptly ended.

Valente noted in his transcription of the 16th century language usage that "thick blood" described a bout of melancholy or inaction on Henry's part. He would instruct the *scrittori* to hunt for the missing pages.

The Pole letter excited the normally unflappable Valente. Although incomplete, it was a phantom finger pointing out of the past to the present—hinting at the Cardinal's genuine horror at what was to come.

Valente's musing ended with the first shadows creeping across the courtyard. There were no lights in the Tower of the Winds. If there were no electrical wires there could be no electrical fire hazards, nothing to endanger the ancient tower and its treasures beneath.

The priest hastily left the room and carefully made his way down the Tower staircase. There would be great excitement when he showed his find to Bishop di Montevecchi; much greater than he could ever dream of.

CHAPTER 22
A SUMMER HOUSE OVERLOOKING THE STRAIT OF SICILY

Salemi had been gazing at the dappled waters of the Mediterranean. He watched the slight sea swells disappear into the cobalt haze of the horizon. Not far beyond that bending, blue curtain was Africa, where the first Salemis had emerged under the glittering swords and shining banners of Islam. The sun beat down and occasionally he heard the splash of a fish breaking the calm surface.

A slight breeze from the hills massaged his hair and carried away the sweat from his body. It was a glorious day to be alive. He planned to snorkel and dive, then enjoy a light lunch of smoked eel and warm potato salad. His family's seashore villa was a sanctuary for the priest. A shelter from the dirt and dysfunction of the world.

Then he saw Carleto, the son of the postmaster, hiking down the rocky outcrops from the village, jogging through clumps of red poppy, waving a telegram in his hand.

The vacation was over. The Vatican had spoken. He was to get the noon plane to Rome, with enough clothes for a long stay.

ROME — THE VATICAN CITY

Bishop Luca di Montevecchi had decided to mentor the young Sicilian priest after listening from the darkened wings of a seminary auditorium to a student debate in Palermo.

The mercurial young man had not only strength of advocacy and wit but an inner fire in his slim athletic body.

The Bishop had instructed an aide to supply a full background and academic report on the young firebrand. He might have plans for this precocious islander.

What he discovered was a story of tragedy, resilience and determination — a crucible that had produced a spirit of raw steel which could be forged into a worthy weapon for the Church.

The young priest's pedigree was superb, yet star-crossed. His father, last of an old Sicilian landed and professional dynasty had been a heroic and ferocious government prosecutor. His fight to break the strangle-hold of the island's Mafia gangs had ended as his wife had tearfully foreseen; his body shredded and atomized by a powerful car-bomb outside a Palermo courthouse; his blood staining the magenta tiles of the surrounding roofs on that clear October day.

His mother — the beautiful, blonde daughter of a wealthy Irish-American, Philadelphia family — remained in Sicily. She ignored the calls from her American family to return home with the 10-year-old child. She would stay in Italy to honor the only man she would truly love. The boy would be a testimony and a tribute to her martyred husband.

From the redoubt of the Vatican di Montevecchi had tracked the progress of the young priest, Joseph Salemi. The young Sicilian's intensity of purpose was ameliorated by a natural charm and humor.

Salemi had the tenacity and aggression of his murdered father and the obstinate belief and overarching faith in the Holy Roman Church his mother had bequeathed him.

The Bishop's professional interest slowly and irresistibly became avuncular. At first he had allowed the Sicilian every opportunity to fail, every chance to flinch in the face of battle; but the priest's obduracy and resilience had been noted.

When the young priest had inevitably hit a bureaucratic wall, di Montevecchi had moved quickly to loosen a few bricks and wait patiently at the other side for his little bull-dog to emerge. Salemi became one of the youngest men to gain the rank of Monsignor.

Now the time had come to invite the tenacious priest to join his secretive cadre in their holy mission.

A short stroll from di Montevecchi's apartments, in a subterranean chamber under the Vatican Radio building, a small operations room had been set up. Two men spent each morning from 6 until 2 in the afternoon collating the disparate information that came singing into the computers and fax machines.

A museum theft in Frankfurt, an auction in Incanabula in Zurich and a grotesque ritualistic murder in Buenos Aires. All were grist for the watchers in the brightly lit cellar — its walls and surfaces painted a light blue to soothe tired eyes.

It was here that the minutiae of the world were picked up and gleaned, and mostly discarded. Very occasionally a pattern would merge, only to unravel when thoroughly analyzed. But now there was a growing visible thread that might spark renewed interest in the Henry file. It was certainly worth getting a man out in the field. Someone to apply synthesis and scrutiny and, above all, daring to the project.

The Bishop had chosen Father Joseph Salemi for the task.

CHAPTER 23

Salemi left the buzz of traffic, the heat and the crowded dusty street and entered a hotel doorway. After a greeting by a uniformed doorman, he turned towards the black marble bar.

Le Grand Hotel had long been an oasis of gentility in the Termini District of Rome. It casts its cooling shadow over the Via Vittorio Emanuelle Orlando just off the Piazza della Republica.

In this stately refuge of first-class service and refinement, di Montevecchi had long held court. He had loved the old hotel opened in 1894 by Cesar Ritz and had used it for decades. Despite his disapproval of the 1999 renovation he continued his patronage, no doubt heavily influenced by the fact that the wine cellars still carried the private vintages of red Tuscan wine from his family estates.

A closet boulevardier, he loved to observe the rich and famous who passed through its marbled rooms. He was an admirer of beauty in all things and, at heart, a romantic.

He remembered the American movie star Elizabeth Taylor sitting in the old bar lounge late one night in the 1970s — just di Montevecchi and she, at separate tables. She had smiled at him and lifted her glass in a silent, polite toast. She always took a suite that occupied half of the first floor, he had been discreetly informed by desk clerk.

Now, di Montevecchi was sitting at one of Le Grand Bar's red velvet banquettes. A beam of reflected sunlight warmed a plate of rice-papered macaroons. A cognac was in his hand. He rose and embraced Salemi.

The young priest smelled the scent of cigars and ash on di Montevecchi's broad chest.

Apart from their wit and intellect, the two priests were as different as could be. The older man Falstaffian, quick to smile or scold; the young priest intense, and shy with strangers.

Di Montevecchi spoke the pure, flawless Italian of his native Sienna; Salemi the sing-song, impure accent of Sicily. Yet these men of the church were formidable in tandem.

"So," di Montevecchi beamed as he hugged Salemi, "How is my little mezzarazza?"

Di Montevecchi had long ago coined the word, meaning half breed, as a fond nickname for his younger friend, a reference to his Sicilian father and American mother.

Salemi laughed. "I was fine eating honest Sicilian food. Now you drag me back to Rome. My waistline will grow again."

In a display of surrender, he reached over and unwrapped a macaroon from its paper tissue. "I know you like your comforts, but why are we here in the lap of luxury?"

The smile left di Montevecchi's jowly face, which seemed to have a permanent 5 o'clock shadow.

"We needed to talk away from the mice," said the bishop. Di Montevecchi had long claimed that even the poorest mouse in the Vatican recesses and darkest corridors was under the control of a cardinal or a Vatican committee. The "Mice" were what he called the gossips and worse that inhabit any closeted community.

Di Montevecchi could rarely resist a touch of theatricality when he thought the occasion called for it. He paused, sighed dramatically and announced: "They have found something very interesting in the Secret Archives. It may confirm something both wonderful and terrible.

"It seems the old Cardinal was right. He knew something was going to happen."

For an hour, the two priests huddled over the table. Risking di Montevecchi's look of disapproval, Salemi ordered the bar's cocktail homage to Cesar Ritz, a gin and sambuca in a coffee frosted glass.

Di Montevecchi glanced at the Cartier tank watch on his broad wrist and then at an ever observant maitre D'. The man nodded and telephoned the concierge on a house phone.

"We have much to do and you have much to learn," he warned Salemi, enjoying the air of mystery. Ten minutes later, a black Lancia limo from the Vatican fleet purred up to the hotel entrance. They headed to the crowded bridges across the Tiber and the Vatican City beyond.

CHAPTER 24

The limousine stopped at St. Anne's Gate, where a blue-uniformed Swiss Guard looked into the car, smiled a greeting to di Montevecchi and waved them through. The Bishop instructed the driver to drop them at the Vatican Garden. A plump squirrel darted across their path and vanished into the lushness of a grove of bushes.

Three of the gardens' tribe of cats froze and watched warily as the Bishop and Salemi passed.

The unusually heavy summer rains had intensified the colors of the garden to a vibrant green. They found a bench in a deserted part of the gardens. The Bishop lit a cigar, blew a plume of rich Cuban smoke into the scented air and began the education of Salemi in the secret project.

Another euphemistic phrase. There would be no appeal elsewhere if failure loomed. Salemi spoke for the first time. He knew what to say.

"Your Eminence, I have always welcomed any opportunity to give all that I have for the Holy Mother Church. No sacrifice will be too great. If I fail, it will be my responsibility, my disgrace alone.

Salemi had deliberately exaggerated his Sicilian brogue. Let these haughty Roman Cardinals think they were dealing with some ardent peasant. Cardinal Benedetto barely let him finish. He was not fooled. He knew that Salemi recognized the now patent game of artifice. His voice strengthened, grew louder.

"You know more than a little about your true mission. So far, there has been little more than a theory bordering on a fairytale; a tantalizing dream stitched from a spider-web of theory.

He leaned forward into a beam of sunlight, once more the avaricious predator.

"If I believe the recent reports, we may have an opportunity to confront, and God willing, intercede with a dangerous prey. That is your task. To meet him, however fleetingly, and invite him to rejoin us and change history."

There was a sudden metallic clang, probably from the aging steam pipes underneath the chamber. Salemi could have sworn it was the Cardinal's talons flexing and contracting in expectation of failure.

CHAPTER 26
NEW YORK

Throughout the world, as invisible as any nation's spy network — *nostri occhi* served the church and its trusted leaders like Bishop di Montevecchi. This multitude of "eyes" had a great advantage over their secular rivals. They worked within a giant, global franchise that had taken millennia to build.

Wherever Rome's agents traveled there would be a cardinal, a bishop, a local priest a church and powerful members of the one billion strong faithful to help and inform. Executives in business and government could open doors—or close them to enemies if need be.

In a quiet apartment in an 1860 brownstone, Father James Orr looked down at the autumn leaves of tree-lined Gramercy Park. The old priest often thought he was becoming part of this sedate bywater of old Manhattan. He was an old curiosity just like the historic brownstones and the private park.

The classic house had been willed to the church by the last aged member of a now extinct New York dynasty.

His duties were few these days. It seemed everyone would be glad if he would accept full-time retirement. But the mother church and her sacraments were his life blood. No matter what, he would serve her.

The telephone call from di Montevecchi had been as abrupt as it was welcome: "Are you ready for action, old Irishman?"

"Holy Jesus! Is that you, Luca?"

"Yes it is, James. I am sending a man to you. He arrives tomorrow in New York. See if you can help him. He will explain everything. Matters of importance to us and our quest have to be organized. I know I can count on you."

Orr felt a renewal of energy and vanished optimism rise. He had not been written off.

He was still needed. Wanted by a very important man for what must be a significant mission.

"What level of organization are we talking about?" Orr was all business now. His concentration was almost palpable at the other end of the transatlantic line.

"Is it a New York thing, or does it reach further? What would you like me to organize first?" Orr asked, trying to control his excitement.

Di Montevecchi understood the old priest's bubbling enthusiasm. Orr's value, his quick intelligence and depth of experience had been overlooked by the Cardinals and Bishops in America.

Di Montevecchi said gently: "First of all, I want you fresh and rested until my man arrives. It's not only your famed organizational skills we need. We want your brain and historical knowledge.

"All will be explained to you by Monsignor Salemi."

Di Montevecchi chuckled: "I'd love to watch you play poker with him, you old fox. It would be an education for anyone watching. He is somewhat of a Sicilian firebrand, but you will get on well together, you two."

Di Montevecchi continued warmly: "If you need anything else, call me on the private number. We must meet soon, my old friend. It's difficult to find priests to laugh with these days, I miss your irreverence."

Orr put down his receiver and moved to the window overlooking the lush park below. He could not resist offering a prayer in happiness and relief.

He was needed, still needed, by the Holy Mother Church. He felt a welling joy spread through his being.

In a chamber of the Vatican, the Cardinal challenged di Montevecchi: "You are staking a lot on an old man."

"I know. I felt his desperation to be useful. That and his intellect will serve us well. He is a better servant of Christ than many of us." Di Montevecchi had spoken.

The Cardinal saw that his strong-minded Bishop would brook no criticism.

"Let us pray so," he said sourly.
He disliked the ebullient Bishop who seemed to appear and disappear in the corridors of Vatican power like a will o' the wisp. He disliked di Montevecchi, but he knew better than to take him on directly. If a miracle happens and he succeeds, then the Cardinal would share the glory. If not, di Montevecchi can wear the mantle of failure and disgrace.

CHAPTER 27
WASHINGTON, D.C.

A faint scent of a floral Penhaligon scent carried on a damp breeze greeted Taylor as Ann entered his apartment. She did not offer a handshake, and he could see she was still upset, but in control.

Taylor indicated a chair, but Ann looked toward the bay window overlooking the canal and moved toward it.

"I'd rather stand, if you don't mind. See what kind of a view you have."

She looked out at the little bridge with its procession of tourists. Taylor could not help noting the firm curves of her body. He waited for her to build her confidence to speak.

She began her apology hesitantly but then grew more articulate.

"I feel such a fool. I was upset but that is no excuse. Please forg..."

"That won't be necessary," Taylor interrupted. "You were in shock. It's perfectly natural. Jeez, anyone would be upset. A lot of hardened professionals couldn't have dealt with what you saw."

He offered her an olive branch.

"Perhaps you can help now by telling us all you know about your friend."

Ann sighed and her graceful form seemed to sag. She turned away from the window: "There is something I didn't tell the police. But I know in my heart that it wasn't what killed him."

Taylor waited silently. There was no point in showing frustration or anger. Just listen.

"Secrets?" said Taylor.

"You have to remember Gerry and I shared a lot of confidences together. He was like a brother, and the best friend I had. We told each other about our troubles and our dreams. We looked after each other when we could." Her voice was pleasing, easy on Taylor's ear.

"Gerry had a sort of dark side to him. Don't get me wrong — he would never harm anyone or anything. But there was this side that I could never understand. I don't think he really knew what drove him there, but he would try to rationalize it.

"One night I called at his apartment early. He had given me a key for when I cat-sat during his vacations.

"I could hear the cat. It had crawled into a cupboard and been shut in. Normally I would never have gone into his bedroom. We respected each other's privacy. It was unspoken, but understood.

"I opened the door and, sure enough, the cat jumped out. It took me a few seconds to register the contents of the cupboard. Lots of leather, leather hoods... I think you know what I mean.

He'd only hinted once before of that side of himself."

"I didn't tell the officer who questioned me at the theatre. But it's been preying on my mind. Perhaps it should be checked out. Maybe he met some madman who wouldn't leave him alone or stalked him?"

Taylor knew how difficult it had been for her to describe her friend's perverse sex life, even though, from an investigative viewpoint, her sense of loyalty was misguided.

"I'm sure the officers would check all that out as a matter of course. We'll let them know what you have told us. I don't think you have caused any harm."

Taylor pulled a yellow legal pad from a desk and handed it to Ann.

"Let me make you a coffee or a drink of some sort while you write down any names or descriptions of Gerry's friends. Anything you think might help, however fragmented."

Taylor moved to the recessed kitchen area.

"What's your poison?" he said, trying to lighten the mood.

"A beer, please," Ann replied.

A beer, thought Taylor. This is my kind of gal.

CHAPTER 28

Ann left Taylor's apartment and found herself on the pavement of M Street. She felt a mixture of uncertainty and relief. She dreaded what the inquiries into Gerry's S & M activities might uncover.

What posthumous judgments on his secret life they might trigger. Yet she knew that if the murder investigation was to succeed, they had to check all possibilities.

Sooner or later, they would have stumbled upon his dark side. As soon as they searched his apartment they would have found the cupboard with its sinister leather gear and chains.

This FBI agent seemed to be sympathetic. She decided he could be trusted. He wouldn't deliberately blacken what was left of Gerry's tainted memory.

The skies had cleared, and she decided on the short walk from Georgetown to her apartment at the Watergate. She walked over the canal bridge and down to the river. On the riverside, a handful of people ate and drank at one of the open-air restaurants. Seagulls swooped for scraps on the river walkway. She watched four rowers skull up towards the Key Bridge at Rosslyn. She could hear the grunt of exhaling breath as they pulled in unison, their oar blades dripping rainbows in the afternoon sun.

Everything was pleasant and peaceful. Gerry had often met her here. He loved the river and would call and ask her to join him for a lazy Sunday brunch at one of the cafes. They would get slightly drunk and share dreams and plans. It all seemed empty now that he was gone.

She crossed the Rock Creek Parkway and walked up the hill on Virginia Avenue to the Watergate Apartments, nodded to the doorman and entered the elevator. Joining her was a neighbor, a senior Senator tipped as possible presidential material. They exchanged pleasantries and the Senator asked after her grandfather.

That was one of the problems of being from an old establishment family. She was judged as a Powell, not as plain Ann.

She entered her duplex apartment. The gray concrete balconies over-looked the apartment building's swimming pool. Gazing across the Potomac, she could see the Georgetown riverside restaurants and their ant-like customers, the river snaking down from Rosslyn and its cluster of skyscrapers.

She glanced over to her left to the balconied end rooms of the Watergate Hotel.

She spotted a flash of light from just inside one room. The screen door to the room was open. Just inside, she could make out the figure of a man. He had field glasses in his hand. But he was not looking out over the river. He was looking at her apartment building. He saw her register his presence and turned back inside to the shadow of the room.

"Get a grip on yourself, Ann," she whispered. “It's just some curious tourist.” But a cold, uneasy feeling remained.

CHAPTER 29

After Ann had left, Taylor called Liddell and arranged to meet him in a Georgetown bar. He told him about the victim's fetishistic life style. They agreed it should be pursued.

"How did your wacky blonde actress come across?" asked Liddell.

"She's no bubblehead," Taylor replied, more strongly than he intended to. "She's a nice kid who's lost her best pal."

Liddell interrupted: "Oh, dear are we falling for her, John?"

"Screw you!" said Taylor. He laughed and hung up.

The cat had entered from the shop below. He sniffed the air, where the faint scent of Ann's perfume remained.

Mickey's Bar was an 80-year-old corner saloon just off the main commercial drag of Georgetown. During the day it was packed with tourists drinking the house punch as they lunched on the bar menu of snack food.

In the quieter evening hours, the locals ventured in. Liddell and Taylor sat at an unsteady table between two stained and scratched wooden dividers.

They ordered two large bottles of Grolsch beer and Liddell drew a set of reports from his aluminum case. Both men had learned to distrust computer e-mails.

"The facts as we know them," he sighed.

"Oh, yes. The facts," echoed Taylor, sharing Liddell's faint sarcasm.

Liddell rested his huge fists on the 2-inch-thick document and said: "Let me sum up. The victim was still alive after being pulled under the stage. He had been stunned and disabled by a blow to the cervical cord. He was then dragged into that hellhole and tortured.

"The killer slowly butchered his limbs. His tongue was cut out. His ears were excised. The medical exam shows tremendous force which caused spinal shock, effectively immobilizing him. The weapon could have resembled a butcher's cleaver or heavy hunting knife. They have microscopic shards of metal from the weapon or weapons embedded in edges of the bones. They have a pool of bloody water deliberately tainted with bleach or some harsh chemical which will pollute any DNA, underneath a water standpipe at the rear of the stage. Presumably the killer carefully removed his clothes before torturing the victim, then washed the blood off his naked body.

Taylor asked: "Does it sound like an angry lover? An S&M killing?"

"That will have to be checked out. We have undercover officers blanketing all the gay bars, eavesdropping on conversations and picking up leads. But our behavioral science people say there is one flaw to that supposition. They think an angry lover would have mutilated the private parts of the body or removed the sexual organs of the victim. They were intact and apparently unmolested."

"Plus, a sexual killer would have taken some sort of trophy from the immediate murder scene. Instead, he goes upstairs and steals a book, which has nothing to do with the victim.

What about the Embassy murders and Chicago? The victims there were hacked to bits pretty damned good," said Taylor.

"The lab boys are now checking bone samples and wound paths from those who were killed on the Embassy grounds. We'll compare them with transparencies of the wounds from the Chicago and Theatre killings. They are looking for metal fragments from the weapon or weapons embedded in the bones. Then they will try to match them to all the murders. If there is a link, they'll let us know immediately. But meanwhile we will just presume they are all linked until something proves us wrong."

The men were about to order steak sandwiches from a young waitress when Liddell's cell phone rang. The conversation was brief. Liddell stabbed a broad finger at the tiny phone to hang up.

He leered over at Taylor: "Do you fancy a taste of leather and perversion tonight? That was

Joe Carlson of the D.C. Vice Squad. He's found the leather bar where Gerry boy used to play."

"Let's eat first," said Taylor resignedly.

The bar was behind a strip mall just across the Maryland border. The windows were varnished black and only a small lilac neon sign inset in a corner of one advertised TOM'S.

Liddell and Taylor found Detective Carlson parked outside in an unmarked police sedan.

Lean, with a leathery angular face, Carlson broke into a grin when he saw Liddell. Taylor was introduced.

"It's early yet, but the guy we want to speak to comes on duty in half an hour," Carlson told them.

In the gloom of the bar, it took a full 60 seconds for their eyes to adjust. Above the bar was a crude mural, which looked to be copied from the notorious Mapplethorpe study of a leather clad man kneeling with a gleaming black whip handle inserted in his anus.

The bar smelled of stale beer, urine, leather and a sweet earthy odor Taylor couldn't place.

Taylor made out a back saloon through the murk and caught the gleam of steel-barred cell doors. The bartender wore leather cross straps and black leather chaps. A studded codpiece enclosed his genitals. Gold rings pierced his nipples.

There were three other patrons in the bar. They talked quietly together. A mixture of black, highly polished boots, leather and dangling chrome chains.

"The fun doesn't start until later," the goateed barman told Liddell. "But I can guess you fellas aren't here for fun. Right?"

He looked at Carlson: "Like I said, Stone should be in any minute now."

For once Taylor didn't feel like a beer, but he and Liddell pretended to enjoy a Budweiser, no glasses offered.

Taylor went to the toilet off the saloon. The locks had been wrenched off the stalls. A huge 10-foot by four-foot metal sink, more suited to a mortuary, stood on a 3-foot high concrete table in the middle of the room. Carlson had told him that was where voluntary nude victims lay down to be washed in streams of urine. He shuddered and wandered back to the bar.

Stone was a giant of a man. Bearded, his head shaven bald. He had an incongruously high-pitched voice.

"Yes, I knew Gerry. And, yes, we did get it on a few times. But everything we did was consensual."

"We're not accusing you of anything," Liddell counseled.

"Who else did Gerry mix with?" asked Liddell.

"Very few people. He wasn't really promiscuous. Oh sure, he would stray occasionally and get wild. But he was very careful who he got down with. If he thought there was any risk of real danger, he would back out. He was sensible that way. He would not just allow himself to be topped by any stranger."

"Topped," asked Liddell.

"The dominant is the top, the submissive is the bottom," explained Carlson.

The trio in the corner suddenly voiced whoops and cheers. Liddell and Taylor swung round and saw an odd couple enter the bar. A large gray-bearded man with a leather cap and leather chaps. He was holding a dog collar attached to the neck of a thinner man dressed only in a leather pouch and black boots. They joined the men in the darkness of the corner and moved into the saloon out of view.

Taylor found himself yearning for the fresh evening air outside.

"Can you give us a list of other bars he may have frequented?" asked Carson.

"He could have gone to any of them, but this is the one he seemed to frequent consistently. He might have met some nutcase — God knows there are enough of them out there. But the way he was killed doesn't sound like it involved anyone in 'the scene'.

"We get our kicks out of consensual dominations, control and sex. Leave no marks is the general rule. Our people don't get off slaughtering some poor bastard and butchering him like a carcass of beef."

They thanked Stone and the barman and went out to their parked cars. It was silent outside save for the distant hum of cars on a thruway. The neon sign buzzed quietly. A small animal stirred in the dumpster outside the bar.

"Why do I think we are wasting our time here," said Taylor.

"Why do I think you're right," Liddell replied.

"Still, we know he liked that sort of life. Could it be he refused to play with the wrong guy? A guy who came back after him with a hatchet?" said Taylor.

He yawned. "Let's get the hell out of here, amigo," he said to Taylor.

CHAPTER 30

He lay in a grassy burrow by the banks of the river. The fast-flowing water cast its customary spell on him. His senses were rushing. The rich smell of a rotting log, the scent of wild roses and clover. This was the place he chose to replenish himself. The way always led to the chuckling water.

He was back where he felt comfortable, listening to the wild birds. Insects droned and wisps of dying plant life silently offered themselves to the breeze.

He heard tentative movement through fern and underbrush. A small deer, perhaps.

Make the day perfect, the voice whispered. Let's kill it. Let its warm blood drip over our hands. Memories of home.

The dark evening would be used to plan the next steps. Much to do. Weapons to be sharpened. People to hunt, a great, deadly game to be played.

CHAPTER 31

Taylor awoke the next morning, his esophagus complaining about the stale beer and junk food from the night before. He had decided to call Ann and relate what they had found out at the leather bar.

Officially it was none of her business, but he felt sympathy for her feelings of loss. Or was it becoming more than that. She was certainly one hell of a good-looking woman.

He rang the Watergate apartment, but there was no reply. He was just heading for the shower when his phone rang. He cleared his throat and thought about how he would greet her. He was hailed by Liddell's bass voice.

"We're on for the Embassy at 11 a.m.," Liddell gruffly informed him.

Liddell had arranged to meet the Scotland Yard Detective Superintendent on loan from London who had drawn the Embassy murders enquiry. It may be in the heart of Washington, but it was still British territory.

The State Department liaison had arranged a meeting at the small area of British soil set back from the road on a curving, hilly brow of Washington's Embassy Row.

To gain entrance to the chancellery, visitors and staff had to present their I.D. cards, then pass through a clear bulletproof door, which sealed them temporarily in a glass chamber. Sensors would detect any weapons. When security was satisfied, the inner door was opened. Their host was waiting for them. He led them along a corridor past a wide stone balustraded stairway. They turned left and into a bright luxurious morning room near the gardens.

Superintendent Kenneth Roselove was a tall, elegant man with a dated, imperial moustache tracing his upper lip. He spoke with a southern English accent.

He began formally. "Welcome aboard, gentlemen. I have heard great things about you chaps from my colleagues. The more the merrier, as they say."

Taylor had the feeling that the Englishman probably didn't speak that way back in London.

Somehow, when some Brits came to America they became caricatures of what they imagined the Americans wanted to hear in an Englishman.

Roselove went on. "As you can imagine, there has been the most ungodly hue and cry back home about these deaths. The papers are calling for the heads of any of us involved in the Prince's security. It's already cost a dozen men their careers."

“Was the Prince expected at the Embassy?” asked Taylor.

“Not officially,” said Roselove. “There was speculation in the British tabloids that he might break the trip for a night or two in Washington, but nothing was set in stone. Any plans for a quick visit were scrapped after the Chicago incident.

"Still, the Foreign Secretary is being lambasted in the commons and the Lords over how our security was so lax as to allow some madmen inside the Embassy grounds."

"To be fair," said Taylor, "That's a pretty good question to raise."

"I agree," said Roselove nodding his head wryly.

The three men walked into the room and then through the glass doors leading to the gardens.

Liddell looked at the lush shrubberies and weeping willows edging the gardens.

"What about the news stories about the angry Hispanic lover trying to kill his girlfriend. These poor guys just getting in his way."

Roselove's lips tightened into a frown.

"Just that, as I am sure you have already guessed. A convenient fable to buy us time and save a few red faces," he said.

"We have to consider two options. One: It was a rogue terrorist group who had somehow disabled part of the security system but failed to knock out all of the sensors. Their system was down for about 50 minutes that day but unfortunately I have found that was not unusual.

"Or two — and experience has shown me truth can be stranger than fiction — some madman just happened to jump the gates at the right time. Even then the security fallback system worked. He was detected, but not immediately."

Taylor and Liddell looked at several lighter shaded grass areas near a tree. Roselove pushed the tip of his highly polished black shoe through the blades of re-turfed lawn almost thoughtfully.

"That's where the bodies were found," he said. "The original grass and earth cover is down in your FBI lab. This is fresh turf. Not much more here to interest you, I'm afraid."

"It's worthwhile to see the murder site," Liddell said diplomatically.

"Very helpful," Taylor tactfully agreed.

Liddell pointedly looked back to the Residence and the doorway.

They would not gain any insights here, they silently agreed.

CHAPTER 32

Taylor would not admit it to Liddell but almost a year away from the bustle of the agency had left rust deposits.

At the University, analyzing and talking about crime and police work, not doing it, he felt like a sports commentator who knows his subject but never experiences the game on the field.

Liddell had picked him up at his apartment just after 10 a.m. for his official return to duty at the office. As Liddell drove, Taylor crouched in the passenger seat fiddling with the radio to find an all-news station He avoided the sensitive subject of Liddell's son.

Liddell, the former college football player, had always taken his robust health somewhat for granted. It was, therefore, a harrowing emotional blow when doctors told him his 10-year-old son would have a shortened life, threatened by a chronic disease.

As the boy's condition slowly deteriorated, Liddell's bosses at the FBI offered him easier, less demanding casework which would allow him more time at home.

But his work ethic would not allow him to choose that path. He would share the load with his colleagues, making time whenever he could for the boy. Having arranged the best possible care for their son, he and his wife agreed that if the disease progressed more quickly than expected, then Liddell would simply take an indefinite leave or, if need be, quit the agency.

Liddell had brought two plastic containers of harsh black coffee.

"Were working at the headquarters building, not the Washington Field Office," he said.

Taylor's stomach ached and he had an acidic taste in his mouth. He had forgotten the dietary rigors of a detective's life. Eat on the run, eat and drink whatever is at hand. He missed his carefully balanced diets. For all his jogging and exercise he was sure as hell soft where it mattered for a cop. He was disgusted with himself for that and resolved to toughen up physically and mentally.

After clearing security at the FBI building on Pennsylvania Avenue, the two men entered a pastel-colored windowless room with a long conference table and a five-by-three-foot screen hooked up to a computer. Taylor recognized Bill Seurat one of the FBI's most senior managers. Bill was a hardened, experienced field agent. Now he was part of the intelligence and counter-terrorism division within the agency.

The other man was introduced as Ted Kenney, a crime laboratory expert out at Quantico.

Coffee and sandwiches, ordered from the staff cafeteria, had been placed on the table, a cardboard box containing soft drinks beside it.

The men made small talk and asked about former colleagues as they drank and ate hungrily.

The door opened again and Grasso walked in. He smiled at them all, but Taylor could see a tenseness in his movements and demeanor.

When the pleasantries were finished, Bill Seurat began. No more chit chat.

"We believe at least three or more different weapons were used in the murders, if — and it's a big if — we can assume they are all related.

"Some appeared to be stabbing wounds; others deep cuts and slashes. Some bones looked like they had been sliced by a butcher's cleaver — immense damage to the body tissue, muscle and skeleton.

"It took a lot of energy and sheer ferocity. If it's a group of killers, that might account for the seeming disparity of weapons used.

"If it's one guy, from the level many of the body blows were delivered, he must be well above average height and strength."

"Sounds like we're looking for a giant loaded down with weapons or a band of bloodthirsty Ninjas," said Liddell dryly.

"Can we take first things first," asked Taylor anxious to bring the group focus back to the cases.

"What do the Chicago killings tell us? Why were two lovers, having an illicit little affair, hacked to death at a tony Polo match."

Seurat pushed away a swatch of black hair from his forehead and frowned. "We have thoroughly investigated the two victims and anyone who knew them.

"The male, Carson, had a murky background. He was in over his head with the crowd that belonged to the Polo Club. He was facing some scary margin calls, and was losing his shirt regularly in Vegas."

"The dame," Seurat began, then looked apologetic when he remembered Taylor's initial connection to the case. "Sorry, John, the girl seems innocent enough. She was married, the husband played around. It looks like she thought she would get even with him. Friends say she had always been faithful to him in the past. He was accounted for at the time of the murders. His alibi checks out."

"So we're back to they were in the wrong place at the wrong time?" asked Liddell.

"Looks like it," said Seurat.

"What about the Royal connection," said Taylor. "That seems to be the thread. The Prince and his people certainly got out of the area in a damned hurry. What do the Brits believe?"

"Outwardly they have kept a stiff upper lip, and all that," said Seurat. "But there has been a security shake-up ever since. They have complained bitterly to the State Department and the Secret Service that such atrocities could occur during their visit. Officially they blame our lax security for allowing a double murder near the Royal presence.

"But unofficially they are very concerned about the bloody arm found in his pavilion. The blood spread over the flag or standard or whatever they call it. They worry that could have been a personal message for him."

Seurat continued: "The link became even stronger when the Embassy killings surfaced. The victims again were in the wrong spot at the wrong time. They were also hacked to death. The details of that investigation, which is still being updated, are in the green folders in front of you, gentlemen."

Seurat went on: "Now we come to the Theatre murder.

"Once again, we can only surmise at what happens. Curtis was into the S & M scene. Perhaps he planned a kinky session under the stage, which got out of hand. Maybe he met someone who wasn't playing his kind of sex game."

"But the people who knew him said he was only interested in safe consensual S & M," Taylor pointed out.

"Correct," said Seurat. "But they found traces of marijuana and cocaine in his body. Slight levels to be sure, but they were there. Maybe he got high and experimented with the wrong guy. Drugs and sex — the oldest recipe for disaster."

"But again we have another link with Royalty. The Royal book stolen from the library upstairs. It was definitely in its case the day before the murder. So once again we have a link, however tenuous, to English Royalty."

"Well, thank God the Prince is back in England in some castle or palace or wherever he hangs out," said Liddell.

"Not for long," said Seurat cryptically. "He refuses to put off a visit in January for his postponed visit to Florida—another f-ing Polo match. The State Department and his own security people are having kittens over it, but he won't back down. So the pressure is really on to find whoever is behind this long before then. We have been authorized to procure whatever we need for this manhunt."

"Our behavioral science guys are trying to profile the killer or killers. We have booked space on the computer to see if we can identify a behavioral pattern in all this. They are looking internationally as well as just the US.

Seurat glanced at Grasso, who motioned him to sit down. They waited for questions but there were none. Grasso nodded to Kenney, a florid-faced, green-eyed giant with fading red hair.

Kenney had kept his silence up till now. He was more at home in a lab than a conference room.

He stood and moved to a computer and illuminated the wall screen.

For 40 minutes he showed crime scene photos, mutilated corpses and body dissections. As he scrolled the autopsy photos, he zoomed in on glittering objects in some of the bones. Then he showed ultra-magnified slides of the gleaming fragments of metal left by the weapons.

"We are trying to find out everything about the metals involved — type, manufacturing process and age, if possible."

"We are still comparing fingerprints from the Chicago and Theatre murder scenes. There are literally hundreds involved. That will take time."

Grasso rose and thanked Seurat and Kenney. He addressed them all:

"I don't have to emphasize the pressure that is on us from the powers that be. I have every confidence in you. You'll get any help you need. On a personal note, I'd like to welcome John Taylor back."

Then lowering his voice, he added: "A warning just among ourselves. Be very careful what you say to anyone. Power plays and old interagency rivalries are roiling. Don't give the bastards any fuel."

The men implicitly understood that, of them all, Grasso had the most to lose. His career would implode if they didn't get results. To a man, they would do their damnedest to succeed.

It was now 12.30 p.m. and the meeting ended. Liddell had decided to return to Quantico with Kenney for further lab work.

Taylor volunteered to go back to the theatre to talk to staff. He had to admit to himself it did occur to him he might run into Ann.

CHAPTER 33

The expert on the historical manuscripts and books at the Croft library was employed by the rich University which endowed it. She appeared to Taylor to be surprisingly young. He had expected an elderly, stuffy librarian. Rachel Phillips was in her late 30s, handsome and quick to smile.

He had peeked into the theatre on his arrival, but the stage was dark with no sign of the actors. A blackboard straddling an aisle announced a rehearsal at 4.45 p.m. in bold chalk letters. He had climbed the stairs to the library where Miss Phillips was waiting for him.

"The book that is missing is irreplaceable, quite priceless," she told Taylor. "But of course, it means nothing when one weighs it against the death of a young man."

"What made the book so special," asked Taylor. "Was it its age? Its content? Was it written by a famous man?

"No, Mr. Taylor. It belongs to the very beginning of the 16th Century. It just qualifies as an incunambulam — being printed just before 1501, and it belonged to a child. It's a gilded and illustrated Book of Hours.

"Richly handwritten and painted, it offered a prayer for every hour of the day and special texts for important dates in the ecclesiastical calendar.

This particular book was probably read every day by the young boy who became Henry VIII of England.

"The guy with the wives," Taylor smiled.

"That's the one," replied Miss Phillips. "So you can see its importance. It's a beautiful book; its covers are jewel encrusted and it was probably one of his most cherished possessions as a child."

"What are the chances of getting it back?" asked Taylor.

"Not very good, I'm afraid. We have notified the international insurance groups who run a special art theft security network and, on your advice, your own special FBI art recovery unit. They have issued descriptions of the book to art dealers, libraries and collectors throughout the world, International police art theft specialists have also been alerted.

"But this book is so distinctive it would be impossible to sell it publicly. There are a few underworld dealers who might buy it and sell to private collectors. I'm afraid it could just disappear into some private hands and that's the last we'll see of it."

"How difficult was it for the intruder to steal the book?" said Taylor.

"It had been in a glass case .The lock was smashed open. It seems the thief made his way up from the theatre wing. I think he must have been hiding down there until the security people left.

We are limited in the amount we can budget for security," she sighed.

"There were actually many books that arguably were more valuable than the Book of Hours. None of them seem to have been taken. It looks as if the thief ignored them. It's very puzzling to us."

Taylor thanked the young woman for her time and walked downstairs to the theatre lobby. It was 4.30 p.m. He was just in time to see Ann enter the building.

She was wearing a white blouse open at the neck revealing a thread of gold chain. Her long legs showed off snug light blue jeans. He was pleased when she broke into a grin on seeing him.

"How is everything," she said. "Anything new?"

Taylor found himself automatically pulling his stomach in and straightening his posture.

"Were charging ahead, but it looks like a long road. When does your rehearsal finish? Perhaps we could meet for a drink or something and I'll try to fill you in."

"I can't tonight," she said. "I have things to do."

"Not to worry," said Taylor and made to leave, feeling slightly foolish at such a clumsy attempt to meet her.

"What about tomorrow," she called back with a disarming smile. "Dinner?"

"You're on," Taylor said. "I'll telephone you to confirm a time."

"Great," she said. She disappeared into the darkened theatre, leaving a wisp of perfume in his nostrils.

CHAPTER 34

Taylor spent the day sifting through the files and dossiers he had been given during his visit to FBI headquarters. Reading the material and the in-house memos, he began to realize the huge scope of the investigation and the myriad police forces involved.

At 3 p.m. he lunched on tomato soup, milk, and a cheese and lettuce sandwich. No beer today. That was becoming a bad habit. He called Ann and left a message on her cell phone. Like him, she preferred to monitor calls at her leisure. He would meet her in the cocktail bar of the Watergate Hotel at 7 p.m.

He followed up by making a reservation in the hotel restaurant He found himself unashamedly trying to ensure she would realize he was more than just some hard-nosed cop.

Taylor sipped a Manhattan as he waited for Ann at the small, horseshoe-shaped cocktail bar of the hotel. The bar, on a raised platform and tucked into a corner overlooked the lushly carpeted lounge and the canopied entrance.

He savored the bite of the drink and nibbled on pretzels from a glass bowl on the bar. Opposite him three British television executives engaged in noisy and forced conversation. They were there for a sales campaign to American distributors.

He could tell she had arrived by following the barman's admiring gaze toward the entrance. Ann looked stunning. Her golden hair shining, her full but shapely figure clad in a form fitting, above-the-knee, sleeveless dress. Her honey skin seemed to glow. She carried a small Gucci purse. Gone was the troubled, unkempt actress. He was looking at a sophisticated woman; a strong, glamorous woman. He suddenly felt out of his depth.

She smiled and walked towards him. He felt awkward and didn't know how to greet her. She solved that by lightly taking his arm and offering her cheek. He bussed it briefly, feeling heady from the scent of her.

"Shall we just go down to the restaurant?" she asked.

Taylor had booked a table at the hotel's Aquarelle restaurant.

"Perfect," she said. "I'm starving."

After tipping the barman, they crossed the center of the lounge and turned down a stairway to the lower levels of the hotel and the restaurant.

Taylor was about to identify himself to the Maitre D' but was cut short.

"Miss Powell," he beamed. "Delighted to see you again. How is your grandfather?"

"He's fine, thank you," she looked at Taylor subtly putting him at ease and added: "And so am I."

The dinner was excellent. They both had a chilled Red Pepper Gazpacho soup. The soup was light but spiced to perfection. Taylor ordered the premium Hereford Beef filet mignon and was delighted when Ann tucked into grilled lamb chops and Merques sausage. Taylor could barely pronounce the name of the red wine she approved from the sommelier but it was light and easy on his palate.

Throughout the meal she had asked questions about the murder inquiry, which he had answered guardedly. Then, over lavender honey ice cream and coffee, they began to explore each other's lives.

He found himself telling her about his career beginnings in New York and his disgust with the cronyism in the police and then to his dismay at the former FBI political infrastructure. He had leapt at the one-year arrangement with the University, with its secret promise of a way out of the Agency, then ran into the same damn politics. He talked about his work and then his frustration at the University. He cut himself short. God! He sounded like such a whiner.

She listened intently, gently anchoring his confidence.

She told him how she had been drawn to acting to conquer painful shyness and a loneliness that never quite went away. The fact that her parents died when she was a child. She had grown up in a large house, an only child. Make believe and imagination had been her childhood playmates.

Her grandfather was still alive, in his 80s but still active in various charities the family had funded. Scion of an old colonial family he had served a term as Lt. Governor of their state.

They had cognac and she suddenly wrinkled her nose and began laughing.

"Oh God, I think I'm drunk."

"I'm not far behind you," Taylor said. He signaled for the bill.

"Do you think I could see you to your door, Miss."

"It's still early," she said. "You can walk me to the door, walk through the door and have a nightcap," she teased.

CHAPTER 35

Now it was morning. Their lovemaking had been full of lust and need. A voyeur witnessing their joining would have described it as almost desperate, even brutal. But their sensuous struggle and soaring climax had been deeply satisfying for them.

She had risen first and Taylor was once more lost in admiration as he saw the flawless body through the shower glass as she bathed.

He moved downstairs to the kitchen of her duplex. The sun was sparkling on the waters of the Potomac and dappling the white ceiling.

He found eggs in the refrigerator. Taking a glass bowl from the cupboard, he covered the base with water then broke four large eggs. He salted and peppered them, then scrambled them pouring them into a skillet with melting butter. On each of two plates he placed a slice of toasted bread and poured the eggs over them. The coffee was percolating, a jug of tomato juice was cool and fresh and all was well with the world. She joined him and he enjoyed watching her hearty appetite.

There was no tension, no awkwardness

following their carnal night. He felt a contentment steal over him. It was Saturday and even cops are allowed a day off, he thought.

"Let's plan a lazy brunch, somewhere," he said.

He smiled at Ann but was met with a frown. The old guarded look had come back to Ann's face.

"I don't think so," she said almost coldly. Then, "I'm sorry, really. I have things to do."

Taylor felt the warmth slipping away and wondered where he had gone wrong.

Christ! I'm too old for these games, he thought. But he smiled and said: "That's OK. I've got enough to keep me busy. I'll call you later."

"Maybe tomorrow," she corrected. "I've got to get dressed now."

He felt like a little boy who had just been dismissed. He quickly dressed and shouted a cheerless goodbye as he left the apartment.

After the quick walk home across the bridge to Georgetown, he let himself into the canal loft.

The red light was pulsing on his answering machine. She's changed her mind," he hoped.

But it was Liddell, asking him to call back urgently and stop turning his fucking cell phone off.

He called the agent's Virginia home.

"You called, Master," Taylor joked.

"Yeah. Something's come up," said Liddell. "We've got a lot of puzzling but possibly promising stuff coming in over the computers. We've got search engines combing the world."

"That all?" asked Taylor.

"No. They have discovered something that could be quite sinister. Someone, somewhere in the world, is running a similar search program. These are not random hackers. They are organized and are being fed secret pass codes at the highest levels. It's coming out of Europe and it doesn't look like the British."

"We'd better get everyone together on this one," Taylor advised.

"Yup. See you later," Liddell's gruff voice seemed tired.

CHAPTER 36
NEW YORK
(Two months earlier)

The white, red and green fuselage of the Alitalia jet speared through the scattered cloud cover over the wetlands and factories of northern New Jersey and landed at Newark Airport a few minutes before its scheduled 2 p.m. arrival.

After passing customs and immigration, Salemi went to the main hall. There, a uniformed chauffeur held up a sign for "Salami." He didn't bother to correct the man.

Storms in the plains had disrupted air traffic from St. Louis and Chicago, and the airport was filled with frustrated passengers angry at delays. Baggage in hand, Salemi and the driver went straight to the limousine.

Just before curving into the Lincoln Tunnel, the road revealed a spectacular view of the south tip of the island of Manhattan. Salemi never failed to be stirred by the classic silhouette of the city skyline. But, with sadness, he still pictured in the cognitive recesses of his mind the old ill-fated twin towers of the World Trade Center.

They emerged into the bustle and noise of the West Side and crawled behind cross-town traffic to a private, church-owned, red-brick building on Madison Avenue near St. Patrick's Cathedral.

There, an Auxiliary Bishop greeted Salemi, barely hiding his surprise at the visitor's relative youth compared to his title. Standing quietly next to a shrouded window was the small, slight figure of an older priest.

A man in his late 70s, Father James Orr had apple red cheeks. His eyes were blue gray, intense but mischievous, hinting at the brilliant mind behind them.

The old priest and Salemi shook hands.

"We presumed you would want private quarters," said Orr. "I'll take you there myself. The driver can bring your bags later. It's a grand day for a walk," said Orr with a slight clap of his hands.

The two men left the Cathedral and walked north for a block, then turned east toward the river. Just before First Avenue they stopped at a brownstone, its ground-floor windows barred.

Orr fished for a key. A friend of the Church lets us use it," he said mysteriously.

Inside, Salemi found a large stone kitchen stocked with food. Throughout the house, furniture and wooden floors were highly polished. The faint smell of lilac-scented wax permeated the house.

Insulated windows reduced the traffic noise to a faint buzz.

The men entered an elegant living room on the second floor. Its contents looked as if they had been unchanged for 100 years.

"Bishop di Montevecchi sends his warmest regards and his prayers," Salemi told Orr.

He decided to quickly reassure the older man and went on rather formally. "As for myself, I am honored to have the opportunity to work with you.

"It is a very important cause and the Bishop tells me you are the one to help us with this journey."

"Journey?"

"One way or another, we believe this is a journey; a very dangerous one, but one which could be most important for our Church."

Orr leaned forward in his armchair and pulled a cigarette case from a jacket pocket.

"I'm your man," he said with a slight Ulster accent, his eyes shining with enthusiasm. "You don't mind if I smoke. I'm a bit long in the tooth to give it up now."

"Whatever makes you comfortable," Salemi said resignedly. "We have a long, busy road ahead of us."

"You'll find the computers have been installed and are up and running. They are in a dayroom upstairs that we have converted into an office."

Salemi noticed that two sets of desks had been placed at either end of the large room. The old man was making sure he got involved. That was all right; he would need all the help he could find.

The following day, Orr arrived at the brownstone bearing coffee and hot buttered bagels from a neighborhood deli.

Salemi had carefully sifted the material he carried and gave the old priest a heavily bowdlerized version. For the moment, some things must remain a secret from the old man.

Orr reached in his pocket for gold-rimmed half glasses and perched them rakishly on his nose.

He read intently for 10 minutes, a puzzled expression growing on his face.

"Forgive me, Monsignor, I'm not clear on this ... this matter.

"I see a pattern of killings, suspicious deaths and art and weapons thefts in Europe. Do we believe they will happen here, in the U.S.?"

"I think they have begun already," said Salemi grimly. "I think they have begun in Chicago."

"I'll call our travel agency right now," said Orr.

The old priest leaned forward and without using the arm rests seemed to jump from the chair onto nimble feet. There was no apparent age in these strong legs.

The athletic move was meant to impress Salemi. He smiled — it had. Di Montevecchi was right. The old man would be an asset to their quest.

CHAPTER 37
WILCHESTER, MASS.
(The present)

He had hidden in the tall grasses and white flowered weeds at the side of the abandoned railway line. The sinking sun glinted off the old factory windows that now housed the museum.

He needed more instruments of death. Old steel for fresh blood. Possessions from his time — a talismanic link ensuring his return.

Just before twilight fell, he had jimmied a long-forgotten basement door. The rotting planks which had been nailed over it cracked and splintered easily, sending a covey of spiders scampering over his hands and along the cracked brick and iron walls.

He had watched the last visitors leave; followed 20 minutes later by the curators and the volunteers who staffed a small historical bookshop inside the museum.

Now he made his way through long-ago abandoned rusting objects to creaking wooden stairs and a trap door. At the third strenuous push, the seal of grime and rust broke and the door lifted. He emerged in a corridor of the museum and climbed stone steps to the second-floor balcony.

Below him, glittering like ice, were hundreds of spears and swords; weapons of every description, every historic period. Bills and halbeards from Germany, swords from Rome and Carthage and Japan.

Looking down in the dying light, he saw the sinister silhouette; an effigy of a full size courser, with a crouching knight holding a sharp tipped lance.

His eyes adjusted to the light. The black horse and knight's armor was intricately embossed and engraved. His hellish dragon-winged helmet, in the Austrian style, was limned by a dark purple wall banner.

All along the walls of the two floors were armor and weapons from the ages. At intervals, signs were posted: "Do Not Touch Weapons or Armor."

The truly valuable pieces were kept in glass cases and arranged by time period. He paused and slipped into the shadows against the wall. Someone's footsteps at the other end of the hall.

He smashed a case and felt the polished wood and leather handle of the axe. The noise of breaking glass brought the stranger hurrying toward him. Perfect.

As the man, tall but slight, stepped past him he spun out of the shadow and chopped the axe into the startled victim's knee. As the man clutched the gaping wound he backhanded his fist into the victim's throat, rupturing his windpipe and silencing his scream.

The janitor fell, trembling from shock and the inability to breathe.

He knelt and looked at the janitor's face. A mask of fear, agony, shock; life draining away.

He put his arms under the struggling body, pushed up with his legs and launched the janitor over the balcony. There was a muted grunt as the body was impaled on the lance of the ghostly tournament figure below.

The evening was proving satisfying in unexpected ways.

CHAPTER 38
WASHINGTON, D.C.

"Who the fuck could be duplicating our Web searches, and why?" asked Taylor.

They had all gathered in the afternoon in the drab conference room; Grasso, Taylor, Liddell, Bob Seurat and the lab man Kenncy.

They were angry and frustrated at the news of outside interference.

"We've been trying to track them down since this morning. Our computer boys say so far they have covered their trail pretty effectively. But the source of the pattern search is still a mystery," Seurat replied.

Liddell knew that sources like the FBI's DNA database of over half a million criminals were off limits to the public. But he had little knowledge of how much was out there for the public.

"How difficult is it for a normal Joe to put together an efficient Web search?" asked Liddell.

"It's getting easier every day," said Seurat. "New Web sites are flowering each week. You can call up one site that will tell you the movements, destinations and passengers on board all private jets in the world. You go on-line with Nasa satellite and view, within one square foot anywhere you want on earth. There is so much out there it is almost impossible to keep current.

"But our sophisticated search patterns would be above the resources of the normal computer hacker. We have entree to secure files around the world. That's why this mystery twin search is so disturbing.

"What about the British?" said Taylor. "They've got a lot at stake."

"The liaison man at the Embassy claims it's not them. But he concedes one of the cloak-and-dagger branches of the Brit government might be doing their own covert checks. MI5, MI6 or some like-minded bunch.

"The director is going to put pressure on State and the British Foreign Office. If it is them, and they find something, we want to know, pronto," said Seurat.

"Could it be the news media?" Kenney asked.

"There is always that chance, but it is unlikely they would engage in such a widespread, sophisticated program. We are talking about combing through incidents of this violent nature throughout the world for the last 20 years. We are gathering data on all thefts of precious library materials, anything that might shed light on the crimes.

“We are going through extensive lists of criminals and psychos who might be our boy, or boys. It doesn't help, of course, that we have never had an eye witness or a description of the killer."

Seurat described a massive computer search. Killings with the slightest similarities were gathered over the Internet and collated by analysts.

Taylor shared the unease of the men at not being able to strictly control the crime enquiries. Interference by unknown or even known sources was anathema to their professional pride.

He tried to lighten the mood and quipped: "Well, the good news is we might be able to tap into their Web search and find out what we have neglected to do."

He was met by a fleeting, hostile stare from Seurat. Liddell deflected the barb by turning to Ted Kenney.

"Anything new on the weapons, Ted?"

"It seems we are dealing with a range of cutting and stabbing implements. The medical examiners involved in the cases have all — to some degree or another — made transparencies of the flesh wounds. We have tried to match them with a range of weapons, from plain axes to machetes. The fragmented metallurgical evidence is still being tested. We should be able to eliminate some weapons, speculate about others. But we are talking about minute slivers of metal embedded in bone."

"What about one of these Japanese Samurai swords?" offered Liddle.

“We're checking that. The countless folds and tempering method involved in forging these weapons is unique. We should know one way or the other in the next few weeks.

“We have armor experts offering comparison samples from historic weapons from all over the globe. As you can imagine that’s a lot of swords, axes and knives.

Grasso thanked Kenney for his information and went on to the next subject he had scribbled in a memorandum book.

"Psychological profile." he began.

"We now have undercover men staking out the murder spots and grave sites of those corpses released and buried, in case their killer — if he is a loner — goes back. They believe the killings—if linked- are most likely the work of one man.

"Many of these types cannot resist going back, stealing a look at these areas, even symbolically rolling in the dirt.

"If it is one man, he is obviously very strong and athletic, capable of great speed and fueled by powerful emotions and aggression.

"The target could be the Prince of Wales, except for the theatre murder. Again, the only tenuous link there is the Royal book stolen, but that may fit in with his attention to things Royal. We believe it is important to his profile.

"It could be that he is some crazed Royal memorabilia collector who doesn't mind killing anyone in his way. He killed near the Prince's pavilion, which contained some personal effects of the Prince. The Embassy also had some precious Royal artifacts, and the theatre library. That's why we are adding a list of break-ins and thefts from buildings containing Royal possessions or historical relics. They would also fetch a fortune on the art black market," Grasso went on.

"Finally we have the question raised by the Theatre murder. Is there a gay lifestyle link?

"We have discovered that one of the victims in the Embassy murders had gay contacts — the Chancery servant Jules Pettifer. Scotland Yard turned up numerous contacts in London who reported he was homosexual. However, that, rightly, did not affect his security clearance in any way. We are trying to find out if he had any sexual encounters in the Washington area — and if he visited the S & M scene here."

It was a Friday afternoon, and the weather forecasters had called for a warm Indian summer weekend.

Grasso stood up to signal the meeting's end.

He looked at weary faces of his team and decided: "I think we should all take the weekend off.

Reintroduce yourself to your families. Do some gardening, clear your mind."

"Aye to that," said a weary Seurat.

"What about you, Oh bachelor one," Liddell asked Taylor.

"I've promised to go up and see Dr. Samuels in New York. I'll see him then just laze around. Maybe take in a Broadway show, Watch the girls jog in Central Park. Just kick back," said Taylor.

"Can't be bad," said Liddell.

CHAPTER 39

The rush-hour traffic had begun in mid-afternoon. Thousands of commuters taking an early exit from their offices to catch what promised to be the last pleasant summer weather.

Taylor eventually found a cabby who under Washington's peculiar taxi laws picked up a couple and deposited them at a Dupont Circle hotel before driving on to Georgetown.

Taylor decided to cool his frustration with a long, stinging shower. He dried himself and called Dr. Samuels in New York. They arranged to meet at the doctor's apartment building.

Then Taylor called the Beekman Hotel, his favorite home-away-from-home on East 49th Street in Manhattan.

As it was an off-season weekend, they had room for him. They would even upgrade their old customer to a suite facing the river. They looked forward to seeing him in the morning. Taylor hung up and opened a beer. It was cold and frothy. He made a mental note to visit the Heidelberg Restaurant up in what used to be Manhattan's Germantown, the Yorkville area at East 86th street.

There he would sit in the bar and drink cold, foamy Erdinger Krystal Weissbier.

The telephone rang and he started from his reverie.

"Have I gotten you at a bad time? It's Ann."

Her voice seemed warm, friendly, the opposite of her recent, apparently hostile farewell.

"I'm sorry if I was a bitch the other morning. I don't know what to say. Anyway, I don't want you to get the impression I have any regrets, or anything."

There was a silence, which Taylor drew out, as if to scold her. But he was jubilant that she had called.

He decided to be direct. "When can we get together?"

"Whenever you want," she said brightly, a palpable relief in her voice, which caused Taylor's heart to bound.

She went on: "I had planned to visit a friend down in Virginia to do some horse riding. But that looks like it's fallen through."

"Will you settle for a carriage pony in Central Park tomorrow?" he asked with a laugh.

"You kidding?" shrieked Ann.

"Never more serious in my life," he replied, meaning every word.

They decided to meet at Union Station and share breakfast at one of the gallery restaurants in the thriving mall of the railroad station.

Ann had been happy to go along with traveling by train, not air. It seemed all very civilized and unhurried to her. The way a relationship should develop. Though she felt a growing hunger for his muscular hard body and had no regrets at their hasty lovemaking a few days earlier, she liked the idea of restraint. At least outside the bedroom.

After their first night of frantic love making she had awakened and panicked. She had insulated her feelings, her vulnerability, for too long. She did not want the risk of disappointment. But now, here she was, and she was enjoying every second of being with him.

At the stroke of 10 a.m., the silver Acela pulled slowly away from the platform and began its two-hour and 45-minute journey north to New York.

They both read newspapers sitting back in their First-Class seats, occasionally watching the countryside fly by. They felt warm and relaxed in their mutual company. Almost like old companions.

Taylor found himself speculating on a future with this beautiful woman.

As they stepped onto the platform at New York's Pennsylvania Station, a Skycap took their two light traveling bags. Thirty yards behind them, a man jumped lightly from the rear of the train carrying a garment bag. He watched them closely. Keeping his distance, he followed them through the crowds to the yellow-cab stand up on street level.

The tall red-brick building, once an East Side landmark, had a view of the East River and the bridges spanning it. Still an elegant anachronism, it was dwarfed by the ugly glass rectangles of the UN Plaza building next to the United Nations gardens. Just to the south loomed the 861 foot, black glass cube of the Trump World Tower.

Ann and Taylor were shown to a small suite on the upper floors. They both felt awkward when the porter retired from the room.

She broke the ice by circling his neck with her arms. The sexual heat in both their bodies rose and he strongly guided her to the queen-size bed, hastily ripping off the heavy bedspread and throwing it to the floor. Their love making was quick, intense, almost ravenous.

Afterward, they dozed for 20 minutes, letting a soft breeze from the river cool their exposed bodies.

"I have to see the doctor, now," said Taylor, rising from the crumpled bed.

"Was I too much for your heart?" she laughed.

"Very droll," smiled Taylor. "I have to see Dr. Samuels to brief him.

"Oh, the poor man. You take as long as you need. I can plan some shopping this afternoon. I'll grab a salad in between doing the stores. When do you think you might be finished?"

"I'll head back here for 5 p.m.," said Taylor. "Have fun till then."

Taylor had been to the doctor's Central Park West apartment many times before. These had been jovial occasions. Drinks with the doctor's neighbors before opera evenings at the Met.

Now the building seemed as faded and forlorn as the doctor himself. It would not be long before realtors swooped in and gutted it for the legion of showbiz and Wall Street types who were throwing millions at park properties. It was an old building and still carried the luxury of doormen who operated the clanking elevators.

The Doctor, as was his old world custom, insisted on meeting his guest at the elevator and formally thanking the operator.

He was aging, badly. His cheeks sunken, his eyes bleary and liverish. He had always been a moderate drinker in Taylor's company. Perhaps that had changed.

Most of the rooms in the vast apartment were unused. Dust covers were draped over furniture. Like many fate had condemned to loneliness, the doctor had made a snug retreat within the emptiness of his home. He had moved a small bed into his large library and for most purposes lived there.

They talked briefly about old times, current times, then the Doctor sighed, lit one of his cheroots and looked expectantly at Taylor.

"All we can say for certain at this point, Daniel, is that the husband had nothing to do with it. He's not much of a man, not much of anything, but you can rest assured it wasn't him.

"In fact, it's looking as if Lucy was just in the wrong place at the wrong time."

He searched for the right words, un-hurtful words. "We think she might have had some sort of ... date with the other victim."

The Doctor interrupted him. "You can call it what it was. Lucy had a mind of her own. She was a strong, independent woman like her mother. If her husband was playing around, she would feel free to do the same," he said.

"But why all the mystery, the stone-walling from the police?"

Peals of laughter from the park and a passing police siren spilled in through a half open window. The doctor rose and shut out the unwelcome sounds of humanity.

"Why?" he asked once more.

"Daniel. It seems she may have stumbled into something very big; a whole series of murders involving a very important target. You know the English Prince was there at the time. There is a possibility he may have been the murderer's intended victim. There have been more killings in Washington that we think may possibly be linked to this."

Taylor struggled to explain the star-crossed spatial and time coincidence that had cost his friend's daughter her life.

Samuels saw his discomfort and held up a hand, as if that could calm Taylor's mental turmoil.

"What you have told me helps. Believe me, John, I could never have rested if that bastard she married had harmed her. Now I feel no guilt about allowing that marriage. But I have the guilt of outliving my little darling. That — I will take to the grave."

The Doctor had offered Taylor a beer, but both men felt an unspoken need to end the sad meeting.

"Perhaps we could have brunch tomorrow," said Taylor, rising to leave.

"If not tomorrow, some other time, perhaps, John."

“Sure," said Taylor. "I will stay in touch."

As he crossed the street into the park, Taylor could not restrain his relief at being released from that dark mausoleum which had become the Doctor's apartment.

The contrast between that gray retreat and the green, gold and red of the changing leaves in the park reminded him of leaving the gloom of a tunnel and walking into bright sunshine.

Around him, New York was at play on a warm, inviting day. A buzz and whir of roller-bladers, cyclists, joggers and carriage horses animated the park.

He walked south-eastward past the dusty baseball diamonds and the strolling families. His heart felt for the Doctor and his timeless grief but it was a beautiful day, and he was on his way to spend the night with a beautiful woman. Life has to go on, he rationalized. And life and the future were looking decidedly inviting to him for the first time in years.

When he got back to the hotel, Ann had still not returned. Probably marching back from Bloomingdale's with her hands full of the store's famous brown-bag packages, he surmised.

He left a note asking her to meet him at the open-air terrace at the top of the hotel tower. It would be a perfect spot for a beer and a cocktail before steaks at the Palm Too on Second Avenue.

He sipped a beer and watched the traffic crawl north along First Avenue.

In the late afternoon, the long light washed the surrounding buildings the color of rose-gold. Purples, reds and blues slowly tinged the brick and stone. A light breeze riffled in from the river

It brought back memories of happier days in New York — lazy days exploring the museums, his favorite paintings at the Frick Collection.

He looked down at the southern tip of Roosevelt Island. He thought he saw a figure move in the shadowy ruins of the fenced-off, long abandoned ruin of a plague and smallpox hospital.

Then a hand gently touched his shoulder. He looked up to see Ann silhouetted, her hair back-lit by the falling sun.

He remembered the Impressionist painter Claude Monet's haunting belief: "Everything is ephemeral, but sometimes the ephemeral is divine."

CHAPTER 40
ROOSEVELT ISLAND, THE EAST RIVER.

He felt strangely at home here. He smelled the salt coming off the Atlantic water that raced into the tidal basin known as the East River. Seagulls quarreled with a flock of crows in a swirling black and white dance over some fish scraps on the rocky outcrop of the island.

The screams of the birds echoed down to the ruins and joined the other screams he could hear.

The tortured voices of those who had agonized in the 19th Century mental asylum fire, the moans of the diseased and insane banished to the rocky islet. Voices caught in time. They, in turn, prompted his own demons. The whispering began again—incessant, demanding.

He needed re-assurance he would return.

He would kill again within an hour.

CHAPTER 41
METROPOLITAN MUSEUM, FIFTH AVENUE

Elspeth de la Tour was tired yet happy. One more week should see her back in England to put the final chapters of her history of arms and armor safely into the hands of the University Press editors.

She had just been told that a BBC documentary producer wanted to contact her about a possible television series on her work. The months of travel and study seemed to be paying off.

A consultant to the Royal Armory in Leeds, England, she had arranged to visit the vast collections of the Metropolitan Museum.

The museum staff had warmed to the earnest, petite Englishwoman. Her polite way of dealing with them and her determined efforts to lift and handle some of the heavier weapons without assistance endeared her to them. Throughout the summer a van had shuttled weekly across midtown from the vast museum warehouses on First Avenue bringing the items she requested.

After a few days, they trusted her to work alone and unsupervised. She came and went without fuss, working in a ground-level room at the rear of the museum, adjoining Central Park.

That balmy afternoon, while it seemed most of New York was enjoying the Park, Elspeth worked under the artificial light of spot lamps in the basement area. She had selected a series of early 16th Century weapons and laid them on a large, gray, metal gurney. She had received permission to photograph them for the illustrative plates of her book.

She was becoming impatient waiting for the commercial photographer who had been approved by the museum authorities.

She walked to the park side of the basement and tripped open a metal fire exit door. The sunlight blinded her at first.

She pulled off the cotton gloves she was wearing to protect the metals from destructive human skin oils and pulled a crumpled pack of cigarettes from her shirt pocket. She lit one. The cigarette smoke lingered in the sweet fruity air. Autumn was almost here, she decided.

She frowned. Where was that damned photographer?

She returned to the basement leaving a crack in the door where light sliced into the shadows. It would be quicker for the photographer to come this way than work his way through the maze of offices and exhibitions above, she thought. She returned to the gleaming objects. She heard the faint noise of the moving door and from the periphery of her vision saw the chink of light widen into a swath, then abruptly vanish.

At last, he's here.

She spoke to the shadows.

"I'm over here, Gene. I'd almost given up on you."

Then some atavistic sense alerted her. Something was wrong. The barely silhouetted figure was too large to be Gene. He was hurrying now toward her from the darkness. She could feel the violent intent, feel its onrush.

CHAPTER 42

Taylor and Ann were awakened by a polite knock on their suite door from room service. They had ordered breakfast the night before when, tired but happy, they returned to the hotel. They had made love tenderly this time. Holding onto each other until sleep crept over them.

It was 9 a.m. and a waiter wheeled in a large carafe of mimosa, two egg-white omelets and mushrooms, coffee and croissants.

The hotel had also provided the late editions of the New York Sunday newspapers.

Ann pulled on a silk gown and wandered into the living room area of the suite where the breakfast had been set up. She grabbed the weighty front section of the Times and poured the champagne cocktail into two glasses.

Taylor was left with the tabloid papers. The murder was splashed across Page One of the Post and The Daily News.

At the same time, the telephone shrilled harshly. Taylor grabbed the receiver.

"Have you heard?" the familiar gruff voice asked.

"I'm reading about it just now, dammit," said Taylor.

"Looks like you will be staying in the wicked city," said Liddell. "I'm getting the noon shuttle up there. Can you fix me a room with the hotel?"

"Consider it done," Taylor said as he started to put the telephone back in its cradle.

"Hold on," Liddell shouted. "There's more. We have a very suspicious death up in Massachusetts, at a museum of weapons and armor, no less."

"It can't be a coincidence," said Taylor. "I'll pick you up from the shuttle. I'm going to drop Ann there for a return flight. See you there."

Ann had noted the sudden tension in Taylor and the laconic telephone call. She looked at the tabloid headlines lying on the table.

"Oh, God," she cried. "Is it him? It won't stop. Will it?"

The memories of Gerry came flooding back and streamed in tears from her eyes. She felt Taylor's solid chest against her head, his arms encircling her.

"We don't know yet. It appears the victim was slashed to death. It could be him. Don't worry, babe. If it's him, I promise you he'll be stopped. But first of all let's get you back to Washington, well away from this horror. I'll have to stay."

"I understand," she said, regaining her composure. Then her fighting streak re-emerged and Taylor felt proud of her.

"You just get the bastard. But be careful. Promise me."

"I promise," said Taylor, already impatient to renew the hunt for the killer.

CHAPTER 43

The New York field office of the FBI dropped off a powerful, deep-blue sports utility vehicle in front of the hotel at 11 a.m.

It took Taylor 20 minutes through light traffic to reach the Marine Air Terminal at La Guardia where the shuttle planes arrived.

He kissed Ann goodbye and watched heads turn as she moved with graceful, athletic strides up the sloping walkway past the small square coffee bar to the departure gates.

A meaty hand pinched his arm. It was Liddell.

"Did they send us a car?"

Taylor pointed to the sparkling new vehicle, double-parked near rows of yellow cabs.

"It's all ours," he said. "Very efficient boys in New York. Very impressive."

Taylor got behind the wheel. He pulled out of the terminal and remembering his N.Y.P.D. days, impressed Liddell by taking shortcuts through the streets and avenues of Queens.

"Tell me about Massachusetts," he said.

"It was red-flagged by the computer search pattern. A suspicious death with a high alert factor. It occurred in a museum of arms and armor just two days ago."

Like most trained criminologists, Taylor and Liddell did not believe in coincidence.

Taylor blasted his horn at a yellow cab cutting across his path and returned the finger greeting from the taxi driver.

"The New York's coming out of you," laughed Liddell.

"Sorry, Eugene. Please go on."

"The museum is in a former mill in Wilchester. A temporary guard was found impaled on the lance of a tournament exhibit. He appears to have fallen, jumped or been thrown from a balcony above. His leg had been half severed by some sort of weapon.

"The guy's 38, a continual loser. Problems with booze and drugs and an ex-wife. He has been known to ramble in local pubs about ending it all. The museum officials are checking for any missing weapons or armor. So far, one weapon, a type of axe, is unaccounted for, its glass case smashed.

"There are signs of forced entry at one of the basement doors adjacent to a rail line. Wood boarding had been removed. But the local cops say that the disused rail line is frequented by transients and scavengers. They may have taken the wood for a lean-to or campfires.

"I was going to suggest we take a run up there, then this Met stuff hit the fan."

Taylor took the Midtown Tunnel, and turned right onto Third Avenue. At 44th Street, he headed over to First Avenue, made a left turn, swung out to the far lane and up five blocks to the hotel, where Liddell registered.

Liddell made a telephone call and within 40 minutes a local FBI Agent Carlos Badillo and a liaison officer from N.Y.P.D. HQ in downtown Center Street arrived in an unmarked police car.

The four men were at the museum 15 minutes later. They parked in the Museum's underground car park and were ushered by detectives into the basement murder area. Blood still soaked the floor. A technician was measuring spatter marks. Another photographed the stains and a third marked their position on a chart.

Taylor looked at the crime scene, then at photographs of the victim.

"It's getting even more scary, Eugene. This prick is out of control."

"I agree," said Liddell grimly.

"But where's the link with Royalty here? Is it the weapons or the armor."

Taylor turned to Geoffrey Landon, a slight balding museum official who seemed about to be overcome by nausea.

"Any ideas, Mr. Landon?"

"We do have some famous armor here," said Landon.

"Complete suits that were made for or worn by European kings and nobles.

"These are either in storage or on display upstairs. But there was nothing down here that could be described that way."

"And the victim?" asked Taylor.

"They have to be the tops in their field to work with us here," Landon sniffed.

"She was a presentable woman. A competent scholar. Very dedicated. She had been here for seven weeks. A true expert. She was a consultant for the Royal Armory in England, A great loss to the field of arms and armor."

He checked himself and added: "Of course, her death is a greater loss, I mean, an awful thing."

He excused himself. They could hear him trying to stifle involuntary retching as he walked swiftly into a corridor of the basement.

Liddell glared and Taylor raised an eyebrow and counseled him: "Don't be too angry at him. I'm sure he really feels for the woman. He's been in academia too long, that's all.

"He's still a pompous little shit," growled Liddell.

Liddell turned to the liaison officer, Badillo.

"Murder weapon or weapons?"

"She was hacked pretty good as you can see in the crime shots. We've got people and the museum staff checking every item in the arms department. It looked like someone took a butcher's knife to her. They are going to work right through the night to inventory everything. As soon as we know, you will know. We already think at least two weapons might be missing.

Taylor asked for and was given a complete plan of the museum and the exits, entrances and storage areas. He had not realized how huge the building was. With the treasures it contained, security was formidable. But wherever you had thousands of members of the public visiting every day, and a huge number of technicians and staff, there would always be the chance to slip through the defenses. You might not be able to steal a masterpiece, but it would be possible to get into the building's recesses.

The men walked to the most obvious exit point — the slatted metal door leading out back.

Crime scene technicians were on all fours, bagging anything small or large that was in the yard. Several cigarette butts had been placed in separate plastic bags. They would be tested for DNA. One never knew what piece would fit the eventual jigsaw puzzle. Trace amounts of blood were collected from the concrete path leading from the door.

The warmth of the weekend had faded. The temperature had dropped 20 degrees and a West wind warned of a cold front on the way.

"Let's get a drink back at the hotel," said Taylor, "and try to work out what the hell is happening."

They bid Badillo and the other agent farewell and decided to walk down Fifth Avenue and then East on 57th.

Both were deep in thought, and kept their silence. Both were proud professionals and their frustration was mounting. They were being made to look like fools.

CHAPTER 44
CENTRAL PARK

Darkness had fallen and the park beckoned. The tingling danger of dark ill-lit paths, secluded, shadowy glades and unknown fellow travelers seeking that fleeting, illicit thrill.

The two men entered the 37-acre area known as The Ramble and began their ritualistic sexual odyssey. The daytime bird watchers had long gone. The men had walked these dark dells and woods many times. Now their arousal came from the anticipation of what was to come. What would be offered to them, who would want them and in which rough way?

The darkness, the sounds of leaves shifting in the wind and small animals moving through grass and brush heightened their senses. It was all too hard to explain to their straight friends. An intoxicating cocktail of adventure, anticipation and sexual surrender.

They crossed a small bridge over a stream, heard, then saw two dark figures embracing violently under a tree. The lovers were so intent on each other they noticed no one else. Nearby, a solitary older man rhythmically stroked his genitals and looked yearningly at their act.

They left the pornographic tableau and went deeper into The Ramble. It was there that terror came into their lives.

A tall, unkempt figure emerged from the shadows. His forehead and angular nose reflected the yellow hue of a mist-haloed ornamental lamp.

The two men did not hesitate. This was definitely not what they had in mind. They increased their pace. Best to get past him as quickly as possible. This was the wrong sort of danger.

As they drew close, the wild man started to unbutton his grimy raincoat.

"Oh, God, what pathetic thing is he going to flash us," whispered the older of the men.

The axe blade arced and sliced into his groin. He screamed with pain. His young companion, muscled from fastidious hours in the gym, tackled the wild man and battered him into submission.

Within the hour, the assailant was in a holding cage at the Central Park precinct station. His weapon lay in a plastic evidence bag on the steel desk of the night commander.

Taylor was awakened at 3 a.m. by Liddell's sleep-shattering call.

"There's been an axe attack in the park. The weapon looks like the one missing from the Met. And what's more, they got the guy who was swinging it."

"Jesus. When can we get there?"

"There's a patrol car downstairs. It's waiting to take us there. Everyone is scenting headlines on this. The senior Manhattan assistant DAs are all flocking to the stationhouse like its bonus time on Wall Street. The Federal prosecutors won't be far behind. Let's get there quickly before they fuck everything up. I've called the night men at Quantico. They are standing by to help."

The car drove cross-town and entered the damp winding road that cut through the park from Fifth Ave to Central Park West. The car's headlights startled a horde of rats, which scrambled wildly away, disappearing into drainage pipes in the moss-covered walls on either side of the road.

To their left, they found the gabled brick exterior of the 19th Century stationhouse and pulled into a Police Only car park.

Inside the converted stable they introduced themselves to the senior prosecutor and were greeted by Frank Dornblatt, the detective now in charge of the Met homicide investigation. Dornblatt remembered when the stationhouse in the park was so run down that rats, squirrels and mice regularly shared the cramped quarters with the officers, and damp seeped through the tattered walls. The joke then was that the precinct house had been opened in 1870 and last renovated, according to station wags, in 1872.

Now, just a few years after a modern re-decoration, nature and the park's rodent inhabitants were trying to reclaim it.

Dornblatt offered them coffee in Styrofoam cups and ushered them down a stone passageway into a small office.

“The good news is we think we've got the Met killer, and it's someone we know." said Dornblatt.

"The bad news," he paused, "for you, is that he doesn't fit your picture of a serial killer. But I'll let you judge for yourselves."

Dornblatt stood up and led them down a stone corridor along green painted walls to a holding cell.

"Behold," he said wryly.

Taylor and Liddell looked through the bars at the sorry sight that was Arthur Garimov.

He had once been handsome, now in middle age he wore the scowl and the liquid cloudy eyes of an ill-nourished alcoholic.

His face was bruised and bloodied. One ear looked to have swollen to three times its normal size. His clothes were ill fitting and had come from the city's welfare charities. He was fidgeting and talking to himself; a staccato unintelligible dialogue with some invisible being.

He laughed shrilly then began spouting random numbers and the names of planets, as if explaining some astronomical proposition.

"Who gave him the beating?" Taylor asked, hoping it wasn't some overly enthusiastic young beat cop.

"Relax," said Dornblatt.

"He jumped the wrong two guys. Who says fairies aren't tough. The younger guy beat the shit out of him. The axe didn't hit any arteries and the old guy will recover. His nocturnal activities will he sharply curtailed for a while, though."

"What do you know about Garimov?" asked Taylor.

"He's an old story around here," Dornblatt sighed. "And I mean that literally. He's even been written up in the local press. He's schizophrenic. He threatens people living in the East 80s near the park and gets himself locked up. The court sends him to the psych ward. Six months later, the shrinks say he's fit for the streets if he keeps taking his medication, which of course he doesn't. It's a crazy circle that was bound to end with someone being killed. Now the fucking do-gooders and ACLU lawyers have enabled another fucking murder. It's all a farce."

Dornblatt went on: "It looks like the Met murder was a crime of opportunity. Garimov is shuffling through the park and he spots a chink in the Met security. Slips through an open door, grabs a weapon and attacks the female victim. The weapon looks like one of the items listed as missing from the museum. We are trying to track his movements, trying to find out if he has traveled out of the New York area."

He led them back along the corridor to a small locked room. He opened it and pointed to a table.

"Here's the weapon. Have a look, if you want."

The gleaming axe lay in the glassine bag. Blood had pooled in the corners of the bag. The blade and wooden handle were streaked red.

No one said anything. Outside, in the darkness of the park, they heard an owl hoot loudly. In the walls they heard the scampering of the mice that plagued the old police station. They were deep in the countryside in the middle of a bustling city.

Dornblatt shook hands with them as they prepared to leave.

"The Met is sending a curator round at first light, to confirm it's the missing weapon."

"Thanks for everything," said Liddell.

He and Taylor suddenly felt very tired and very old. New York had just been a red herring, a blind alley. They were no fucking nearer to finding the serial killer than they had been weeks ago.

"I'm too tired to think anymore," said Taylor. We'll meet for breakfast tomorrow and see about getting back to D.C."

"No one said it would be easy," said Liddell.

CHAPTER 45
ROME

As Elspeth de la Tour was being slaughtered in Manhattan, an event occurred 4,000 miles away in Rome that would lead Monsignor Salemi out of the shadows of his covert role.

Yet again Bishop Luca di Montevecchi had been called to the Secret Archives by excited *scrittori*. Once there, he was shown a fire-scarred metal box rescued from some long forgotten cache willed to the church. Inside, in the dense 16th Century Tudor script written in his bold unique hand were fragments of journals written by Henry VIII of England.

After intensive, repeated analysis and interpretation, their contents were related to di Montevecchi.

Returning to his apartments he reached for a telephone.

NEW YORK

Salemi noted a triumphant timbre in the flawless Siennese voice as it informed him: "We have new letters — from Henry himself!

"God is guiding our hands, Joseph. Henry talks of his great journey!"

Salemi listened, somewhat taken aback by the obvious excitement of the usually unflappable Bishop. He took brief notes and assured di Montevecchi that all computer and fax lines were clear to receive.

He crossed the room and took Father Orr gently by the shoulder.

"Perhaps, just perhaps, we have justification to approach those we have been following."

WASHINGTON, D.C.

Ann watched a white-and-yellow motor cruiser round the bend of the Georgetown Channel. The crew, a middle-aged man and young woman were wrapped in neon green weather suits. A sharp wind had made the river choppy and forbidding. She was sitting on her apartment balcony, in jeans and a plaid shirt. She had draped a cashmere sweater over her shoulders against an early fall chill.

Her mind was racing. Things were happening too quickly with Taylor. She was deeply attracted to him. In the past she had favored black-haired Mediterranean-looking men; an attraction of opposites. Taylor was light haired, blue-eyed like herself. Still, he was a man she could fall in love with. She wanted him, but was also alarmed at the commitment she felt he silently demanded.

Self doubt washed over her.

Tears welled in her eyes and she muttered a silent "Damn."

What was wrong with her? Why couldn't she enter a relationship with any sort of confidence?

Over the years she had had more than her share of suitors. She knew she was attractive, more than good looking. She was confident of that.

But somehow her relationships had all ended badly. Harsh words or, even worse, an apathetic "I'll call you." The coward's way of signaling the end.

She stood up and threw the sweater onto a lounger, as if her doubt could be discarded with the garment.

She missed Taylor already and wanted him back in Washington.

Oh, let it lead where it may, she promised herself and moved inside the apartment to call the New York hotel.

Taylor's room phone rang six times and she left a message on his voice mail. "Just checking in with you. I'll call you tomorrow afternoon."

She found it difficult to advertise tender feelings or thoughts on recorded messages.

But from the warmth of her voice it would show him she was thinking about him.

She moved to a comfortable leather chair next to a desk in her library area. It had belonged to her father. On the desk was a letter from the family estate lawyers. It had arrived over the weekend — a decision should be made about the estate in

Virginia. Her grandfather now spent most of the year in Bermuda. Did she wish to dispose of the property, the lawyers wanted to know.

She had loved the farm deep in the Virginia Hunt Country near the battlefield at Bull Run. Wooded hills and quiet country bridle paths mixed with pasture land.

She decided to visit the scene of so much of her past. Rest, reflect, and then press on with the future.

CHAPTER 46
NEW YORK

Taylor and Liddell were still downcast as they mechanically ate a late breakfast in Taylor's suite. The arrest of the mentally ill Garimov had seemed to derail their investigation.

Taylor pushed away a half-eaten omelet and poured black aromatic French Roast coffee into a cup.

He sipped the coffee and tried to buoy Liddell's spirits.

"These things happen with any investigation, Eugene. We've just got to put it behind us and get back on track again."

"Sure, John, but you have to admit it felt good for a while back there, thinking we had the bastard."

The telephone rang. It was Dornblatt.

"I'm glad I caught you guys before you went back to D.C. There's a new wrinkle in this mess. I think you will want to hear it for yourself. Can you come to the museum? I'm with Landon, the arms and armor curator."

"We're on our way," said Taylor.

The trip through the late morning traffic was marked by a chorus of angry horn blasts as Taylor wriggled through the congested streets.

They arrived at the museum and parked in the underground garage.

A secretary met them and took them to Landon's office, where Inspector Dornblatt waited with the curator.

Taylor forced a smile onto his lips and shook Landon's hand.

"We met at the murder scene, Mr. Landon. We appreciate your help."

Landon lifted the glassine package containing the bloody axe.

"What can you tell us, Mr. Landon?" asked Liddell.

"This axe appears to be identical to the weapon missing from our collection, gentlemen. A 16th Century battle axe forged around 1510 to 1540. However, I have to stress the word 'appears'."

He seemed to enjoy the puzzled expressions on the agents' faces. He went on.

"The dimensions are almost the same, but its construction is minusculely different. It was made by a different armorer.

Add its total weight and we have a different weapon altogether. This is not the weapon stolen from our collection at the Met."

Taylor and Liddell exchanged glances. Perhaps they were back on the rails again.

"How can we find out where it did come from?" asked Liddell.

Landon placed the weapon back in the cardboard evidence box.

"Oh, I already know that," he said quietly.

"It matches exactly the description of a weapon stolen last week up in Wilchester."

Before Taylor and Liddell could ask, Inspector Dornblatt anticipated their query.

"Garimov's movements? We are checking it out, but he appears to have had a quarrel with the staff of a men's shelter the day the Massachusetts museum says its axe went missing and its janitor was killed. It's highly unlikely that he could have managed to travel that far, let alone organize a break-in and theft, then gotten himself back to New York in his mental condition."

"Has anything he's told you made sense yet," asked Taylor.

"He's still rambling. He says the world is coming to an end. He may have something there. They are trying to calm him down enough to be arraigned. He makes no sense."

Liddell and Taylor left their car in the museum car park. They walked up an access road near 79th Street and into the park and the rear of the museum. Its walls of glass and concrete jutted into the landscape of trees, lawns and paths.

"I see two possibilities, John. One, Garimov is wandering around the park and finds the axe, hidden or thrown in an isolated spot."

"Or," Taylor interrupted, "some bastard gave him the axe just to throw us completely for a loop."

The agents walked under a red-bricked, arched tunnel towards a stone obelisk.

A large bird flapped its wings noisily somewhere back in the tunnel. Taylor instinctively looked back and caught a glimpse of a man's figure turning abruptly on his heel and walking quickly away from them.

Both men were skilled in field surveillance. Their instincts told them they were being followed.

Taylor spoke quietly, normally, to Liddell.

"I've got a very strong feeling I've seen that figure before." He searched his memory, trying to visually flag his quarry.

"Got it! At the Croft Theatre. He was in the crowd. Did not look like the usual gawpers. Something about him. Very intense."

"Do you think he knows you made him?" asked Liddell.

"Only one way to find out. Why don't you leave the way we came, then double back. See if he follows me."

Liddell patted Taylor on the shoulder in farewell and said loudly: "You have your walk. I'll see you back in the hotel this afternoon."

To anyone observing them, they looked like two out-of-town businessmen planning an afternoon of free time. Taylor raised his hand in a goodbye gesture and walked slowly deeper into the park.

Liddell walked quickly, back through the tunnel and turned left towards the 84th Street exit. There was an artist painting a side view of the museum.

He was mixing a deep green to depict the thick ivy beginning to climb the grey walls of the building. Liddell crossed Fifth Avenue, turned right on Madison Avenue, then doubled back on 79th Street and re-entered the park.

Taylor had said he would walk slowly from the east side of the park in a south-west direction.

Liddell raced up a hill, feeling the burn of too many cigarettes in his lungs. He looked around for any signs of Taylor. Shit. He had lost them. He moved quickly on. Keeping the towering, sun streaked buildings on Central Park South in his sights.

Taylor had stopped to look at a gathering of in-line roller skaters. A loud incessant beat came from a boom box next to a decrepit expanse of tarmacadamed ground. A group of young women and men in brief hot pants circled in an impromptu conga line. Other skaters, mostly men, went through mindless exhibitionistic poses.

He's here, watching me, Taylor sensed. Taylor slowly followed the circling line of girls with his eyes. There. There he is, just back in the trees near the statuary. Damn him, he's looking right at me.

Taylor was not used to being the hunted one. He wanted to charge and lash out at his silent pursuer. But a confrontation in this crowd would achieve nothing more than making him look like a crazy attacking an innocent bystander.

He turned and headed west, often detouring up hills and through clumps of trees along the way. Red and gold leaves had begun to carpet the ground.

He wandered around a 15-foot high rock outcropping, one of the many giant boulders of coarse metamorphic schist scattered throughout the park.

Clouds were threatening to push in from the south and the few late-season sunbathers who used the rock had collected their blankets and left.

He strode quickly round the base, scrambled up and crouched within a four-foot-deep fissure about 12 feet above the dusty ground. Within minutes he heard the faint scuff and crackle of feet on dead leaves. He peered over the blue-grey rock surface. It was him. It was his first close look at his pursuer.

He was an inch short of 6 feet. He wore a dark wind-breaker and black slacks. Hard to tell how well muscled he was under that loose Jacket. Christ! Was this the killer? Taylor had never shied away from a fight. In fact, like most successful combatants, he actually enjoyed fighting. But, he was no longer young, and God only knew if there was a weapon under that baggy nylon windbreaker.

Where was Liddell? But it was too late now to have doubts. It was time to act.

Taylor jumped from the rock and broke his fall by driving one knee into the small of his pursuer's back. The man should have fallen like a sack of bricks but, on contact, he allowed his knees to buckle, then his feet and legs to rotate. At the same instant an elbow crashed into the bone behind Taylor's ear. Like a stone skipped on the surface of a lake, Taylor ricocheted off the hard body and landed heavily on the ground. He had been winded in the fall. His breath came as a whistle.

At that moment, Liddell burst through the trees and yelled: "FBI. Freeze. NOW!"

The man's black piercing eyes glared at Liddell then softened. He offered Taylor a hand up. Taylor angrily dashed it away with his own bloody and scraped fist.

"Easy, gentlemen. Please let me explain. My name is Joseph Salemi. We follow a mutual cause."

Salemi held his hands wide apart and smiled at the tall, heavy black man pointing the automatic handgun at his face.

He knew he only had seconds to defuse the explosive moment. He couldn't blame these men for their present actions.

A woman walking a Pomeranian dog appeared from the other side of the rock, saw the sinister tableau and turned on her heels.

Salemi knew it would be only minutes before the Park police were summoned by the terrified witness. He knelt down in the crackling grass and leaves. Taylor was back on his feet, anger coloring his cheeks. Salemi sensed he was getting ready to attack.

The scent of the grass and rotting leaves mixed with his keen sense of danger. The large black man with the handgun and his furious companion were supposed to be professionals. He hoped they re-acted in a disciplined manner.

He repeated: "Gentlemen, please forgive my following you, but I assure you we are all on the same side. We are hunting the same killer." His voice carried a faint Mediterranean accent, his English tinted by slight British overtones.

Salemi pointed to his windbreaker pocket. "Please," he gestured. "I have papers that may help identify me."

Liddell moved close and stood over Salemi. Taylor told Salemi to lean back and sit on his hands. He reached into the jacket and took out a sheaf of documents in a waterproof pouch.

Taylor looked in amazement at the papers he had taken from the stranger, who appeared calm and stoic, gazing coolly at Liddell's gun muzzle.

One document made of what felt like vellum, was marked with the white and yellow papal flag and the silver and gold seal of the Papal Arms.

It identified the wiry, compact man kneeling on the grass as Monsignor Joseph Salemi, an envoy-extraordinary of the Vatican State. He also carried a Vatican passport and a private telephone number to the Vatican Embassy in Washington.

Liddell passed the pistol to Taylor and pulled out his cell phone. He dialed a number at FBI

Headquarters and relayed the suspect's name and the Vatican Embassy number. That message was relayed to the State Department liaison to the FBI. It would take about an hour to investigate, the FBI agent was told.

"Gentlemen," said Salemi in a friendly voice. "My knees are aching and I need a drink. I promise you I will give you my parole while you check me out."

The old-fashioned, usage of “parole" struck a humorous chord with both Taylor and Liddell. It was disarming. Was it calculated to achieve that effect? They would have to remain sharp and alert with this guy. But to remain fixed in this dramatic grouping would only draw attention to themselves. They, too, did not want the spotlight that would follow if the park police arrived.

"Get up on your feet," Taylor ordered. "We're going to take a walk. You have a lot of explaining to do."

The men followed a path which took them past the Wollman Ice Rink, where loud rock music blasted the teenage skaters and shattered the tranquility of the park.

The noise from the rink was augmented by the sound of police sirens. Two heavy-set and muscled young cops approached them, bulletproof vests straining their dark blue uniform shirts.

Liddell moved towards them and showed them his FBI ID. That seemed to reassure them and they radioed to their dispatcher.

The trio followed a path down to the Pond in front of Central Park South and sat on a bench to await the phone call from Washington. Salemi sat in the middle. The agents' arms rested on the back of the wooden bench. Three men enjoying the view of the pond, its ducks and the marsh birds in the rushes. But they were ready to wrestle Salemi to the ground if he made a wrong move.

WASHINGTON, D.C.—EMBASSY ROW, MASSACHUSETTS AVENUE.

At the Apostolic Nunciature, the Holy See, Giovanni Rinaldi picked up the secure phone in his office overlooking the rear gardens.

"Giovanni, its John Sadowsky. Have you a minute?"

Rinaldi, an elegant Roman from a long line of Italian diplomats remembered Sadowsky from the Washington social circuit.

"Of course, John. How can I help?"

"Have you heard of a priest called Joseph Salemi? He's supposed to be visiting here from Rome."

There was a perceptible pause on the line, then Rinaldi said: "Salemi?"

He stretched out the name, Sah-lay-mee. Sounds like a Sicilian name. But, why do you ask?"

Sadowsky noted that the Embassy man had conveniently ignored his initial question.

The languid voice and flawless English accent of the diplomat continued.

"Is this man in trouble?'

"Not yet," said Sadowsky, alert to Rinaldi's tone of feigned disinterest. Two could play at that game.

"It's a simple request from the New York Police Department. He was pulled over in Central Park. It looks like a mistake. He resembled a felon they had warrants on. He produced some official Vatican documents including a Vatican passport, to identify himself. It's all routine, so far."

"Let me call you back" Rinaldi purred.

Five minutes later, Sadowsky's telephone rang.

"We can confirm he is one of ours, so to speak. A priest. Nothing more. A priest who delivered some routine documents to us and is now on vacation. He is on leave of absence from his duties, which are minor, in Rome."

Now Sadowsky's interest was really aroused, but he replied calmly: "Fine, Giovanni. Sorry you were bothered on something so insignificant."

"It is always a pleasure to help, even in the smallest of matters." the silky voice replied.

Rinaldi replaced the receiver of his telephone. He reached into a desk drawer and pulled out a lined writing tablet.

A few minutes later he rang for his secretary. The languid voice had gone. "Have that encrypted at once and sent to the Cardinal in Rome." he ordered.

Trouble had entered his tranquil social life of diplomacy in Washington. And he didn't like that at all.

Sadowsky placed a call to Liddell's cell phone. It was answered after one ring.

"They know him. He pans out. He's on leave of absence, on personal business. Nothing else."

"I see," said Liddell.

"What story has he given you?" asked Sadowsky.

Something about Sadowsky's tone rang warning bells in Liddell's head. He had never trusted the State Department or the Secret Service for that matter.

"Oh, just as you say. He's here unofficially. Vacation. I guess we grabbed the wrong man. We'll apologize to him and send him on his way. Thanks for checking it out."

"No problem. We'll forget about it," said Sadowsky.

Sadowsky replaced the telephone in its cradle and frowned. He knew that fewer than 600 people in the world possessed Vatican passports. He moved to another console and buzzed his assistant.

"Get me an appointment with the chief. We may have a little investigating to do."

CHAPTER 47
NEW YORK, CENTRAL PARK

"Okay. So you are who you say you are. What the hell are you doing following us?" a steely Taylor asked Salemi.

They were walking past the horse carriage ranks opposite the Plaza Hotel. A wind spiralled the dry dusty flakes of horse manure into the air. To Salemi, it was not an unpleasant smell. Country lanes, echoes of a timeless rural life.

A blast from a yellow cab brought his attention back to Taylor's question. The two American policemen were still on edge. Hostile.

"I understand your anger. It will take a while to tell you. Let's find somewhere away from the traffic noise. This street corner reminds me of Rome. Cars buzzing everywhere."

Taylor hailed a cab and gave him the address of the hotel. The three bodies were crushed into the ridiculously small area that passed for passenger seats in the modern New York taxi fleet.

It was just before lunch time when they arrived at First Avenue. They decided to take the elevator to the rooftop restaurant bar, which was just opening.

They sat on the terrace overlooking the rush-hour traffic of First Avenue. They ordered German beer.

"Now," said Taylor. "Our patience has run out. Speak to us."

Salemi looked at his two escorts. "I think I may know what is driving the killer. But it may seem fantastic to you. You will just have to hold off your cynicism until you have heard everything I say."

Salemi's first phrases of English had a hesitancy of timing. But like most linguists, his pace picked up as he eased into the English part of his brain.

"What do you know about the workings of the mind?" the priest asked quietly.

Taylor and Liddell glanced at each other. Each had studied the methodology of the Behavioral Science innovators at Quantico. The FBI criminal personality profiling program proved so uncannily accurate, it often seemed like witchcraft to the widespread police forces it assisted.

Taylor told the priest of their FBI profile training. The dark eyes widened and the black eyebrows were raised.

"I'd love to study that sometime. But I am talking about," he paused, searching for the right word, "a more clinical assessment of the killer's mind. Who he is — or, more to the point, who he thinks he is.

"And if we accept this, we must seriously consider if it is possible he is being controlled by ... well that is a giant step I won't inflict on you at the moment."

Taylor was intrigued by the priest's reticence and was about to press him when Salemi continued.

"In short, gentlemen, I and my colleagues have been tracking a man we believe is responsible for the U.S. killings and many more around the world."

Liddell banged down his beer glass and eagerly asked: "You mean you have an identity? You know who he is?"

"No. We believe we know who he thinks he is. And we believe there is a chance he really is that person."

The priest sensed their growing confusion.

"Let me take you somewhere. Perhaps the puzzle will fall into place there."

"Where would that be?" Liddell asked, a tinge of sarcasm in his voice.

Salemi stood up, leaned over the stone balcony and pointed North, up First Avenue.

He laughed: "We could hit it with, how do you say, spit from here"

Taylor shook his head at the realization that someone had been shadowing them and working on the murders just a few blocks from their hotel.

He drained the last of the Beck's and nodded to Salemi.

"Let's go," he said.

CHAPTER 48

Salemi opened the door to the brownstone and announced: "We have guests, Father Orr!"

A moment later the smiling pink face of the old priest appeared above the bannisters of the staircase leading to their improvised office upstairs.

"So they didn't break your neck or shoot you, Joseph," he grinned.

Orr had no idea how near Salemi had been to that fate.

The two investigators were ushered up the stairs and into the priests' den.

Taylor saw that the office was richly furnished. Deep leather chairs mixed with oak and walnut furniture. An old but lush Persian carpet spread across the polished wood floor. Father Orr had scavenged through the ornately furnished house and had his finds installed in the work room. Orr had advised Salemi he worked better in comfortable surroundings.

Salemi allowed him his little luxuries. He had come to regard the wry old priest as invaluable to their hunt.

Taylor thought Orr looked almost pixyish. A little over 5-foot-4, he had a full head of snow white hair. His facial skin looked almost translucent. His cheeks were splashes of red. He carried the lines and jowls of age but his blue eyes were striking. They could be the eyes of a boy; bright, shining with intelligence and observation.

After being formally introduced, Orr pointed to four leather padded chairs near a large fireplace. He placed Edinburgh Crystal decanters of brandy and Scotch on a low table and switched on a lamp stand.

The outside light was fading fast and the corner was in deep shadow.

With the weather change had come dark clouds and a damp chill that slowly crept into the old brownstone. After the hot summer, the at-first welcomed, cool breezes were now uncomfortably cold. The first heavy raindrops began to tap and streak the windows.

Salemi crossed the carpeted room to the marble fireplace and took a wax coated spill from a bronze cylindrical container on the mantelpiece.

He struck a match to the taper and touched it to a nest of crumpled newspaper underneath a frame of thin sticks and large logs. As the sky darkened, the fire grew brighter.

Sitting in the time-worn leather armchairs with the taste of old Scotch on his tongue and wood smoke in his nostrils, Taylor felt removed from the frantic scramble of Manhattan. He could have been in some great country house. The old building was expensively soundproofed against the blare of midtown traffic.

Not for the first time since he had encountered Salemi, he wondered if he and Liddell had dropped through some Lewis Carroll inspired trap door. There was a note of surrealism to the situation.

But there the two priests were, acting like perfect hosts, fussing over their guests before the topic of the evening was tabled — murder.

A log crackled and spat a flaming jet of resin and Salemi began.

"We are, in our different ways, in pursuit of the same man. I must ask you to give me your word that, at least for the immediately foreseeable future what I say goes no further. Why will become clear in time."

Taylor saw the flush of anger on Liddell's broad face and heard him explode.

"Let me remind you. You are interfering in a U.S. government criminal investigation. You could find yourselves in jail, clerical collars and all. You are in no position to impose conditions. For two cents I'll..."

Taylor quickly moved to lighten Liddell's threat. He cut in.

"Let's hear what they have to say first, Eugene."

He looked at his angry partner.

"O.K.?" he pleaded.

Liddell sank back into his chair silently.

Salemi resumed as if nothing important had happened.

Taylor couldn't help admitting a sneaking regard for Salemi's unshakable aplomb.

The intense, articulate Italian continued.

"Our story begins over a year ago when a document was found in the Sacred Archives in the heart of the Vatican."

"The what?" asked Liddell.

Orr leaned forward in his chair. The firelight danced off the gold-rimmed glasses hanging on a chain from his neck.

He explained: "It's a library. A very old library that contains books, manuscripts and letters from the span of history. It holds many secrets, many still untold."

Salemi picked up the story: "One of the library staff, a full-time researcher, if you like, came across a startling letter in a box of manuscripts and letters from the era of the English King Henry VIII."

"The one who chopped his wives' heads off," volunteered Liddell.

Orr smiled and said: "Quite so. Quite so."

Salemi continued: "A search was launched into the letters and journals of various powerful contemporaries. We were initially interested because they were written at a time of great moment and import to our Church in England.

"Taken altogether they offered a new, tantalizing insight into that period and hinted at some great hither-to unknown event in the King's life.

"A day or so ago a new letter was found or should I say a part of a letter—from Henry himself

“This one initially attracted our attention because it was written in English by the King’s own hand. I say that because of the over 1,000 Henry letters held by museums, libraries and universities, 80 percent were dictated to clerks and only signed by Henry.

"Many of these are in Latin or French. A good portion of the surviving English letters are billets-doux from Henry to Anne Boleyn, who, as Mr. Liddell has pointed out, certainly had her head chopped off. These letters are held by the Vatican.

"All of these letters have been studied, analyzed and annotated by historians through the centuries.

"But the new find in the Secret Archives has not been seen since shortly after Henry wrote it. This particular letter was sent to a girl who was to become his next wife — Lady Jane Seymour. They were betrothed the day after Boleyn’s execution. By the way, Mr. Liddell, she died naturally of blood poisoning a few years after the marriage; 12 days after giving birth to a son by caesarean operation.

”But its subject is not love. It's a bloody nightmare describing terror, vengeance and what we believe is a description of the future. A first-hand description as mad as that seems!

"First you have to understand that, to the 16th Century man, Purgatory, Heaven and Hell were manifest, real places. All over Europe the wealthy built chantries in churches where monks and priests would be employed to say prayers for the dead. Each prayer hopefully fractionally reducing the hundreds of years their benefactor would spend in Purgatory.

Henry believed in witchcraft, black magic and that the skies could rain real blood. He believed that frightening apparitions and the wildest chimera stalked the world.

But even his contemporary beliefs can't account for the letter fragments we have discovered. Henry was one of the best educated men of his time and regarded widely as a very astute and intelligent man. If anything, he was supremely practical, an analytical man who saw through the artifice of his time.

His descriptions of events are profoundly different from any popular magical portents. Although written in the style and phraseology of the Tudor period, it is not the voice of a 16th Century man. This was not some feverish dream he recorded. This is an account of an extraordinary journey he is convinced took place"

"This letter goes far beyond contemporary superstition. It relates fragmented remembrances of what could possibly be interpreted as our modern world. And if one applies that interpretation, one of the fragments eerily paints a picture of the crime scene at the Polo field in Chicago!"

There was silence save for the crackling of the logs in the fireplace. Outside it was quite dark and the rain had softened what little noise entered the room.

For once the ebullient Liddell was speechless. Taylor stared at the two priests.

"I know it sounds like madness; madness from Henry and madness from us for believing it. But Henry claimed his journey began after a near fatal jousting accident when he was knocked unconscious.

"The actual accident, on January 24th, 1536, is recorded by historians and really did occur. He was unconscious and thought to be near death for over three hours. Messengers were sent from the tiltyard, fully believing that he was in fact dead. When he came to, his reign of terror began.

That letter describes his journey into the future "to cleanse with blood the pretenders" and his enemies then his safe return to Tudor England.

He talks of his "talismans" — objects he needed to relate to; to maintain a mystical link to his own age. Talismans that would ease his spirit's return after he had completed his killings.

"We have compiled a list of thefts from museums and private collections around the world in the last few years. There is a pattern to it if you believe the Henry letter. Each of these thefts was of weapons or articles belonging to the Tudor era.

"A tournament helmet, reputedly worn by Henry and in private hands in Wiltshire, England, had a square of the velvet padding inside removed.

"Imagine that. A burglar breaks in, smashes the case with the metal helmet in it and just takes part of the silk and velvet padding. Goes to all that risk for something that may have touched the King's head."

"There is a similar trail around Britain and Europe and we fear a number of unexplained deaths. A priest killed at a monastery in the Pas de Calais which held Henrician manuscripts. Bodies that were disposed of and are just now turning up. I'll give you a list of what we have found. But the information is still coming in."

He continued: "We are trying to isolate incidents and suspicious deaths, which would fit in with what, we admit, must appear a fanciful scenario."

Taylor noted that Salemi's English was almost flawless and his grammar sounded very British. Must have been educated somewhere in Britain, he guessed.

But what those slightly accented tones were telling him was unthinkable. He could just see Liddell and himself trying to explain back in Washington that they were hunting a ghost. It was ridiculous. But yet he realized the priest was deadly serious as he described the perverse fairytale.

He was all the more surprised then when the usually pragmatic Liddell cried out enthusiastically: "The prayer book!"

"The prayer book stolen from the theater in Washington. That fits right in. Damn, it was even owned by Henry when he was a boy."

Then the big man frowned and seemed embarrassed.

"I don't believe what I'm saying here. It's Looney Tunes. We're about to tell our boss we think the killer is a time traveler. Look out for a long-dead King who likes to cut people into pieces. This IS madness. Time travel. They'd send us to the funny farm, and I wouldn't blame them."

Orr, who had been gazing into the flames of the fireplace, quietly spoke: "You know," he said in a measured resigned voice, "some of the greatest physicists of the past 100 years believe time travel is not impossible: highly improbable, but not impossible.

"Even Aristotle thought that time was circular, not the straight flying arrow most of us think of today. Einstein's Theories of Relativity provide for the possibility of time travel, of a fourth dimension. The physicist who inspired Einstein, Hermann Minowski, argued that space and time were not separate and that it formed a continuum. An inseparable continuum.

"Other physicists believe it is possible to have a parallel world. They believe wormholes in which some sort of time travel could be achieved to be out there.

The most recent studies using quantum mechanics indicate that a time traveler would only be able to travel in an undeviating path down a trail of events that already had happened. He could not change what had already happened. But the same theories do not deny the possibility that a time travelers could travel into the future and, along the way, change history.

"This of course is a very simplified explanation of complicated equations. Quantum physics. Trying to explain the physics of tiny particles at best deals in probabilities, not exact measurements.

"It's true that the physical movement of a human body would be impossible using today's science.

"But what about the mind? If space and time can run in any direction, couldn't the mind? All it needs to act out its will is a bodily host.

"Physicists talk about a winding path of time travel, a meandering river. First it guides you through space time, where you can spend as long as you want. When you arrive at the final twist or bend in the path, it shoots you back. To those around you, you have not gone anywhere because you return almost instantaneously to your body.

"History is full of examples of time slips, incidents in which rational human beings have found themselves witnessing history. They recall details they could not possibly have known.

"There is the famous account of two Victorian women who turned off a path in Versailles and saw a 17th Century court at play. They described buildings that had been knocked down 200 years before.

"Then there was the couple in Haiti who one night saw a 17th Century French street, the lanterns swinging from the house gables in a sugar cane field, before it abruptly disappeared.

"They were all rational people, embarrassed to recount what they saw. Scores of these encounters exist. No doubt thousands more are out there, untold.

"I could go on all night. The bibliography on time travel and time slips is huge. But I think we must accept that there is certainly a possibility of time travel — at least through the human mind. We have not even begun to understand the possibilities of the mind."

Taylor let out a whistle of breath and lifted the Speyside single malt Scotch to his lips. He inhaled the mellow, flowery bouquet and swallowed.

"You are saying that somehow the spirit, mind or whatever of King Henry has traveled here and is getting some madman to slaughter innocent victims."

"Yes," said Salemi. And we have his possible target. The man who will be the future King of England — the Prince of Wales. A man whose forebears come from a completely different Royal line. Completely unrelated to the Tudors. In the killer's demented view, a false claimant of the throne."

"Some sort of revenge," spluttered Liddell, who was feeling dizzy with all the wild information his mind was being asked to process. The son of a noted California mathematics professor, he had earlier bristled at the implied presumption that quantum theory would have to be simplified to him.

He collected himself and said: "Homicidal revenge or some other belief we have not figured out yet."

Taylor decided to splash some ice water on this talk of ghosts and time travel.

"Or it could just be some nut who thinks he is Henry VIII, couldn't it? Someone suffering from delusions of grandeur. The mental wards are full of Napoleons and Caesars — all firmly believing they are the real thing."

Salemi looked calmly at Taylor.

"But that doesn't explain the Henry letter — the descriptions in it. The possible reference to the scene in Chicago. Polo came out of India centuries after Henry's reign. Details never released by police. The blood on the Prince's standard. Explain that to me."

Taylor sighed. “I can't explain it," he admitted. “But look at the so-called prophecies of Nostradamus. They are so vague you can make with them whatever you like.”

Then a hard edge returned to his voice: "But if we are discussing explanations, how about explaining what your interest is in all this. How long have you been shadowing us? In short, what the hell has it to do with you or the Vatican? What do you gain by helping us track down this madman?"

Salemi met his glare. Again that unruffled composure, Taylor noted.

The priest assured him: "We are purely interested in the phenomenon posed by the possibility it is somehow Henry's spirit. I serve a very old congregation of the Holy Church which is continually reviewing such historical anomalies.

“History is full of strange quirks like this. We simply wish to gain a better understanding and, if our efforts can help identify the killer and save some lives, all to the better."

Taylor would have bet money right then that Monsignor Salemi had some Jesuit training in his cupboard. He had long admired the talent for debate and sometimes sophistry from the Jesuit trained mind.

"What do you really want, in this case," he interrupted.

Salemi smiled as if a child caught out in a harmless fib.

"We want to have the chance to talk with the killer when he is caught to see if he was in fact influenced by the spirit of Henry VIII.

"What does he know of Henry's frame of mind at the time of the accident, if anything? If Henry had somehow been channeling to the host, those insights into a man who changed the course of Catholicism in Britain and Europe, it would be exciting and invaluable.

"To those who study the history of the church it would be a fantastic glimpse into the mind of Henry."

Taylor allowed Orr to refill his whisky glass and splashed ice water into it. He would let Salemi's explanation pass for the moment.

"Then why don't you allow us to do our job and apply to interview him in jail or whatever mental hospital he ends up in."

Salemi looked at Orr as if making a sudden decision.

"We believe there are some among you who want him killed. They want no trial. They want no lengthy evidence that could prove embarrassing to them. I'm talking about senior officials entrusted with the security of Britain and the U.S."

He went on: "We have ears in many places, Mr. Taylor. Believe me, what I say is true. You and your colleague could be in some danger yourselves."

A log collapsed and flames yellowed the wall.

Taylor and Liddell frowned and drank their Scotch. Both were thinking the same thing. What the hell have we got ourselves into?

"Can I see the letter?"

"Here is a copy," said Orr, pushing an e-mail facsimile across the table.

Taylor looked up at Salemi. "Supposing, just supposing we consider seriously your theory about some malevolent time traveler or someone who thinks he is. You say the Chicago murders are referred to in the King's letter. It might not do any harm to revisit the Chicago killings from that point of view."

"I agree," Salemi said. "It may be that some ritualistic part of the murders, some arrangement in the killing ground, an unsuspected clue might fit in with the Henry theory. Would he have left some warning sign for the Prince?"

"I know a man, a friend of our bishop, an expert in London," said Orr.

CHAPTER 49 — NEW YORK

Salemi walked the two agents to the door. His offer of an umbrella was politely turned down as the rain showers had slowed to a faint, occasional drizzle. He shook hands with the men and returned upstairs.

Orr ended his conversation with his friend in London and replaced the telephone receiver. He looked at Salemi, who had an unspoken quizzical look.

"He'll do everything he can to help us. He is a good friend not only of myself but of Bishop di Montevecchi, and a loyal son of the church."

Salemi glanced at the empty spirit glasses left by the two FBI agents on the fireside mantelpiece He was not sure how much of their story the agents believed but they seemed like highly intelligent men with minds at least open to all possibilities.
The old priest's face was flushed; whether by excitement or the liberal dashes of Scotch, Salemi couldn't tell.

"You asked him about 'his contacts'," Salemi said.

Orr replied: "Moberley's been out of British intelligence for years but he still has them. It's a club they only leave feet first. If you agree, I'll send him some of the key computer pattern searches. With his unique knowledge of historical arcana and genealogy, he might see something we wouldn't. It's worth a try."

"I agree," said Salemi, "But will he unwittingly drop some clues to his chums in MI5 and 6. Can we absolutely trust him not to favor old loyalties?"

Orr looked offended.

"Down through the centuries, this man's family has suffered oppression, even torture and death, to remain loyal to the Holy Church. He is beyond suspicion. He is....."

Salemi interrupted: "I'm sorry, Father. Please forgive me. I have unshakable trust in your judgment and your and the Bishop's London friend. There is much on my mind. It's been a long day and we have so much more to do. Your help has been invaluable, my friend."

The old priest nodded his head. He was tired now. He stood and told Salemi: "I'm off down to the pantry for some milk and a sandwich. Can I get you anything, Monsignor?"

"Thank you, no," said Salemi. "I will sit up here for a little while and think. God Bless you, Father James.

"And you, Joseph," said the old priest, his shadow disappearing down the corridor.

CHAPTER 50

Taylor and Liddell had walked briskly north from the priests' brownstone through puddled streets and an autumn mist. The rain had tailed off and they decided to grab chili and burgers at a popular bar on Third Avenue.

They sat in the back room sipping coffee while their order was made. The dark room with its red-and-white checkered table covers was crowded and noisy. No one would hear what they said.

Liddell laughed uneasily and asked: "Did all that really happen, or did I have a nervous breakdown? Tell me it's a breakdown, John."

"No such luck," said Taylor.

"Christ! What are we going to tell the bosses? They're liable to yank us off the cases, and I couldn't really blame them."

"Yeah, right," said Liddell. "We'll spend the rest of our careers in Bangor, Maine, picking up the transatlantic assholes who get their flights diverted there for threatening stews who cut off their boozing privileges."

"You'll meet people from all over the world that way," said Taylor.

Liddell glared, then returned to the problem facing them.

"Just what are we going to do?" he asked. "What do we tell the brass?"

"At this moment, as little as we can get away with," said Taylor.

"We don't want to admit that the priests have been following our moves for months now. Let's just say they contacted us and volunteered their theories. We are examining them along with all the other wild scenarios that have been proposed to us. Grasso is under the grinder, too. He'll be happy to report upstairs that we are considering a broad range of motives in these cases. Even fantastic ones like some psychopath who thinks he's a dead King.

"I must admit the priests have amassed a lot of compelling data. We can be fairly certain that the target is the Prince. But if he is in London, where is the killer now?"

An elderly waiter roughly grabbed their empty chili bowls, smacked two plates of hamburgers and fries in front of them and went wordlessly on his way.

"Good to be back in a real New York joint," said Taylor.

"Whatever we decide, they'll want us to personally report back in Washington," said Liddell.

He added slyly: "Now that shouldn't upset you too much, lover boy."

"Watch it," growled Taylor. "She's a lady. Don't you start stereotyping her."

Liddell looked at his friend and saw his sudden vulnerability.

"I know that, John. She's a beautiful woman in every way," he said softly.

The agents finished their meal, paid the waiter and moved into the front bar where they lingered over drinks. Later they walked out onto Third Avenue and then East toward the river and the hotel.

They had decided to play along for the moment with Salemi and Orr. Taylor had volunteered to be the liaison with the priests. He would contact the younger priest twice a day for any updates. They would vaguely promise to reciprocate with their own information. But, as far as they were concerned, any information offered from their side would be harmless.

They crossed First Avenue and walked up the gradient to the hotel.

"Have a good night's sleep, John," said Liddell.

"I won't have a good anything until I find out everything there is to know about the priests' interest in all of this. For all their noble concern, they are holding something back. I'm positive of that."

"I couldn't agree more. Good night," grunted Liddell.

When Taylor opened his door, he saw the red message light blinking on his bedside telephone.

He retrieved Ann's recorded message and subsequent hang-ups. He looked at his watch. Too late. He'd call her in the morning and plan to meet her back in Washington.

He fished out the fax of the Henry letter that had so excited the priests.

He had read long-winded prose before, but the density and endless clauses in an English he barely recognized quickly defeated him. That form of English was alien to him and definitely not to be attempted last thing at night with tired eyes and mind. He would take the priests' word for its contents.

He was asleep within minutes of his head hitting the pillow.

CHAPTER 51
WASHINGTON, D.C.

Ann had called the New York hotel again. Once more the voice mail asked for a message. She abruptly hung up. She was reluctant to call his cell phone. That should be for business only, she felt. She was annoyed with herself. It was 11 p.m. Here we go again, she thought. You are starting to chase too hard. You'll put him off the way you scared the last man who meant something to you.

She could hear the wind shuffle the dry leaves across the river on Roosevelt Island and remembered their romantic evening looking at the similarly named isle in New York's East River.

Across the Potomac the lights in the Georgetown basin twinkled in the wind.

She felt lonely. She had made some big decisions and needed some comforting reassurance from someone — Taylor preferably.

Earlier she had steeled herself and taken a taxi to the theater. But she could not bring herself to enter the darkened playhouse.

She lingered in the outside corridor and called out to Ken, the director.

"My dear Ann, I've been worried sick about you. How are you?" he began.

Past experience told her he couldn't give a damn about the rich kid's feelings, but this was not the time to tackle him.

She felt released by her decision.

"I'm sure it won't make any difference to the company but I don't think I can come back here. I've written a note to the board thanking them and you for all your help."

The sly eyes met her gaze and his head tilted in reluctant acceptance.

"Are you sure, Ann? We will all miss you." Then quickly, too quickly, "...but I understand. It's your peace of mind we have to think of. I'll tell the other cast members. You'll still come and see us, I hope."

He looked at his watch.

"Sorry, Ann. I have to go. We'll keep in touch, yes?"

"Of course," Ann told him, happy that she would not have to deal with the bastard ever again.

She arranged for what little possessions she had left at the theatre to be boxed. A makeup kit, some posters and pictures. She would send a messenger for them in a few days. She left a neat, handwritten note on the Players' notice board thanking everyone. She had cited Gerry's death as a final decisive factor but in her heart she knew it was a partial excuse. She never wanted to see the theater again.

In the evening, she had gone to the Watergate Hotel for soup and a moist omelet with a half carafe of Muscadet. She was feeling heady from the alcohol when she returned to her flat. She wanted to speak to Taylor but she couldn't reach him.

She sat in her study, vainly waiting for the telephone to ring. She was falling hard for Taylor. Something she had thought unlikely at first meeting. He was unlike any of the men she had dated. Hardened from the streets and dealing with criminals, he was different from the socialites she was used to in D.C. and Virginia. But there was something about him that excited her. A mix of strength and tenderness. She was damned if she would let that go."

Tomorrow she would talk to him. He would get some time off and he would join her down at the family estate "Foxlair" at the weekend. They would take the relationship from there.

CHAPTER 52

The trees were signaling the carotin-fueled color changes of fall and everywhere the rich earth smell of decay filled his nostrils.

He returned to a solitary life. His meals were prepared by the cook and left on a table for him to a precise time schedule.

He had reduced the estate workers to a skeleton staff. They had strict orders to avoid the big house unless personally summoned. The estate manager was given instructions by telephone.

In the mornings he rode a large bay stallion, which tugged and wrestled against him, working the muscles in his arms, shoulders and back and thighs.

He would ride to the north part of the great park then through the trees to the river. There he would strip off his riding habit and plunge into the chill, slowly meandering stream. The current soothed him better than any massage. He floated on his back looking at a pair of cardinals in the tree branch above him: the male bird a shimmering blood red. Like the wandering vagabonds they were, they would soon be gone.

Another few weeks of training, gathering strength and, like the birds, he would once more leave the estate.

CHAPTER 53
LONDON

Sir Moberley Johns was the last member of one of England's aristocratic Roman Catholic families.

He had been born and grew up at the family seat a few miles from Sherborne, Dorset. The horrors of public school were made manageable only by the certainty of holiday interludes at his enchanted birthplace, a crumbling anachronism in a changing world.

He had played and day-dreamed along the dusty wings of the huge house. He had hidden in the priest holes and the private chapels his ancestors had secretly constructed centuries before, when their faith could cost them their lives.

He remembered that day, long ago, when he had motor-cycled up from Oxford and his graduate studies to see the death blow delivered to his home.

His father's face, ashen, defeated, would always cloud his memory.

Death duties and taxes had eaten up what was left of the once great manor and his desperate father had applied to Britain's National Trust in a last ditch effort to save the house. With those government funds, the great house might live on.

But there would be no tax payer relief to save their home. A Trust inspector tried to break the news gently to Moberley and his father. Pointing to the ruined 14th Century tower, the crumbling Tudor main hall, he slowly shook his head.

"I'm sorry. It's just too far gone. I couldn't justify the expense of repair."

"I was afraid you would say that. Thank you so much for your time and effort," his father had replied courteously.

It was the last time the grief-stricken old man mentioned thc house. Nine months later, he died.

Now, 30 years later, Johns himself felt like an anachronism. He free-lanced as an auxiliary herald at the College of Arms in the ancient Roman heart of London.

In a second-floor office, within a stone's throw of the walls of the Tower of London, he labored.

The work could be varied and some of it still excited him. Each year, when Royal and political honors lists were issued, the parvenus, quick to advertise their knighthoods and ennoblement, called for their coats of arms.

He would patiently assemble armorial bearings which heraldically represented the background or interests of the new knight or Lord. Using watercolors, artists would illuminate the escutcheons, bars, fesses and ordinaries onto vellum.

If he was lucky, really lucky, his months would be brightened by a request for identification of some arms or heraldic device on some valuable painting or manuscript.

Like some timeless Sherlock Holmes, Johns could tell the historical period and the families and subject histories from the heraldic details of the work.

Here he would spot a badge on a background piece of furniture which belonged to the Medicis. A bee motive belonging to Napoleon, or the red dragon of the Tudors. The number of legs on a dragon motif could decide which famous family was represented. He could look at a score of box-like "quarterings" on a shield and trace the historic lineage of the tiny pictorial testimonies, each one representing a family tie.

This afternoon, he had returned home to his riverside cottage by the banks of the Thames, across the river from Kingston on Thames.

The 18th-Century house, willed to him by a maiden aunt, was roomy. It nestled under trees with a small private lawn reaching to the river.

Johns was lying on the grass watching the late-evening incoming tide push tiny swells into the dark river when he heard the telephone jangle from the open windows of his kitchen.

He tried to ignore it, but it rang incessantly. He ambled over to a wall telephone just inside the trellised door at the back of the cottage. The climbing roses had almost faded.

"Moberley, that you?"

The clear, ageless voice, with the faint Ulster accent was readily identifiable.

"Hell's teeth! A voice from the past. How in God's good name are you doing, Father Orr?"

CHAPTER 54

On the southeast wing of the great house was one of four ivy faced turrets built on a whim of the owner in 1877.

In the topmost room of one of the 120-foot stone cylinders, a small library housed the present master's most valued possessions.

Light from a stained-glass, latticed window projected a kaleidoscope of blue, green, red and yellow diamonds on a polished oak desk.

Here he spent many afternoons, cut off from the world in his lofty tower.

The staff were never allowed in this section of the building. With over 100 rooms to maintain, they were happy not to be responsible for this section of the sprawling house.

On the table, the light fired the gold filigree and red and blue enamels decorating a small leather and vellum Book of Hours.

He reached past it to a shelf crowded with similar leather volumes and brightly hand-painted manuscripts. He gently pulled down a slim volume containing sheets of music handwritten on yellowing vellum. He opened it and saw familiar staffs and bold musical notation. His anger flared as he saw within the huge illuminated initial of one page a hand-colored image of a falcon pecking at a pomegranite. Once, its crude message had amused him. Not now.

He took a small steel rod inset with a diagonal razor blade and carefully sliced the page. It was a 16th Century motet- a sacred choral piece meant to be sung without instrumental accompaniment. It had once been a favorite. Not now. He searched in a desk and found a fountain pen. He filled it with red Waterman ink. His letters were distinctive, a bold, square Tudor Script.

He and his host were now indivisible, a deadly symbiosis of old and modern, a mix of the ruthless cunning of a timeless hunter and the technological artifice of the New Age. He would travel to the coast several hundred miles to the East, to one of the crowded barrier islands. There he would post it. It would be in London in a week. Then more fear would be upon them.

CHAPTER 55
LONDON, ST. JAMES'S PALACE

The brown paper package was logged and opened by the Prince's security staff after passing through a plastics explosive detector.

The single, aged sheet of paper inside with the carefully caligraphed staffs and notes was puzzling. Written boldly across the page in what looked like Old English to the examiner was the challenge: "None more from this treacherous house."

The staff were used to all manner of crank letters, but now security had been tripled. Everything in the slightest way unusual was sent to the head of security, a Scotland Yard Commander, on loan to the Royal Protection Squad.

The envelope and its contents were placed in a glassine bag and hand-carried up the wooden stairs to the Commander's office, on the same floor as the Prince's working apartments.

Within the hour, calls had been made to the Home Secretary and the Foreign Office. They in turn called a number in Washington.

CHAPTER 56

Two days later, just yards from St James's Palace, Moberley Johns sipped a rare single malt whisky in the hotel bar off a quiet cobbled Mews. The bar, part of a small but famous hotel, was famed for one of the best selections of Scotch whisky in London.

The entrance was under a narrow archway hardly visible from the busy road that swept past the Palace. Only the tight wheel radius of London taxi cabs could negotiate the open cul-de-sac at the end of the mews — or an expert horse and carriage driver.

It was 3.30 p.m. and the bar was deserted, save for an American couple gazing at a London tour Baedeker.

Johns' friend looked into the oak-paneled saloon, nodded to Johns and sat down beside him. The tourists left to talk to the hotel concierge. The barman's intuition and acquaintance with the tall, elegant man with the thin military moustache who entered the bar prompted him to excuse himself after pouring a large gin and tonic for the newcomer.

Sir Moberley and Dennis Buxton-Smith CBE were alone.

The saloon was quiet, save for the muffled voices in the hallway and the sleep-inducing ticking of an antique grandfather clock against one of the walls.

Buxton-Smith pushed a copy of the music sheet across the table to Johns.

Johns' thick eyebrows rose in mock surprise. "Music?"

"So it would appear," Buxton-Smith said dryly.

"And?" Johns said.

Buxton-Smith barely concealed his irritation at Johns' posture of naivete.

"I am going to get quite cross, Moberley, if you continue acting like the village idiot. You know damn well how this ties in."

Johns tried to make amends.

"Sorry, Dennis. Your people were on the mark. This is certainly a fragment from a Tudor song book.

"In fact, I would link it to three specific Tudors. It's from a Book of Music, one of a handful we know to be in existence believed to have been compiled for Anne Boleyn by her musician and accused lover Mark Smeaton. He was the poor fop who was tortured by Cromwell and the King's command to falsely admit an affair with Anne. The poor bugger was promised his freedom if he claimed adultery with the queen. He did his unsavory part at her trial but was executed anyway.

Johns returned to the music book after Buxton-Smith glared at his digression.

He recalled: "A similar book was stolen from a private collection in Shrewsbury a year ago. One other, a more famous book, is safely in the hands of the librarians of the Royal College of Music.

Johns examined the color facsimile of the page.

"How interesting. A threat scrawled over a Tudor text. The hand colored initial is most interesting, though.

"It's a rather tasteless and vicious jibe against Catherine of Aragon who was losing the King to the younger, coquettish Anne Boleyn.

"It shows a falcon, Boleyn's badge, furiously pecking at a pomegranite — Queen Catherine' of Aragon's family badge.

"It was obviously compiled when Anne's fortunes were in the ascendant — around 1532 — and Queen Catherine was basically exiled to a country palace, ignored and insulted by Henry. Four years later, Henry beheaded Anne Boleyn."

Buxton-Smith sipped his gin and frowned.

He sighed. "So, now we have cryptic links to Anne bloody Boleyn and Henry VIII. What the hell is going on?

"The security for the Royals is unprecedented. It's been kept fairly quiet so far, but sooner or later some rag's going to get a hold of it. Then, God help us all."

The stress of the situation was imprinted on his once handsome, aquiline face.

"Can these 'friends' of yours give us any further information?"

Johns had told the government agent as much as he thought relevant to the safety of the Royal family, an institution he fervently believed in. His duty to safeguard them was above all things. But he also had a duty to the church. Both causes could be served faithfully.

"My friends, as you call them, are anxious to give you all they gather. They also have an informal relationship with U.S. official investigators."

Buxton-Smith smiled wryly.

"It WOULD be useful to compare what we get officially from Washington with your friends' information. But tell them to make damn sure they don't interfere with any official work. The tumbrels are waiting for the unwary, Moberley. I'd rather one of them wasn't mine."

"Look, Dennis, I'm only too happy to help. Have you thought of listing the colleges where Tudor script is studied? Perhaps we could go through the students for the last few years. Check against aberrational individuals those with mental problems, at least to get it started."

“It was started this morning, Moberley. We would welcome any further suggestions you can offer."

"Oh, I'll have quite a few, old man," said Johns, reaching for his whisky glass.

CHAPTER 57
NEW YORK

Salemi shielded the paper bag full of hot buttered bagels from the steady drizzle and skipped up the steps of the brownstone.

He unlocked the door, entered the gloomy hallway and shouted to Father Orr in the upstairs office. The old man's voice was impatient. He came to the head of the stairs.

"Where have you been, Monsignor? We have received an important call. There's work to be done."

Salemi opened the bag and let the scent of bagel and melting butter rise to Orr's nostrils.

"You're forgiven, Joseph," said Orr wrinkling his nose dramatically. "I've just made a fresh brew of coffee."

Salemi effortlessly mounted the stairs and asked: "What news and from where?"

Orr looked pleased.

"Our man in London has come up with a nugget. It could be the killer has finally communicated — by air mail, no less."

Salemi listened as Orr recounted the conversation with Moberley Johns.

The younger priest frowned.

"Why haven't Taylor and Liddell passed that information along to us? I understand their latent distrust, but I thought we had an agreement to mutually cooperate."

"Perhaps they haven't been told or if they have, it will take some time for them to trust us," Orr said. "The British are probably keeping it to themselves. They don't want to alert the FBI to the American origin of the package. I know these people.

For them it's important to control all aspects of the investigation and the protection of the Royal family."

Salemi countered. "Yet they have shared it with Moberley."

"As far as they are concerned, Moberley will always be one of them," said Orr, "A brilliant, eccentric, but loyal member of the English establishment. Besides, he is one of the foremost experts on the historical period that seems to haunt the killings."

Salemi looked thoughtful then asked.

"What help does he need from us?"

"He's pretty confident the British intelligence boys will keep him up to speed — to a point. But, he suggests we push ahead with our own inquiries. And he wants to know which schools in the U.S. and Canada teach Tudor script.

"However as the document was stolen in England he thinks the killer may have lived there."

Salemi nodded.

"I think our English friend may be right."

Orr crossed the room and picked up a coffee flask from a side table.

"Are we going to tell Taylor and Liddell?" he asked.

"Certainly," said Salemi. “If they are hiding the information, it will remind them we are abreast of them. If they don’t know, it will prove how valuable we can be to them. They will trust us even more. And they will realize they cannot trust their superiors in Washington, or the British."

"Bravo," said Orr dunking a bagel into a cup of sweetened coffee.

CHAPTER 58
VIRGINIA

Ann felt slightly ashamed. She was acting like a teenager. It was the third time in half an hour that she had left the house and walked to the head of the driveway, hoping to see Taylor's car crest the hill and turn into the estate.

What if the bastard doesn't come? I'll kill him. There she went again. Fight the insecurity, girl.

A gray saloon car appeared over the hill and slowed as it approached the farm entrance. It turned into the driveway and she saw a flash of Taylor's fair hair.

God. It was going to be all right. The doubts were scattered like chaff. Here he was, a big grin on his face, arms encircling her.

They did not bother to take his overnight bag from the large government car. Nor did they take a tour of the house. Taylor happily allowed himself to be led directly to Ann's bedroom.

That evening they dined simply and lazily over a beef casserole Mrs. Green the housekeeper had prepared for them. They sipped Beaujolais by a log fireplace.

They reveled in their satiety. Their bodies were tired from lovemaking but irradiated with feeling. Neither had felt this way before. Neither dared to mention it; frightened to call down some vengeful God—to shatter their fledgling romance.

They spoke of little details of their past lives, making light of tragedies; covering every defeat, every heart break with humor. Sadness had no part in this relationship.

Then Taylor broke the bad news to her.

"I'm so sorry, Ann. But I have to go back to the trenches tomorrow."

"You shit. You didn't tell me until after you hauled me off to bed." She glared at him, then laughed.

"Okay, okay. You can go, but you better haul your ass back down here within the next couple of weeks," she said.

She was surprised at her own reaction. The old Ann would have sulked, shown anger. She liked the new, emotionally mature Ann.

She sensed he had been dreading telling her. He was keenly aware of her feelings. That mattered to her. She was happy to show she respected his, and the pressures that went with his job.

She was happy. This relationship was going to work. She felt it.

"Can you tell me about it?" she asked laying her head on his thigh. One side of her face was bathed a pinkish yellow from the fire; the other side in soft shadow.

Liddell called me on the way down here. There's been a development in England. The priests have gotten some new information, possible evidence. We're going up to New York to meet with them. I don't know how long it will take. I'm sorry."

"Don't be," Ann whispered. "We have lots of time ahead of us."

Then she jumped up and reached for the wine bottle.

"Just don't dare go to London without sending for me," she smiled. "I've got a Harrods card I haven't used for years."

"That's a deal," said Taylor laughing, relieved and warmed by her understanding.

He would now do anything for this lovely woman. This was a relationship that would grow. For the first time in his life he felt he had found home.

CHAPTER 59 — WASHINGTON, D.C.

"Limey bastards!"

Grasso was barely able to contain his rage. Liddell and Taylor sat silently waiting on the calm after the storm.

They had met in the lounge of the Willard Hotel. Grasso did not want any record of their conversation somehow picked up in the FBI HQ.

Grasso had expected some of the other agencies involved in the investigation to play territorial games, but this was just plain recklessness.

His anger was further fueled by the insistence from the State Department liaison that nothing was known of the mailing from the U.S. to the Prince.

Grasso unclenched his fists and focused on the two agents.

"We are getting immense pressure put on us to solve this. At the same time, there are people at the top tying one hand behind our back, keeping information from us.

"So, fuck them. We play them at their own game."

"John. How well do you trust those priests?"

"About as far as I can throw them," said Taylor.

"But there is no doubt they have important sources of information, special contacts beyond the scope of our normal police networks. They want to help us. But I can't help feeling they have a hidden agenda."

Grasso turned to Liddell.

"Eugene?"

"I agree with John. I vote we use them, but I still don't trust 'em."

Grasso looked round from the bar. It was noon and the regulars were beginning to fill the room.

"Okay. Get your asses up to New York. Work closely with these two comedians. Report only to me. Go wherever the search takes you. I'll fix the expenses and logistics this end. Good luck."

It was the first time they could recall the stoic Grasso ever wishing anyone 'Good luck'.

Jesus, if Grasso felt that way, perhaps they really needed it.

CHAPTER 60
NEW YORK

Grasso had ordered Taylor and Liddell to base themselves in the Millennium UN Plaza Hotel at the eastern end of 44th Street.

The United Nations Security Council was in emergency session and world leaders and foreign ministers gridlocked midtown Manhattan traffic with their motorcades.

Many stayed in the Tower of the hotel, their rooms overlooking the green glass of the UN and the vivid color splashed flags flying from the long line of metal staffs fronting the United Nations grounds.

With the dignitaries came massive security. Agents from all countries liaised with the Secret Service, the FBI and the N.Y.P.D. to ensure their safety.

Outside the hotel, government cars from all the agencies idled on the cordoned-off 44th Street. Surrounding streets leading to the U.N. were blocked by huge grey sanitation trucks loaded with sand. The sidewalks were lined with steel interlinking barriers. Inside the hotel, a special block of rooms had been set aside for federal agents.

It was the perfect cover for Taylor and Liddell. If need be, Grasso could claim they were on security detail while waiting for a break in the murder cases. They would be lost in the human circus and confusion surrounding the hotel.

They arranged to meet the priests at the brownstone and walked north along First Avenue.

Orr opened the door of the house for them and said jovially: "The good Monsignor awaits you upstairs, Gentlemen."

Salemi rose to greet them and motioned to a color facsimile lying on the main table.

"Our contact in London faxed that to us last night. He thinks it is very important. I agree with him.

The priest's dark eyes sparkled with intensity.

Taylor picked up the sheet of music and tried to decipher the scrawled blood-red script written diagonally across the music staffs.

Salemi read the brief formal message in Tudor English

"What house does he mean?" asked Liddell.

"It could be a reference to the Royal Family as in 'The House of Windsor.' That's what the Brits think anyway and that's why they are keeping it to themselves."

"But it was posted in the U.S., presumably by the killer," said a puzzled Liddell.

"Or by an accomplice," said Taylor.

"Which could mean the killer is in Britain somewhere, planning his next attempt," said Salemi.

"Is there any chance of seeing the actual

package and postal stamps that the music came with?" said Liddell.

"Our man in London says that's not possible. The British won't let it out of their hands. He did find out it was posted in Hilton Head, South Carolina," said Orr.

Taylor shook his head slowly.

"I don't think that will take us very far, even if we got a copy of the franked package envelope. Hilton Head is a popular resort; particularly at this time of the year. Heavy postal volume. I am sure the person who mailed it will be pretty much untraceable."

Salemi told the agents of Sir Moberley Johns' suggestion to track down students of Tudor history, primarily those who had learned early Tudor or Elizabethan script.

"God, how many colleges have Shakespearean courses and history departments?" asked Liddell.

"Quite a few," said Orr. "But we are going to concentrate on the most prestigious. It's as good a place to start as any."

Taylor noticed Salemi glance at his watch, a stainless steel bezeled diver's watch.

"Excuse me," the priest apologized. He crossed quickly to a window, pulled the lace curtain and looked to the street below. "My car has arrived. I have to catch a plane."

"A plane?" Taylor queried, not liking this development.

"To London, Mr. Taylor. Somewhere in England lies the key to all this."

CHAPTER 61

Salemi sat in the business class area of the British Airways lounge at John F. Kennedy airport, reading a day-old copy of Corriere della Sera.

He looked up from the newspaper and smiled as he saw a familiar figure enter the lounge, grab a beer from the free bar and head towards him.

Salemi laughed and said: "Somehow I thought I might see you here."

Taylor looked a little sheepish, then grinned and sat down opposite the priest.

"My boss seems to think we should have a look at things over there in England."

And he thinks you should keep an eye on me, thought Salemi. This, too, could be handled.

"Good," said Salemi offering his hand. "We'll make a good team. I was hoping you would come along, but it had to be your decision."

Taylor had sped to the airport after a short conversation with Grasso.

"The priest's on the move — to London," he had informed Grasso.

"Well, you better go with him," had been Grasso's dry reply.

"Okay, I'm on my way to the airport."

Grasso had made sure a ticket was waiting for Taylor at the BA check-in area.

He had told Taylor: "We'll have funds for hotels and expenses sent to you from one of our special accounts.

"Don't go near the U.S. Embassy in Grosvenor Square. The place is full of God knows how many spooks. The less they know the better.

"Keep in touch with me or Liddell," he had ordered before hanging up.

A boarding announcement for their flight was made. They stood and walked to the rear of the Club Class lounge, where a ramp led down to the gates.

Thirty minutes later, they were airborne, climbing out over Long Island Sound, bound for the northern coast of Labrador and the vast ocean leading to the Old World.

CHAPTER 62 — LONDON

Salemi and Taylor booked into a hotel in Russell Square, an area popular with tourists budgeting their spending money.

From there, the Strand, Covent Garden and the Thames Embankment were an easy walk.

The digital clock on the bedside table told Taylor it was 9 a.m. His body told him it was 4 a.m. in the middle of a sleepless night. He decided against a nap. A shower and breakfast would wake him up.

He telephoned Ann at the farm, remembering to charge the call to his cell phone. Salemi had warned about the ferocious charges hotels impose on the unwary.

She answered on the fifth ring, just as Taylor realized his time blunder.

Her voice was drowsy. For an instant he thought of hanging up.

"Ann," he said softly. I'm sorry to disturb you, I forgot the time difference. Go back to sleep."

The voice on the other end was now alert.

"What time difference?"

"I'm in London. Flew here last night. Didn't have time to tell you."

"Jeez, I've found myself a regular jet setter," she laughed.

Then a serious note.

"You're there on routine stuff?" she asked. "No danger or anything?"

"Purely routine, Ann. We're nowhere near catching this guy."

She sounded relieved.

"Is Eugene with you?"

"No. Monsignor Salemi."

"Good. He should discourage these brazen English hussies from chasing you."

Taylor gave her the hotel name and number and promised to call her each day and hung up. He had arranged to meet Salemi at the concierge desk in the main lobby of the hotel. They had a 10.30 a.m. appointment with Sir Moberley Johns.

CHAPTER 63

A black taxicab threaded through traffic and took Taylor and Salemi past St. Paul's Cathedral and toward the river. The driver pulled smartly into a small courtyard off Queen Victoria Street and deposited them on the porch steps of the College of Arms.

They were 15 minutes early for their appointment with Johns.

"I wonder if he's here yet," said Taylor looking at his watch.

Salemi raised his arm and pointed to a silver-and-blue flag flying on a staff from the building's porch.

"Oh, he's here all right. That's his personal banner," he said.

He saw Taylor's confusion and explained:" All the heralds and the junior rankers, the pursuivants, take turns on duty. Each week a different man takes on all the new business coming to the college.

"On Monday, a new banner will be flying there, and a new herald on duty."

"How many are there," asked Taylor.

"Normally about 13," said Salemi. "They are

all appointed by the Royal Household and are paid ridiculously low annual stipends. “We’re talking about less than $100.

"But once you initially contact the herald on duty, you are normally his client for life. A good percentage of the fee is given to that particular herald. That way, many heralds build up their own private independent practices, like a doctor or lawyer.

"Moberley is unusual in that he is an auxiliary pursuivant. Unlike the other heralds, he is not counted as a member of the corporation of the college—which is part of the Royal Household.

"Father Orr told me that's usually the way he likes things in his public life. He is on the fringes and is invited there when other heralds are ill or business pressures call for him."

At 11 precisely they entered the wood-paneled interior of the 17th Century house.

At the top of the stairs, Sir Moberley Johns stood. Taylor thought the man would be at home on some Victorian stage. He was below medium height and had a heavy build.

His feet were spread apart, his stocky shoulders pulled back, his fists thrusting into his hips.

The face was round and fleshy with clear green eyes. The nose had been broken, the balding blond hair cropped short giving a directness and a sense of the formidable to the man.

He grinned and welcomed his visitors.

Orr had briefed Salemi well. The old priest had described Johns as Churchillian and affable, but no man's fool.

He led them along a wooden passageway above an interior court and into a book shelved room.

"I have heard nothing but praise for your work, Monsignor," said Johns.

"Thank you, Sir Moberley. My Bishop and Father Orr say the same about you."

Taylor vaguely felt he was an outsider in some exclusive club. What work? Which Bishop?

But a beaming Johns turned to him.

"Let's forget the 'Sir' my dear fellows. Please call me Moberley or whatever you like. Mr Taylor, welcome to our sceptred isle."

Then the joviality faded from his pink face.

"We all agree our individual roles are to be kept confidential?"

Taylor and Salemi nodded imperceptibly.

"What do you know of English history, Mr. Taylor?"

CHAPTER 64

Taylor listened as Johns deftly sketched a portrait of the truculent, enigmatic King Henry VIII. Johns' voice was rich and polished and, Taylor thought, quite spell binding.

After outlining a biographical skeleton — the high hopes of a new golden age under the tall, handsome prince in contrast to the stinginess and austerity of his father, Henry VII, the man who fought bloodily to win the English throne and started the short Tudor dynasty — the herald went on to examine the contradictions in Henry's psyche.

"This was a man who loved company and close friendship, yet would coldly execute those intimates who defied his will. He was a devout Catholic, a man who believed in a literal hell and heaven. He attended Mass every day of his life.

"Yet he believed in the superstitions of his day. Witches did exist. And the Devil lurked in the shadows. But his pride, willfulness and obsession for a male heir estranged him from that very church he believed would ease his post mortem path to heaven. The younger Henry was cheerful, gregarious; the older Henry a bloodthirsty tyrant.

“In his youth he was blond, handsome, a magnificent figure of a man. A sportsman and horseman. Judging from surviving suits of personal armor he was well over 6-foot-2, an unusual height for his times. In his decline he became a corpulent, testy creature, his foul-smelling legs deeply ulcerated.

"Now we come to the interesting question: Why is the killer linking this dead Tudor despot or his period with this trail of killings?

"It must be obvious to him that we would eventually tie the murders to the thefts of weapons and Tudor artifacts. He is sending us a message, don't you think? Particularly with the music page."

Taylor knew the historical lecture had been meant solely for him. Salemi had been politely silent. Now it looked as if the priest had roused himself from a daydream.

"I'm sorry, Moberley. You were saying?"

"The message from the killer," Johns patiently repeated.

"Everything points to a planned assassination of the Prince. If this killer is somehow possessed by the mind of Henry, the House of Windsor, formerly the House of Saxe-Coburg-Gotha before the World War against Germany suggested a name change, would be alien to him. A target.

"The Secret Archives journal is incomplete. We are searching for other pieces of the Henry correspondence, which may help us predict where he will strike next.

Taylor found the historical abstractions fascinating, but as a policeman he felt bound to introduce a hard note of pragmatism.

"I think we really have to concentrate on physically finding clues to this man's identity. Do you still feel that the answer lies here in Britain, Sir Moberley?"

Johns laughed.

"Why not? It may be just conjecture, but I believe anyone who is so obsessed by Henry would spend time in England, visiting the palaces and estates he strolled and played upon. Hours meditating in the rooms and corridors he once walked through; touching his past."

Johns went on.

"I have taken the liberty of contacting some of my colleagues in the field of Tudor history; mostly University men who actively teach.

"I hope to hear back from them within a few days. Meanwhile, my cloak and dagger friends have promised to get me an expanded list of thefts and violent incidents, which may come under the purview of our inquiries."

There was a knock at the door and a tall, pretty woman entered carrying a large sheet of drawing paper.

Taylor glimpsed the vivid colors skillfully painted on a shield supported by fantastic creatures on either side.

"Meet Jenny. She's one of our best artists.

"We also have a group of scriveners who draft the armorial bearings. We're quite a self sufficient little company."

The woman left and Johns rose apologetically.

"I did promise to have this completed by tomorrow."

He couldn't resist a touch of wickedness.

"These freshly appointed socialist peers get very upset if their heraldic arms lag behind their new notepaper."

He smiled and escorted the priest and the agent to the door.

"Perhaps we could lunch at my club tomorrow. With luck, I may have something from my contacts."

Salemi gave Johns a piece of paper with their hotel number and the numbers of two cell phones they had rented from the concierge purely for local London area calls.

Taylor thanked his host.

"We'll look forward to dining with you. We'll talk to America during the evening hours. The time difference is in our favor. Maybe by tomorrow we can kick-start our operation over here."

CHAPTER 65
ROME

The waiters at Le Grand Hotel trod very lightly around a certain banquette on this particular afternoon. The normally affable Bishop Luca di Montevecchi scowled into the glass containing a classic Ruffino from his family estates.

Errant service was sharply reprimanded; superfluous attention was met by a dismissive wave of his plump hand.

A cell phone rang in the restaurant. The staff looked anxiously towards the bishop, waiting for signs of anger.

Di Montevecchi had shown outrage in the past at such interruptions.

They were amazed when the Bishop sheepishly pulled a small Nokia phone from the black briefcase on the seat next to him.

"I got your message at the hotel. Is something wrong?" Salemi inquired.

Di Montevecchi made sure no one in the restaurant was within earshot.

"The meddling fools here can't leave us alone. We have been told to stay out of the investigation, at least in the United States."

"But I thought Fiore and Marinello were on our side," said Salemi.

Cardinals Tomasso Fiore and Carlo Marinello were the prelates who had used their influence on the seven-man secret Vatican committee, which had given their reluctant consent to the Henry investigation.

But their five colleagues were more interested in the present — and would end the hunt as soon as it clashed with their political aims.

"Someone from the Vatican Embassy in Washington has stirred up resentment against us. They claim that the U.S. State Department has heard rumors of our operation's existence and that it could cause a diplomatic rift.

"The establishment Cardinals have a watchful eye on America. They have great worries about the health of the church there. They do not want to risk political backlash. They have never been at ease with our quest. In their eyes, this is an excuse to shut us down.

"However, our two Cardinals won't let them — yet.

"Cardinal Fiore has privately told me to cool down the operation. I've told them you are in Europe now and that Father Orr is quietly tending the office in New York. We can stall them for a few weeks, but we need to identify the killer as soon as possible, I don't know how much longer we can hold them off."

The Bishop's frustration and anger were clear. Salemi had never heard doubt or despair in the older man's voice before. He sensed it now.

A positive note was needed.

"I am sure we are going in the right direction," he said strongly.

"Your friend Sir Moberley has the expertise and contacts we need here.

“And the FBI Agent Taylor is liaising closely with his colleagues in the U.S. I think that he, too, is under pressure from officials within his agency."

"Warn him to be very careful. It seems we have powerful enemies on both sides of the Atlantic,” di Montevecchi counseled.

The Bishop took a few seconds to locate a button and shut off the hated cell phone.

He looked thoughtful for a few minutes then looked up at the anxious band of waiters.

"Cognac, my brave fellows," he boomed.

They relaxed. The Bishop was his old self.

CHAPTER 66
LONDON

Taylor and Salemi had left Johns and walked to a loud, smoky tourist pub near the ancient, imposing fortress of The Tower of London.

Salemi excused himself, walked outside and used his cell phone. He had promised to check the hotel for messages for both of them.

After 10 minutes he returned.

"I had to call head office in Rome," he joked. "Nothing fresh there. There were no messages for you."

After a dreary meal of London's idea of Tex-Mex fast food and warm flat beer they had joined the tourist throng and strolled through the portcullis gates, up the cobbled lanes of the castle founded in the 11th Century by William the Conqueror.

Looking down from a high wall toward the Thames, Salemi pointed out water-worn steps leading to a grim entrance accessible only from the river.

"That is the notorious Traitor's Gate," said Salemi.

"Imagine the poor souls who were ferried down the river day and night on the dictate of kings and powerful men; the Gate the last view of freedom before entering the tower for torture and possible execution."

Taylor felt the priest's passion. As he gazed down at the ominous, dank steps, the picture the priest had conjured sent a shiver through him.

They walked eastward up a gently sloping hill. There, on a green in an open square, was the site of the historic executioner's block.

Sitting on a small iron-railed patch of lawn was a marker. That spot where scaffolds were erected was the last piece of earthly contact kings, queens and traitors had knelt upon before the executioner's blade separated their heads from their shoulders.

The tourists made light of the killing ground, laughing at the contrived efforts at humor from their guide, a uniformed Yeoman Warder of the Tower.

Salemi whispered to Taylor: "For some reason most of these guides act like bad stage comics. No where else in the world would they be tolerated."

Taylor was surprised by the priest's sharp tone. But then reminded himself that to a man like Salemi, history was serious business. The priest had a reverence for the past which was absolute and sincere. Taylor admired that.

The crowd was noisy and irreverent. One adolescent skipped over the rail and placed his head on a replica of the execution block. His friends laughed and photographed him.

Taylor saw Salemi's disgust and suggested: "Let's get out of here, shall we?"

The priest shrugged. "I had wanted to show you something of the Tower. But it's like a noisy cattle market. It is a pity it had to come to this."

"I first came here as a boy, when I was at school in England."

Taylor was surprised at the confidence offered by the priest who up till now had guarded any details of his personal life.

School in England would explain the priest's sometimes rigid grammatical style of conversation.

"How did that happen?" said Salemi.

"You mean the Tower visit or school?" replied the priest with a smile.

"I was wondering how long it would be before you ventured into my personal background. It's one of the unique American customs. Within minutes of meeting a perfect stranger in a bar he feels free to ask your name, profession, place of birth, age and salary."

Salemi saw Taylor's mouth tighten and his face redden and laughed.

"Please don't be offended. It's a charming if somewhat ingenuous effort to make a stranger welcome. I understand it all too well.

"My mother was an American. And I was very proud of her."

One chance remark by Salemi had breached the defensive walls of both men. Somehow, here in England their very foreignness formed a bond between them. A shared experience which broke down reticence.

As they walked away from the white exterior walls of the Tower, back through the City, Salemi told of his privileged education in a private Catholic boarding school in Cheshire, England, of studies in Switzerland and Florence, and seminary in Palermo.

"What about your parents?" asked Taylor.

"My father was a prosecutor, a very brave man. He was murdered by criminal thugs. My mother died 10 years later of a broken heart. She was beautiful, from a wealthy family. She could have returned home to America. Married any man she wanted to. But she did not want to leave my father's family or his grave. She had loved him very much."

Salemi was surprised at his own emotional outpouring. The only man he had ever confided such intimacies to was di Montevecchi, his mentor and friend. But the big American had awakened unaccustomed feelings of trust and friendship. Or was he simply a first-class policeman skilled at interrogation techniques, a master of ingratiation.

Taylor sensed the priest's sudden embarrassment. He offered his own token of friendship and volunteered: "My own parents are dead. My mother with a weak heart, my father fell 60 feet at a construction site. I still miss them."

Salemi nodded then looked out to the roadway and hailed a passing taxi.

The taste of their vapid lunchtime beer was still with them.

"Let's go and get a real drink — in an American bar."

"How do we manage that," said Taylor.

"Take us to the Savoy hotel," Salemi instructed the cab driver.

"It's not quite a U.S. saloon, but the American Bar in the hotel makes a very passable Martini," said the priest. Let's enjoy today. The hard work begins tomorrow."

CHAPTER 67

Taylor winced as he swallowed the bitter English coffee and toyed with a triangle of rubbery, toasted white bread. He tried Ann's telephone numbers again. There had been no reply the night before at either the Watergate apartment or the Virginia farm.

He had enjoyed the evening with Salemi. Drinks at the American Bar, then dinner at Simpson's not far along The Strand from the hotel.

He had been fascinated by the priest's personal history and admired his wit and acuity. But he knew he had barely scratched the surface of this enigmatic man. Still, he instinctively knew Salemi would be a good man to have on his side if they ran into danger.

The telephone at the farmhouse was picked up; a woman's voice — Mrs. Green.

Taylor identified himself and asked for Ann.

"Oh, Mr. Taylor. She will be so glad you called." Her voice seemed sad, strained.

"Is every thing all right, Mrs. Green?"

"It's her grandfather, Mr. Taylor. He's dead. She's gone to attend to him. Everything was so sudden. She got the news just after you called from London."

"God, I am so sorry. Where is she?"

"Bermuda. He had a villa there. He loved to be near the sea. Swam every morning. They think he had a heart attack and drowned. It's awful news for Ann. She doesn't have anyone left."

Taylor was moved by the housekeeper's obvious love and concern for Ann.

"We'll get her through this, Mrs. Green. Don't you worry."

He pulled a tablet of hotel note paper to him and fished in a drawer for a ballpoint pen.

"Do you have a number I can contact her at?"

Mrs. Green gave a Hamilton number and added: "I think she will be returning very soon. The lawyers here and in Bermuda are being very helpful to her.

"The old man had left instructions to be cremated immediately and his ashes scattered at sea. That's probably happened already."

Taylor could hear a catch in Mrs. Green's throat and realized she was about to weep.

"We have to be strong for her Mrs. Green. Tell her ... tell her I'm sorry and that I'll keep calling until I reach her. She has my hotel number in London."

He hung up angry at himself. Why couldn't he have told Mrs. Green "Tell her I love her."

He now knew that would have been the truth. In future he would hide that from no one.

CHAPTER 68

The Chapman Club snoozed in a cobbled lane just off Pall Mall. The gray stoned Georgian mansion had cultivated a dated and run down exterior which the club members, mostly historians and writers, approved.

It was a place to relax, to drink amid gentle conversation. In debate, one could be strongly opinionated but never loud.

The vein of genteel self deprecation that mined the club began above the marble Adams fireplace which greeted visitors as they entered.

A brass plaque underneath an oil portrait of Napoleon Bonaparte recorded his famous observation on history: "A set of lies agreed upon."

It was there that Johns greeted Taylor and Salemi just before 1 p.m.

The herald's eyes were sparkling as he shook hands, then led the way into the club's dining room.

As he led them to a window table in the one-third full dining room, he muttered just above a whisper: "Good news. I think I've got good news."

Taylor found Johns' enthusiasm and zest fetching.

They sat down and accepted a typewritten menu with the day's entrees from a steward.

"As you know, I sent the word out to some old pals, and, by God, I think we struck gold," Johns said excitedly.

Taylor kept his skepticism out of his voice. He reminded himself that many a case was cleared after a lucky break.

"That sounds wonderful, Moberley. Let's hear it." Johns had once more insisted that they drop the 'Sir'.

"An old classmate of mine, now a don at Oxford responded to my appeal with a very likely suspect. In fact, as he described him to me, I could barely contain myself."

Salemi was growing impatient. Johns caught his anxious gaze.

"To the facts, Gentlemen. The suspect studied Tudor script and history. He was an American. He was brilliant and intense — too intense for some of his fellow students. After an incident in which he injured himself in a fall he became moody, violent. And most importantly, he was caught trying to steal Henrician documents from the college library. Shortly after, he disappeared before the authorities could punish him."

Johns leaned back in his seat and said triumphantly.

"Well, what do you think?"

"I think you're a bloody wizard," said Salemi, laughing.

Johns beamed and said: "I have taken the liberty of making an appointment with my old friend for 5 p.m. at his rooms in Oxford. He will have all the details for us there."

"Meanwhile" he added, picking up the menu. "I think we have time for a quick luncheon. I recommend the Brown Windsor soup and the roast beef and Yorkshire Pud."

CHAPTER 69
OXFORD

Maximillian Morgenstern was tall, thin, angular and capable of great animation when he shared his passion for history with his students.

With his distinctive profile and long hair curling from the back of his head, a student had cartooned the mercurial don after a famous silhouette of the violin virtuoso Nicolo Paganini. The nickname "Pags" Morgenstern had stuck.

In the gray British light, his college rooms at Oxford were almost in shadow. He turned to his guests and gestured to a round tray on a sideboard containing a decanter of golden sherry and four glasses.

He was intrigued by Johns' companions, an American and an Italian—probably both policemen, though the Italian seemed more than that.

Johns had introduced them as colleagues on a "hush-hush" matter, hinting broadly that they were on secret government work.

Morgenstern was happy to be of help. He lifted a glass of the dry sherry to his lips and toasted: "Here's to Richard Copeland Congreve!"

He looked at the puzzled faces and added with a smile: "That's the fellow you've come about, isn't it?"

He turned to Johns. "I wasn't sure of his full name when I spoke to you on the telephone, Moberley. But I've checked. Congreve's the man."

Salemi and Taylor both struggled to contain their feelings.

Christ, thought Taylor, it can't be this easy but let this be the guy. At last someone they could go after.

Salemi said quietly: "Please tell us everything you know, Dr. Morgenstern."

The don's color rose and his voice became louder, staccato. The teacher emerged and the trio became his students.

"I remember he was a large chap. He was a few inches taller than me and I'm 6-foot-1. A very powerful man. He was much older than the other post grads. In his early thirties I would guess. He mixed well at first with the other students, but refused to join in their social activities. Pub crawls and the like.

"He preferred to be in his study, at the library or on the river spending hours rowing by himself.

"He was very serious about his studies, quite brilliant in his own way. The other masters liked him. He had a quick and probative mind. He could be analytical but he also had the swooping imagination the best historians need. Congreve had become quite the expert on the Tudor period.

As Morgenstern spoke, Taylor jotted brief details in a leather bound notebook.

"Then came the accident — a fall that nearly killed him. It was a miracle he survived."

"What happened?" said Johns, playing along with his friend's love of dramatics. Morgenstern loved to tell a story his own way.

His rooms were in the oldest part of the college, overlooking a quadrangle. For some reason he defenestrated himself. Don't know if it was an accident or something else. But it was a terrible fall — about 20 feet.

"He was still unconscious when he was admitted to the hospital but after a week there he discharged himself and returned to college.

"The accident changed him completely. He became a singularly moody and angry man. He became positively misanthropic. He retreated to his study and was barely civil to his masters. His personal appearance and hygiene suffered. He was unshaven and unkempt.

"Then came the incident at the University library. A security guard caught him trying to smuggle out a Tudor manuscript. He attacked the poor man. It took three men to subdue him. He was arrested and the University was notified. The proctor was called and a search of his rooms revealed a half dozen similar thefts.

"What happened in court," asked Taylor.

"It never got that far. Mr. Congreve was released pending an investigation and disappeared.

He apparently descended from an exceedingly wealthy American family. The family lawyers settled the legal problems and arranged a substantial financial donation to the library foundation. Everybody was happy. I heard the injured security guard was given a generous gift to salve his wounds."

After Congreve disappeared, I was asked to go through the papers he had left. His study was filthy. Documents were strewn all over the floor.

"All of the papers were what one would expect from that kind of scholar — all but one.

"He had kept a handwritten journal, full of quotations and personal thoughts. For some reason known only to him he had written it in Elizabethan script."

Salemi leaned forward in his chair and asked: "Was there anything unusual in it? Anything that would let us know how he was thinking?"

"Nothing that made any sense," said Morgenstern.

"Just one thing that may not mean anything, but it might indicate how the fall and the blow to his head had confused his mind.

"While reading the journal I was struck by a very odd thing. Congreve was a very meticulous man. The book was written in late Elizabethan script up to, presumably, the night of the fall. When the journal entries resumed, they were in a much earlier, bolder Tudor script. A subtle change, but a perplexing one for a scholar like Congreve to have adopted."

Taylor risked the question. "What period of time are we talking about, Sir?"

"It's a script from the late 1400s. It was still in use in the early reign of Henry VIII."

"Do you still have the journal?" Taylor asked.

"'Fraid not, old chap. Everything was bundled up and sent off to the lawyers along with the rest of his belongings. After all, it was his property."

He opened a drawer and pulled out a deep blue folder. He handed it to Johns.

"These are a few notes on his studies and what else I remember of the fellow. I tried to get more details from a friend at the University records office, but it seems all details of Congreve have been redacted. Not even a copy of his student alien visa."

"Would he be fingerprinted?" Taylor asked quickly.

"We don't have anything like that. But his picture would be lodged at the local police station."

Salemi rose and shook Morgenstern's hand.

"You've been very helpful, Dr. Morgenstern."

"We can't thank you enough," Taylor added.

The old don clapped his skeletal hand on Johns' broad shoulder.

"You'll let me know how this goes, won't you, Moberley."

"You'll be the first to know, old boy. Still, a tad secret at the moment. You understand."

"Of course, Moberley. Delighted to help. Good hunting, gentlemen"

The three men sat in the lounge in the smoky bar of a 200-year-old inn on the banks of the Isis—the peculiar Oxford truncation of the ancient Roman name for the Thames —Tamesis.

Salemi sipped orange juice. Johns had insisted Taylor try a pink gin. It made Taylor want to gag.

"It's decision time," Taylor announced. "This has to be reported to Washington. And, in fairness to you, Moberley, I am sure you feel duty bound to tell your people."

"As you say John, that is my duty and I will do my duty. However, I can assure you that this information will only reach a select and small number of intelligence and police operatives in London.

"I'll ask them to find out if there is a student visa identity picture from the Thames Valley Police. Besides, if this is truly our man, the hard digging will start over in the United States. We must consider that he has fled home to America where his family money protects him. It's more of an FBI case at this juncture than a British investigation.

"My chaps in London will need all the help your people can give us. We have a long way to go to match this fellow with the killings, since no one has ever seen the murderer and lived. But at least the Royal Protection Squad will have a photograph of a suspect to look out for."

They looked at Salemi, who had kept silent. They did not have to ask the question on their minds.

"I will tell my immediate superior. No one else," the priest promised."

A young barmaid, a slim pretty girl, passed by Taylor, who pushed his gin toward her.

"Can I have a beer?" he asked. "Just a draft lager will do."

Moberley shook his head in disgust.

Then Taylor slapped his hand lightly on the table.

"Christ! What am I thinking? Moberley, do the British cops routinely take fingerprints of those they arrest?"

His hopes were quickly dashed.

“Not until they charge a suspect. Congreve was never charged.”

CHAPTER 70

Taylor could not believe what he was hearing. They had detrained at Paddington Station late the night before, flushed from their success in Oxford.

He and Salemi returned to the hotel determined to get a good night's sleep for what promised to be an exciting and productive morrow. He had called Grasso in Washington with the good news.

Now Taylor checked his fury as he listened to an agitated and apologetic Johns. The pictures of the suspect and all official details about him could not be found. The records seem to have disappeared from the computer files.

"There's still a chance that they will turn up," Johns said lamely. Our intelligence chaps are demanding a thorough search. They want explanations. There will be hell to pay if they don't turn up."

"What is the police explanation at the moment?" Taylor asked. He was fighting to keep his voice and emotions under control. Things had been going too smoothly. He should have known better.

"Well, the student ID photo may have been discarded when the University notified the police he was no longer attending the college. He would have been one among thousands who pass through the foreign student visa system in any given year.

"The records of the police criminal inquiry into the violent burglary are much harder to explain away. Unless Congreve's lawyers had them redacted from the records as part of their deal."

"Well, we've got a name and the address of his lawyers in New York.

"My people in Washington are on it. Though I'd be surprised if Mr. Congreve is waiting at home to receive us," said Taylor.

He arranged to call Johns later in the day then told Salemi the bad news.

At noon Grasso called.

"We have secured Congreve's home — or should I say castle. It's one of the biggest estates in the Carolinas. It's a very wealthy, old family.

"We found about a dozen estate workers, but no Congreve. He lit out a month ago. The staff say that wasn't unusual. He often disappears for months at a time. They never know when he will come and go. He's the last of the line and lives off the interest from massive trusts.

"He has the money and the means to hide out anywhere in the world. He could have all sorts of fake IDs. So far, we have found no adult pictures of him but are checking for passport photos. We have made a preliminary search of the buildings on the estate. But I've now made his personal quarters off limits to everyone. I want you to take a look at it with your ... friend."

Grasso still found it hard to acknowledge a priest was helping with the investigation.

"Anything more from your fucked-up British cops?"

"No. It could be accidental or..."

Grasso finished the sentence for him. "… or British intelligence has pictures and prints and is playing us for dummies."

"That had crossed my mind," said Taylor.

"Let's pull all the stops out to find the fingerprints. Our boys have taken extensive prints from Congreve's house but we need a positive identifier. Keep after the pictures, but prints are even more valuable.

"If we can match them to any found at the murder scenes we can concentrate solely on him. It will smooth any legal obstacles prosecutors might face in investigating him.

"We are going to pile the pressure on the British from Washington. If they are fucking with us, they'll regret it. Stay in London for now, but be prepared to haul ass out of there at a moment's notice," Grasso instructed. "I want your take on Congreve's lair before the family lawyers try to keep us out."

"They giving us problems?" asked Taylor.

"They will. Bet on it. At the moment they are giving us the bare minimum of co-operation. They have warned us we've got the wrong man; threatened legal action if any of this leaks out. At the moment we are stretching our powers under the Patriot Act to the point of elasticity. The Justice guys don't like it.

Taylor offered: "No one said it would be easy."

"Fuck you and your platitudes, Taylor." Taylor heard the telephone crash loudly at the other end. Grasso's mood matched his own.

CHAPTER 71
COPELAND, NORTH CAROLINA

On the edge of the forest, a mile from the great mansion, was a tree house. Its weathered timbers melted into the gloom and shadows of the old growth woodlands.

Richard Copeland Congreve raised the Bausch and Lomb binoculars to his eyes and followed a gravel road that skirted the ornamental lake.

A distant flash of weak sunlight on the windows of three black cars heading up the long drive to the house. The staff greeting them. Nine men all wearing suits entering the building.

A sudden premonition had urged him to leave the great house just three weeks before. He had taken a large duffel bag filled with the last of his books. Most of the weapons had already been hidden around the estate and in a woodsman's hut deep in the forest.

His last trip had gone well. He had returned to the nourishing safety of the woods he had loved since childhood. They were wild, uncut and, in parts, impenetrable. The Congreves had long ago quashed any attempts at commercial exploitation of the vast timberland.

He had planned to slip unannounced, one last time, into the great house to retrieve what weapons were left when he spotted the cars entering the north gate, where the private rail line ended. It had been built by a Congreve baron in the 1880s to speed up private excursions from the family mansions in Newport and New York.

So. They had found him. He laughed. They would never catch him.

He had homes around the country, homes even his lawyers knew nothing about. He had money, he had power, he had witchcraft on his side. He was invincible.

CHAPTER 72
LONDON

It was Salemi, student of the Machiavellian intrigues of powerful men, who first shone light on the missing identity photographs and case details of their suspected quarry.

He and Taylor had walked along the Thames embankment towards Westminster. The sky was gray, the river slate. It was damp and chill and tourists huddled inside the restaurant barges out of the wind.

The cold weather had not cooled Taylor. He was still angry.

"I'm positive we've been screwed by the Brits," he growled.

"I'm positive you're right," the priest said evenly.

"So what the hell do we do?" Taylor said, annoyed by Salemi's complacency.

"We wait a few hours, perhaps a day. Believe me, the picture and records will suddenly be found and offered to you. I know the Brits. They just want a flying start. They cannot lose face. It's a matter of control. When your bosses in Washington pile on the pressure, they'll cave.

"They won't risk damaging the entire operation. They know they will need your active assistance to get results. The stress involved in trying to protect a Prince who disdains security is enormous. They want to be able to tell their Prime Minister and the Prince that they are the ones who discovered the break in the case, that it is their information which they hand over to the Yanks.

"It's the ideal situation for them. They appear to break the identity of the prime suspect in the murders. If it all goes wrong and the fellow is not caught, it's the bumbling Americans' fault."

He put an arm round Taylor's shoulder as they approached the steps leading up to Westminster Bridge. "Relax, my friend. I am never wrong in these matters."

Standing on the far side of the bridge like a pillar of sand in his camel-hair coat was Sir Moberley Johns.

Taylor looked up at the Clock Tower holding Big Ben. Sir Moberley interrupted his gaze with a wave of his hand.

"You should be looking down. That's where the real history lies."

Johns pointed a leather-gloved finger at a narrow square of lawn below the bridge and alongside the Houses of Parliament.

"That area was the old tilt yard of Westminster Palace. That's where Henry VIII and his nobles jousted and reveled. Just close your eyes and imagine the spectacles that must have played upon that unmarked stretch of grass. The lords and ladies who spent their afternoons there. The pomp, splendor and chivalry.

"But enough of that. Let's eat. I know just the place if you don't mind an occasional division bell ringing to drag MPs from their wine bottles for a vote in the House.

CHAPTER 73
LONDON

The meal had been bland and overpriced; the restaurant noisy, the service indifferent. Johns pointed out some of the power brokers in British politics.

To Taylor, apart from the English food and crumpled, badly styled suits, it could have been one of the Congressional watering holes of Washington he tried so hard to avoid.

There was a constant coming and going across the road outside the restaurant to the Houses of Parliament 50 yards away.

If Johns had been trying to impress his foreign visitors, he had failed.

More annoying to Taylor was Johns' failure to produce the official records on Congreve. He was convinced now that the herald and his cloak and dagger cronies were pulling a fast one. But he was determined to heed Salemi's counsel to remain calm.

If Johns detected tension at the table he did not acknowledge it.

He sipped a claret and declared: "I think I might have found a clue which points again to the Prince being the target.

"I was re-examining the Chicago crime scene pictures you so kindly gave me. This time I focused on the curious swath of blood from the severed limb running diagonally across the Royal arms."

"You mean on the flag hanging on the marquee wall?" asked Taylor.

Johns tried not to wince at Taylor's misnomer and continued

"The, uh… silk representation of the Royal arms, yes.

"Whoever did it took great care to create a straight broad path of blood from the top right to the bottom left. In heraldry right and left are described from the point of view of the man BEHIND the shield."

Salemi seemed interested now. His eyebrows lifted and he smiled at Johns.

"The bar sinister," he said. "It was staring us in the face all the time."

Moberley caught Taylor's puzzled look and explained.

"You have the right idea, Monsignor, but through a popular misconception, the wrong name. I am afraid I must correct you.

Many people believe the bar sinister' is an indication of illegitimacy. There is no such thing. In fact the indication of illegitimacy is a 'baton sinister.' A baton is a narrow band extending across the shield; sinister from the Latin meaning 'left.' Is it not odd that anything that did not fit into the orderly ancient world, like being left-handed, could create the menace the word sinister conveys today. The baton sinister need not mean the bearer's family descended from bastardy. It may mean that the claim to a family's lineal descent cannot be proven or the claim itself is illegitimate.

"But in this case we can assume a more outraged motive for the device."

"In other words, the killer was leaving us a message. Right from the start he was warning us," said Taylor.

"Precisely," said Johns. "We have a murderer who believes the House of Windsor has no claim to the British throne."

"That must make the British government a little unhappy," said Taylor unable to resist sarcasm.

Johns looked sternly at Taylor but let it pass. He understood the American's frustration and was embarrassed over the lack of British co-operation on the police files. He hoped that would soon be corrected.

A quarrel with Taylor would do no good for their cause.

"What news from the Americas?" he asked.

"Very little," said Taylor. "We have secured Congreve's estate. They have found a handful of historical documents and some very old weapons.

"They are cataloging them and trying to match them with known historical thefts. Father Orr in New York is sharing the Vatican's computer patterns involving thefts and incidents involving Tudor artifacts. Orr's files are much more extensive than the Quantico printouts."

The bill came and Salemi insisted on taking it. He pulled out a platinum Banco di Roma card and quickly signed.

"I have some personal chores to do, Gentlemen," he said.

"Please excuse me. I will be available on the cell phone if you need me."

Taylor stood and flicked some breadcrumbs from his lap.

"I think I'll stroll back to the hotel and call Washington, and Liddell.

"How are he and Father Orr getting along?" he asked Salemi.

"I spoke to Father Orr this morning. He seems ready to adopt Liddell. They have become fast friends."

"Talk about the odd couple," laughed Taylor.

The suddenly wintry sun was fast falling when Taylor walked up Russell Square and into the entrance of the hotel. He strode to the front office counter and asked for messages.

The young desk clerk smiled broadly at Taylor.

"No messages Sir, but your wife has arrived. We sent her straight up to the room with her luggage. I hope that's all right, Sir."

Taylor 's head spun and his body flooded with adrenaline. He turned on his heel and raced to the elevator .The doors were closing as he jammed his body into the crowded space.

At a tortuous pace the machine stopped and shuddered at each floor. At the sixth level he slipped out into the corridor and gingerly approached his room door.

He fished the key card from his pocket and pushed it into the lock.

He opened the door three inches and listened. The shower was running, a veil of steam was coming from the bathroom.

He entered and crossed the room. The door to the bathroom was half open. Through the opaque shower curtain he could make out the pink and tan skin, the fetching, perfectly proportioned curves that fed his desire.

"It was Ann."

CHAPTER 74

Ann looked into Taylor's eyes and was troubled by what she saw there.

Less than a week ago it had seemed right. She presumed he wanted her as much as she needed him. Now, with a sickening realization, she saw her unannounced journey as a silly, impetuous act.

Taylor's face had registered surprise, then concern. She saw no signs of delight in the gray-blue eyes. That look was distant, even calculating.

She had sat in the balcony of a restaurant in Hamilton gazing at the cruise ships tied up along Front Street. She had watched a British airways jumbo wheel over the town descending to the Bermuda airport. The airliner would be returning to Britain that night. Her grandfather's ashes had been scattered at sea that morning; the lawyers were in charge now. There was no reason to remain in Bermuda.

The Virginia farm was filled with memories of grandpa. She needed Taylor to hold her and tell her everything would be all right.

During the long Atlantic flight she had rehearsed in her mind how he would show his delight at her unexpected appearance. They would make love, then have a romantic dinner.

Now, as she stood on the tile floor of the bathroom, tears mingled with the shower water streaking her face. She had made a terrible mistake.

Taylor saw the tears, thought they were for her grandfather and held her closely to him.

"Oh Annie, you've been through so much. Let me hold you. I'm not going to let anything else happen to you."

He was surprised when she angrily pushed him away.

"What's wrong, Ann?"

Then it came to him. He immediately sensed that his initial reaction had deeply disappointed her and cursed himself.

She had read his contradictory feelings. Above all he took pride in being a professional and it wasn't done to mix business with what would look to outsiders as lustful pleasure.

You didn't fly in your girlfriend when you were working a case. It would look terrible to Salemi and Johns, let alone Grasso and the bureau.

But this was Ann; she needed him as much he did her.

She turned and pulled on a blue bathrobe.

"I've been stupid. I've made a mistake coming here. I'll be out of here in an hour. I'm sorry."

Taylor held her again.

"Don't you dare think of leaving. Look, Ann I'll admit you surprised me. And I'll admit that as soon as I saw you I started thinking how your presence would affect my work here. I've been preoccupied by the whole damn mess.

"But the hell with all that. I want you with me. I love you."

Ann looked at his face and saw the truth of it.

"I'll stay just a day, John. I promise I won't get in the way.

"I understand if something comes up you have to pursue it alone. I just needed to be with you."

Taylor guided her to the bed and laid her gently down.

CHAPTER 75
LONDON

Salemi saw the stunning blonde with Taylor and immediately recognized her. It was the girl from the theatre. The FBI man had obviously fallen hard for her.

Normally Salemi would be sympathetic. He knew only too well the temptations offered by a pretty woman. He had fought to resist them zealously. But what was she doing here? They were at a crucial stage of the hunt for the killer. What could he possibly be thinking? She shouldn't be in London.

The priest masked his annoyance and walked to the front desk area where Taylor introduced them.

Ann was unaware the youthful, elegantly dressed priest had spied on her months before outside the Croft murder scene. Taylor had confided Salemi's role in the investigation. Together they walked out the hotel into a damp freezing chill. A wind blew sporadic curtains of drizzle, guttering the lights from street lamps and the passing traffic. Passengers in rain streaked, red, double-decker buses were crowded behind misty windows.

They walked to the Covent Garden area and entered one of London's oldest restaurants.

They were shown a booth and a menu of classic English fare. The room was all oak and walnut and mirrors and pewter. The restaurant's own privately brewed beer was served in glittering tankards.

Ann felt obliged to explain her presence to Salemi. She wanted to make it clear that Taylor had no knowledge of her surprise trip.

The priest was charming. His black eyes focused on her. He listened attentively and quickly made light of her visit.

"Please. Never have regrets, Ann. I am happy to meet you at last. You have brought sunshine to this cold dark country. We needed you."

Taylor was grateful for Salemi's obvious attempts to welcome Ann and relieve her anxiety. If he had chosen to, the priest could have made her feel awkward, an interloper.

"Besides," Salemi continued, "we were at a temporary standstill in our enquiries. Your visit is doubly welcome."

Ann noticed the easy rapport that had grown between the handsome Sicilian and Taylor. They were relaxed with each other, in tune, like old friends.

Salemi learned of Ann's loss and said he would offer prayers for her grandfather's soul. Ann was moved by his sincerity and compassion. His rock-like faith somehow eased the pain, as if her grandfather's spirit was, somehow, now in good hands.

The Catholic Church seemed to offer much more comfort for those grieving their lost ones. She imagined it must always have been this way. The timeless beauty of the liturgy for the dead.

Her grandfather had, at age 77, been vigorous in health. He had died while swimming in his beloved sea. The corpse had been found a mile off shore; battered and chopped by shipping traffic. There would be no viewing of the body for his handful of island friends. A cremation and ashes scattered at sea was always his wish.

She wiped a tear from her eye and changed the subject.

"Well, John tells me you have a name for the suspect. Does that mean it will soon be all over?"

She caught Taylor's surprised look.

"Oh, dear! Me and my big mouth. I assure you it will go no further, I weaseled it out of him."

Taylor glanced quickly at Salemi. He expected the priest would be angry at his sharing information with Ann. But he need not have worried.

“You have every right to be told," he said gently. "You have lost a very dear friend to this killer. You have my confidence as well as John's.

"As for the murderer, we have to catch him first," said Salemi.

Taylor was once again grateful to the priest for his empathy.

He reminded Ann: "And we have to have evidence connecting him to the murders. We're a long way from any of that, Ann," said Taylor gently.

Salemi tried to explain.

"I am afraid we are waiting for the British authorities to give us more complete trust. But I think that will happen, sooner or later. Sooner, I think."

A stocky figure entered the restaurant, was greeted effusively by the maitre d' and ushered to their table.

Taylor could see Sir Moberley Johns stiffen and glance quizzically at Ann before resuming his mask of bonhomie.

Taylor introduced Ann to him.

"What a pleasure to meet you, my dear," Johns said.

Salemi explained Ann's presence and how fate had caught her up in the case.

Johns relaxed and offered his sympathies to Ann.

After a suitable pause, Ann felt tears rising at the memory of Gerry, and her grandfather, excused herself and made her way to the ladies room.

Johns turned and beamed at Taylor and Salemi.

"Great news, my friends. Great news! We will have the police data first thing in the morning. They have been miraculously found."

Taylor congratulated Moberly, glanced at his watch, and noted it was only 3 p.m. in Washington. He excused himself and went out to the sidewalk near the restaurant entrance. He dialed up Washington to report to Grasso. Salemi similarly went off to call Rome.

As Ann returned, Moberly smiled and said: "The gentlemen are outside calling their superiors. Such is the modern world. It will be my decided pleasure to keep you company. Tell me, do you plan to see the sights of London?"

Ann frowned: "I may not have the time. John told me he visited the Tower of London. Goodness, just the thought of all these executions. Tell me, was Anne Boleyn executed there?"

"She certainly was," Moberly said with surprising amusement in his eyes.

"Forgive me if I seem flippant, but I am always intrigued with America's fascination with Anne Boleyn or, as Henry VIII's courtiers originally called her, "that Bullen woman."

Ann laughed. "I'm afraid I only know the Hollywood version of Anne Boleyn. What was she really like?"

Moberly was struck by the young American's effortless charm and interest in a subject he knew more about than most so-called 'experts'.

"Actually the real Anne Boleyn would have been very well-suited for Hollywood films, for in her time she was the Tudor equivalent of a Hollywood star.

"She was, in her own way, a superb actress who arrived at the English court and dazzled everyone, including of course the very married Henry VIII.

"She could be compared to today's ludicrously named "super models." She dictated the latest fashions from the arbiter of such matters — the French royal court, which she had attended since childhood.

"With the latest French dances and songs, their superior style and formal manners, she positively lit up the more rustic English court. The King, still young, married for political motives to an older woman he did not love, one who could not provide his needed male heir, inevitably fell hard for this flirtatious and dashing sophisticate."

Moberley paused, sipped his wine and began to apologize.

"Sorry, Ann, I do tend to go on a bit when enjoying good company and drink."

"Oh, no," said Ann. "Please go on. Was Anne Boleyn a great beauty?"

"I doubt, by today's standards, she would be regarded as a great beauty, but in her time, she certainly turned heads," said Moberley.

Johns' formidable recall, which continually amazed his colleagues, was exercised quickly.

"One foreign envoy at the court said she had 'swarthy looks, a long neck and wide mouth, her eyes black and beautiful and take great effect. She well knows how to use them.'

"That gives us a good picture of her from someone who knew her. Others also talk of her beautiful mocking eyes, the long slender neck, exotic oval face, the vivacious spirit. The tall, elegant body. Her intelligence.

"Her enemies, and there were many, once she caught the King's attention, claimed she had the stigmata of a witch—a sixth finger on one hand. It was probably an extra nail growth on the little finger of her hand. Love or hate her, contemporaries could not stop noticing her."

Taylor and Salemi re-entered and apologized to Ann for their absence.

Ann told them: "I have not missed you guys a bit. Sir Moberley has kept me spellbound."

All of the group seemed more at ease and more wine was ordered along with the food.

Ann noticed the sudden rise in the energy levels of Taylor and Salemi. She was happy for them but acutely aware she had no business being with them now.

She would leave in the morning.

CHAPTER 76
WASHINGTON, D.C.

The call had come from Grasso that morning. "Get back here as fast as you can. Prepare to go down to Congreve's estate. We have fingerprints and they match two of the crime scenes."

Liddell would meet them in Washington with a Homeland Security plane for the trip to North Carolina; Salemi was welcome to go along.

British Airways were happy to assist the U.S. Government in freeing seats for Taylor's small party. In the yearly air wars over landing rights between the two countries it would not hurt to grant a small favor for the Americans. Ann had bought her own full-price ticket.

Liddell was waiting for them at the British Airways exit ramp. He beamed and raised a thumb above his head.

"We've got a fingerprint match from the Croft Theatre and Library murder scene and the Wilchester Armory killing and Congreve's mansion," he said softly. He was accompanied by an immigration inspector and a customs agent. The party was quickly cleared to enter the U.S.

Liddell, Salemi and the two officials diplomatically walked ahead as Taylor kissed Ann goodbye.

"I'll call you from down there," Taylor promised.

"I'll be at the farm, John. I couldn't have got through this without you."

Taylor hugged her and turned to catch up with Liddell and the priest.

Liddell knew he should be happy for Taylor. He had long worried that his friend was alone too much, that he needed the anchor and love of a good woman.

When the beautiful actress had approached investigators at the theatre murder scene asking to speak to an FBI agent, he had passed her on to Taylor, hoping the good-looking bachelor would draw more information than he would have from her.

Now he could not help but feel unease about the way Ann had so quickly become an intimate part of his life. Perhaps too many years in the agency had made him cynical. For now he would reserve judgment.

At the private area of the airport, a Gulf Stream jet chartered for Charlotte-Douglas International airport waited for them. They boarded, took off and headed south into a brilliant sky.

CHAPTER 77
NORTH CAROLINA

They landed at Charlotte and transferred to a well-worn Marine helicopter flown by a locally based North Carolina National Guard crew.

In the distance, the Great Smoky Mountains of the Appalachian chain marked the border with Tennessee. They wheeled north-west toward Asheville until they picked up the French Broad River, its polished waters reflecting the western light.

Inside the helicopter, Salemi noticed how uncomfortable and spartan the interior of the aircraft was. Two young crewmen constantly moved about the cramped space with rags, mopping up hot drops of oil which occasionally splattered seats and their occupants.

They looked amused at the apprehensive look on Salemi's face.

"This thing won't fly without hydraulic fluid. Start worrying if we don't find any oil to mop up," said one cheerful 19-year-old.

The rear ramp had been left down and Salemi watched in fascination as the peaks and forests, the faint, ancient Cherokee trails slid past them below. Snow already covered the high ground.

An overall-clad crew member gave Taylor his headset. The lead pilot invited Taylor to stick his head in the cockpit.

"How hard will this place be to find?" said Taylor.

The pilot, a stocky, clean cut 30-year-old pointed with a gloved finger to a survey map resting on the thighs of his petite pretty female co-pilot.

"Should be easy as pie, Sir," he drawled.

"We just follow the river and the railroad track alongside it.

"There's a spur line cuts off to the west. It was a private railroad built for the estate in the 1880s. We follow it for 40 miles right up to the front door. The rich certainly knew how to live in those days."

Within an hour they had picked up the rail line and flew 800 feet above its rusting tracks. Taylor saw the flashing white tails of deer scatter from the track side as the helicopter clattered overhead.

The rail line stopped abruptly just inside the stone pillars of the estate gates. A road wound up a rise to a massive turreted house.

The mansion overlooked a huge lake and several streams. A mile away, cutting through the thick forests that surrounded the house, light reflected off a river. Taylor was stunned by the sheer opulence of scale.

They touched down on a lawn 50 yards from

the house and were met by a local FBI field agent. Liddell gazed up at the massive building. A beard of ivy covered its walls from ground to roof. The portico was white marble. The doors massive and hand embossed. He shook his head and turned to Taylor.

"This guy can probably outspend our yearly budget. He's gonna be tough to find."

Taylor nodded his head and sighed.

"Well, let's see if he has left anything behind for us."

The interior of the house was a reflection of the grandiosity of the late 19th Century industrial baronetage. Huge imported furniture pieces, paintings and mirrors dominated richly carpeted, cavernous rooms. Taylor thought the presence of so many expensive artifacts, greedily scooped from the four corners of the earth overwhelmed the first time visitor. Perhaps that was the deliberately contrived point of it all.

The field agent, a lean Kentuckian called Saunders led them to the southwest wing and up to Congreve's lair.

"The staff say that they were mostly forbidden in this part of the house except for cleaning and maintenance duties. Most of the rooms are closed. He seems to have kept to the tower.

"An ancient elevator clanked up to the eighth floor of the house. A wood-paneled passage led to the actual turret. A winding staircase emerged through three floors — a spectacular triplex apartment designed within the tower.

As they climbed the stone steps, Liddell stumbled heavily and swore. Salemi grinned and pointed.

"Look—a 'trip step.' You normally find these in very old castles in Europe. They built one step much higher than the others. You get into the rhythm of climbing the steps then suddenly your foot crashes into the trip step. You can imagine the effect on heavily armed and armored soldiers trying to mount a sneak attack up a narrow winding tower in the darkness of a medieval castle. Crude, but very effective."

They reached the apartments and Taylor looked around what seemed to have been a library study. Books and papers were scattered along shelves and desks. Some one had left in a hurry.

Taylor and Liddell looked at the disarray and then at Saunders. Salemi browsed through the books and manuscripts littered around the tables and on the polished oak floor.

Saunders waved at the disorder.

"That's pretty much the way we found the room," he said defensively.

"The only objects that have been moved according to a housemaid are a bunch of old weapons, axes, daggers and the like. We were ordered to send them up to Washington for the lab boys to check out.

"We are still looking though. There could be stuff of his anywhere in the house. There are 110 rooms, and God knows how many cellars and storage places. Then there is the estate, over 20,000 acres. We could search for years and still be no wiser."

Taylor saw the agent's anxiety and moved to reassure him.

"It's a hell of a task, Saunders. No one is criticizing you. We'll let you get on with it."

Liddell understood Salemi and Taylor wanted to be alone to sit quietly and try to conjure the killer from his unique lair.

"Why don't you take me on the grand tour of the house," he said to Saunders.

After they left, Taylor and Salemi silently took in the turret library.

Taylor leaned against a wall and pushed one of the stained-glass windows open. Below, in the dusk, the parklands and forests looked wild and forbidding.

Once more Taylor tried to imagine himself in the killer's shoes. Standing in his room, touching his possessions, senses pitched to the room's atmosphere.

The darkness filtered into the room and Salemi became a shadow at the other side of the turret. He thought he heard Salemi whisper something to him. Then he realized the priest was mouthing a prayer.

A chilling atmosphere of evil was present in the chamber.

Both men felt an ancient archetypical fear clutch at their hearts. They could sense a menacing dark spirit all around them.

Without a word, they both made their way to the door and left along the passageway and down the winding stairs anxiously feeling for the trip step in the darkness. As they moved toward where they thought the elevator gate was, the lights snapped on flooding the hallway. An automatic timer had triggered them.

Taylor and Salemi looked at each other in relief. They did not have to explain the dread they had been suffering.

"We'll go through what's left in the morning," said Taylor.

The priest nodded his head.

"Did you feel him in there, John. Did you feel his malice?" Salemi said softly.

CHAPTER 78

They were gathered in the vast kitchen of the house. Banks of dumb waiters, cut into the walls, stood ghostly sentinel on faded memories of countless guests and banquets.

They sat around a large butcher table listening to Agent Saunders deliver a short biography of Richard Copeland Congreve.

"The Congreves rose to power in Pennsylvania and New York. They became hugely wealthy through steel mills and subsequently the railroads.

"The Copelands were land rich but, by the standards of the wealthy of that period, cash poor.

"The marriage between the last Copeland daughter and a Congreve heir owed more to pragmatism than love. But it enabled the Copeland lands to survive."

"Richard Copeland Congreve is the last of his line. We have talked to the staff and old timers in the area who knew him as a child."

His parents both died when he was 20 years old. It was ruled an accident. They drowned in the lake in the middle of the night. There were rumors of a suicide pact. Others said it was a murder-suicide. Both corpses showed high amounts of alcohol and drugs.

"Did Congreve have any friends?" asked Liddell.

"Not that we can find. He seems to be the classic loner. They say even as a child he would disappear into the woods for weekends on his own. He was a secretive, shy boy. He is an expert hunter; spent all his young life tracking animals. He can live off the land. He has hunted in Alaska, South America, Africa and even Borneo. He is absolutely at home in the wild. He is a skilled rower, a powerful swimmer.

"He is a study in contrasts — one side of him athletic, reveling in the outdoors; the other studious, pursuing history, spending days in dusty libraries peering at old documents.

"The staff were pretty terrified of him. They stayed out of his way most of the time. He would come and go unexpectedly. They were happy when he took off for Europe and then college in Britain.

"He returned early this year and stayed off and on. He closed most of the house and quartered himself in the tower. They basically dealt with the estate manager. A trust fund administered expenses and upkeep of the estate."

Saunders pushed a large photo print along the table.

"That's our boy," he said. "It's the only one we could find. Taken 20 years ago, when he was 17.

Taylor looked at the photograph. "A wide, even-featured face stared at him. The eyes were deep set and gray. The hair held sandy highlights and was short. The jaws were strong and even, the chin cleft. He was a handsome young man.

Yet the overall face looked like a mask. There was no smile, only a slight look of disdain toward the camera.

Saunders went on. "When he surfaced early this year, the staff said he had put on a considerable amount of weight. He's a big man, about 6-foot-4. He looked as if he was carrying 240 pounds on his frame.

"But they think he dropped a lot of that when he started his woodsman activities again during the summer. He could be 220 pounds or so now."

"What personal records have we found?" asked Taylor.

"We are still searching. The staff remember computer equipment being installed years ago, but we have found no sign of any. But it could be hidden anywhere in the house. It will take time.

"Phone records indicate there was a dedicated computer telephone line. Depending on which search engines he used we might get a clue as to what he pulled off the Web."

Taylor and Liddell sympathized with the task facing Saunders.

"We'll talk to Grasso," Liddell said. "You need a lot more hands down here to assist you."

“Thanks," said Saunders. "There's just too much to do; too big an area to search properly with what I've got."

Rooms had been aired and prepared for the FBI team. A white communications mobile center had arrived that evening. It would be staffed 24 hours a day.

Salemi and Taylor walked along the gravel path after a dinner of rabbit stew cooked by the wife of an estate worker.

They looked up at the forest beyond the park. They thought they heard the cough of a bear in the distance. The full moon was partially obscured by cloud cover, then shut out completely. Snowflakes began to fall.

Salemi sighed. "He could be out there in the tree line — watching, mocking us," he said.

"He could be anywhere," said Taylor. "But I don't think he will show his hand until the next Royal visit. I'm actually hoping the Prince will get his way and make the trip to Florida in January.

"Till then, we will just have to grind away. Try to get inside his mind. Hope he doesn't kill again. His passport pictures could be with us by tomorrow.

The snow thickened and they turned back to the house. They thought they would be lucky if weather conditions allowed them to fly out in the morning; Taylor to Washington and Ann; Salemi onward to Rome.

The holiday season would soon be upon them. While the rest of the world prepared to relax, to have fun, he would be busy. He had much to plan.

He must go over every inch of the killing fields — in the south and in the north. There was much to do. If all went well he would soon be free.

CHAPTER 79
ROME

Rain slicked the Roman streets hatching a rainbow of colored umbrellas among the crowds of Christmas shoppers. The light was fading and yellow street lights began to claim attention.

Behind the Vatican walls, most of the day workers had left. The rail station was closed and many of the offices, short staffed by Christmas leaves, were shuttered.

Only the Vatican security forces were busy, planning for the multitudes of the faithful who would crowd into St. Peter's Square for the jubilant Christmas celebration.

The dampness soaked into the gardens and the ancient buildings, releasing a rich smell of loam into the air.

Despite the cold, di Montevecchi opened a window and let the wind carry the heavy scent into the wood paneled chamber. He found it harder each day to adjust to the confines of the Vatican. He wanted to be home in Tuscany — walking free in the familiar hills and woods of his ancestors.

There was a knock on the door and a secretary announced that Salemi had arrived.

The man left and the Bishop embraced the Sicilian.

"I won't keep you from your trip back home, Joseph. But I wanted to hear from you in person. We can only trust so much to the telephone, my friend."

Salemi was tired from the trans-Atlantic flight, but buoyed by the prospect of meeting with his mentor and then a few days at the seaside villa in Sicily.

To Salemi the Bishop looked careworn, his face thinner, aging just a little too quickly. He prayed that the older man's health was not giving way.

They would all be better when this matter was resolved one way or the other.

Di Montevecchi motioned to a velvet padded bench below an oil painting of the crucified body of St Andrew.

The image was stark, bloody and disturbing.

The Bishop sat down beside Salemi and said: "So far, we still have the support we need here. But we must have results soon.

"I know," Salemi replied. "It seems the Americans are pinning everything on the Prince's visit to Florida next month. Our friends Taylor and Liddell have been called back to Washington. They are in close touch with me. Every police force in the States has been asked to look for Congreve on a confidential basis. They are being told he is a possible terrorist suspect.

"In New York, Father Orr continues to labor on at the computer. We keep searching for any fresh sign of Congreve.

"Have you heard anything new from Sir Moberley?"

For the first time, some vitality seemed to surge back into the Bishop's massive body.

"Yes," he said. "This morning, in fact."

He rose and stood before Salemi.

"Moberley's intelligence contacts have paid off .There is a top secret plan by the Americans and the British to spring a trap with the help of the Prince.

"He has volunteered to appear vulnerable on several occasions during the Florida trip in January. There has been a massive row about his decision to visit, but the Prince insists. The Prime Minister was opposed to it. Let's face it, the public would have his head if it came out he allowed the future king to be murdered.

"But the Prince has convinced him. The plan is that he will appear to be without proper security on several occasions in seemingly unguarded areas during the tour.

"A small undercover squad of elite SAS men and US Special Forces will be nearby at all times waiting to pounce on the killer.

"We have to hope that your FBI men flush him out before the sharpshooters do. That is our only chance of gaining contact with him.

"My fear is that the British will further isolate the Prince from our friends in the FBI."

Salemi pointed to a telephone on a mahogany desk.

"Is that safe to use?" he asked.

"Only speak in general terms," di Montevecchi warned.

Salemi dialed and, a minute later, Taylor was on the line.

"It's your favorite parish priest, John. We might have a little problem on the invitations to the big party in Florida. It seems that the British delegation might not have enough room for us next month."

Taylor barely paused and said: "I just heard about that myself. But it shouldn't be a problem. The Vice President of the company is a good friend of the Brits and as usual he will be there at all the functions. We'll go in on his invitation. It's no problem."

"Thanks, John. Give my love to Ann," said Salemi.

"I will, Joseph. We are going to spend Christmas down at her estate. We'll miss you. I'll see you in the New Year."

Salemi hung up with relief.

He looked at di Montevecchi.

"He knows. The US Vice President is one of the US polo crowd. He will be constantly socializing with the Prince. The agents will appear to be part of his personal protection. That will keep them near the Prince."

Di Montevecchi beamed and put his arm round Salemi's broad shoulders.

"Some dinner for you, Joseph? That airline food is no good for you."

He picked up the phone and called the limousine dispatcher for a driver. He needed to be free of the dark, echoing corridors that surrounded him. He wanted to dine out among the bright festive lights of the Via Appia. He knew a restaurant there which had the traditional Christmas baccala — salt cod with porcini and artichoke.

A night away from the ghosts and solemn stillness of the Vatican would do him good.

Salemi jolted him from his happy anticipation.

"I think I met Henry's malevolent spirit—at the Congreve estate," the Sicilian said.

CHAPTER 80
SICILY

Salemi gazed out at the twinkling lights of a cruise ship far out in the straits.

Far behind it he could still see the phosphorescence of its wake. On board there would be dining, dancing, the chatter of strangers socializing.

Here at the villa all was silent, save for the moan of the wind and the waves scouring the rocks below.

As usual he was alone. He was used to that. The circumstances of his life had seemed to mark him for a solitary role. In his youth, after his father's violent end and his mother's much slower death, he had welcomed his focused, singular path toward the Holy Church.

But now, with the passing years, his mind turned back to the brief happiness family life had afforded him. His playful, energetic father — animated emotional, expressive. His beautiful blonde mother, the cool patrician American who held everyone at arm's length — except her son, with whom she shared her subtle humor, her tenderness and her adoration of his father.

The approach of Christmas was, he knew, a time for rejoicing in the birth of Christ. A sacred time, a time for reflection and renewed hope. But each year he felt the increasing tug of Christmas past, the early memories of family gatherings, he and his cousins playing makeshift soccer games with bright party balloons in his grandfather's great living room.

He thought of his new friend Taylor, and his beautiful lover.

They would be in her country home now. He imagined them decorating the rooms with bright Christmas favors. There would be a Christmas tree, gifts. Love making before a crackling fire.

He pushed the thoughts from his mind and walked to a cherry wood barrister's desk that had belonged to his father.

There was much to be planned for the next few weeks. He and di Montevecchi had dined well in Rome the night before. They had lingered over coffee and brandy, reviewing what they knew so far about the killer. Salemi's experience at the Congreve estate was touched on only fleetingly, as if both men were afraid to accept its malevolent portent.

One puzzling aspect of the recent murders associated with the Prince had troubled both of them. Why had they all been confined to the United States?

He would ask the Vatican computer team to double check the incidents in Britain and Europe and match them with the Prince's whereabouts at the time. Normally this was one of his favorite seasons to be home. Only a few weeks ago the olives had gone to the mills to be pressed. It was a time for great rejoicing.

But this year he only felt a sense of dread. Somehow he must contact a murderous spirit before its host was killed, and try to change history.

CHAPTER 81
WASHINGTON, D.C.

Taylor and Liddell had spent their days haunting the lab and computer analysts on their return from North Carolina.

Everyone agreed that Congreve was the likely killer. The prints from the Congreve mansion matched partial prints taken off the bloody punch bowl in the Chicago pavilion and those in the Metropolitan museum and Croft Theatre murder scenes.

Transparencies of the victims' wounds appeared to have been caused by similar weapons. Microscopic shards of steel found embedded in bone from the bodies of the Chicago victims and one of the Embassy dead matched. Fluorescent X-rays had revealed the inner structures and allowed carbon dating to the 15th -16th Centuries. The quality and forging process also indicated the early 1500s.

Now all that remained was to catch the killer.

Grasso had been furious when he learned of the British plan to keep his agency away from the Prince during the next American visit.

He had gone straight to the Director and begged him to pressure the State Department and Homeland Security.

He had told Taylor and Liddell of his efforts over a bar lunch near the Capitol.

"I've expressed our fears to the director that we are being cut loose from the investigation. I have to believe him when he says that's not going to happen. What's this crap you're giving me about a plan to ice the killer before he can be tried?"

"I don't think it's crap," said Taylor.

The tables nearest to them were empty. The lunch crowd mostly departed.

"I don't know whether it's just the Brits or the State Department people, but we think they don't want any more embarrassment — the sort of embarrassment that a highly publicized trial would create.

"There's going to be a lot of questions asked about just how efficient their security is. Careers will be ruined at Cabinet levels if there is ever a full public enquiry."

Grasso looked irritable.

"I know all that. But really, John, you're telling me they are going to off this guy just to save face. Where do you get that fucking idea?"

"There's been interference all along, boss. Plus our sources in Europe haven't been wrong so far."

Grasso glared at both of his agents.

"You mean the priest," he said sarcastically.

"Yes, the priest and the very powerful outfit behind him," Taylor reminded Grasso.

"O.K.," Grasso allowed.

"Keep your heads down. I'll see what I can do to keep us in the hunt. I suggest you fellows take the opportunity for some R and R over Christmas. After that, you won't have any time for family or friends if you still have any. Just make sure I know where to find you."

It was the nearest Grasso would get to wishing them the season's greetings.

He stood up and grinned at Taylor and Liddell.

"You got a quarter?" he asked Liddell.

The tall agent nodded and reached into his trouser pocket.

"Good," Grasso said. "You and Taylor can toss for the lunch bill."

CHAPTER 82
VIRGINIA

The scent of wood smoke and horses would remain in Taylor's memory of that perfect Christmas. That and the hours of lazy love-making in the toast warm master bedroom of the main house of the estate.

In the mornings they would ride over the rolling pasture lands, where a local farmer was allowed to graze his small dairy herd. They would listen to the tintinabulum as a bell from the lead cow called the herd together for milking. They would canter down a tree-canopied lane to the local inn for an early lunch. Then back to the farm to read, sometimes to talk. Mostly they were happy just to be near each other. Their feelings, like their bodies were in perfect harmony.

On Christmas Eve, they exchanged presents, an antique gold pocket watch for him, a hunting print for her, chosen by Taylor's friendly landlords.

The next day, on a whim, they decided to travel up to New York. They would visit Dr. Samuels and drop in on Father Orr.

Taylor wanted Ann to meet both men. Some instinct told him that, after the recent loss of her grandfather, the company of older men at this sentimental time would fulfill an unspoken need; perhaps ameliorate her grief.

Ann insisted on booking a room at the Carlyle on Madison Avenue. This time, the trip would be on her, she insisted. Taylor was secure enough in the relationship not to feel his independence threatened.

By his lights she was a very wealthy woman. She was used to a certain standard of living. It was pointless and destructive to demand she conform to his financial limits.

For her part, Ann was aware that her money could be a sensitive issue for the proud Taylor and was politic in the way she used it around him.

They drove up to Washington over icy roads for a change of clothes and mail pick ups then caught the noon Acela for New York.

Snow was falling as they hurtled past tangled forests of trees skirting the Chesapeake. From Baltimore to New Jersey they watched the brightly decorated Christmas displays on the roofs and walls of countless tiny row houses.

NEW YORK

In his vast apartment on the West Side, Dr. Samuels had dusted off his best Harris tweed jacket and had heated a bowl of punch for his guests. They would be the only visitors to his home since the holiday season had begun.

Their hastily announced visit had caught him by surprise.

Taylor had not given him a chance to dither and fob them off. He would have found some excuse not to see them. He had become far too reclusive. Now, he was glad they had insisted. For the first time in months, he looked forward to human contact.

CHAPTER 83
MANHATTAN

Father Orr had celebrated Christmas as he always did, with the poor in the city shelters and the dying in the hospitals and hospices.

From his earliest years in the Church, his intellect and education had attracted the attention of the cognoscenti of power and politics in the Vatican. Some in Rome saw infinite possibility in the brilliant young priest from Ulster. But the glittering stage of Rome could not eclipse Orr's shining vision — that of his pastoral duty to the Lord.

For Orr, that duty was the core of his being, of his calling in the Holy Church. If not to serve God for and among the people, what purpose could there be to his life?

He would always work faithfully at whatever task was given to him by Rome, but always in his heart and in his spirit there were his love for and his duty to the masses of humanity struggling in this world.

While Salemi was away, he had worked tirelessly in the East Side brownstone. Each day he collated the information pouring in from Rome and now from London. Liddell was also delivering possibly pertinent material from the Langley computer search engines.

When Taylor had telephoned him that morning, Orr had offered to send his latest computer collations down to the Washington FBI office. He had been delighted when the agent told him: "Keep a copy for me. I'm coming up to New York. I'll collect it from you personally.

"And I would be very happy if you could make time to join my lady and myself. She wants to meet you. She heard Monsignor Salemi and Sir Moberley and me sing your praises when we were all in London.

The old priest was flattered and delighted. He enjoyed animated discussion good food, wine and company. Taylor's visit would be a dandy excuse.

"Bless you," said Orr. "I could do with a dinner and a bit of crack with friends."

"We'll call you when we get in," Taylor promised.

Taylor had watched with pride and pleasure as Ann had charmed his old friend the doctor. Ann's own sense of grief seemed to diminish when she compared it to this kindly man's cruel loss of his only daughter.

She was touched by the doctor's genuine sympathy with her loss and the obvious love and concern Taylor had for the man. They had drinks and some deli meats the doctor had laid out with great care. She looked out of the window onto a snow-covered Central Park.

She smiled as a large Irish Setter whirled in circles in a snow bank chasing its tail. Parents and nannies dragged children on sleds deeper into the park.

Taylor was pleased when the doctor happily accepted his offer of dinner at a restaurant that night. He wanted Dr. Samuels to meet Father Orr. Perhaps the two men, with their lively wit and zest for debate could continue a friendship when Taylor returned to Washington. He would do his little bit for the cause of ecumenism.

An hour after they had settled into their suite at the Carlyle, Father Orr arrived at the downstairs bar.

Ann had diplomatically said she would join them later. She realized the two men would have business to discuss. Despite the holiday season the cloud of the murder hunt still hung over them all.

Taylor found Orr sitting in a cloth armchair in a corner of the lounge. He was nursing a Scotch whisky. Beside it was a small jug of cold water.

The old priest delivered a firm handshake to Taylor. His eyes seemed as bright as ever.

He inquired after Ann.

"Well, John. Is she 'The One'?"

"Don't be marrying me off yet, Father," Taylor laughed. "You'll meet her soon enough. She was hoping you would have time to show her round St. Pat's."

"The Cathedral? It will be my pleasure, John."

Taylor was anxious that Father Orr did not get the impression his only value was as a tourist guide.

"How is the search coming along, Father? It is proving very important to us," said Taylor.

"I didn't know if it will be of use, John, but I am trying some new avenues of research. I might know something in a few days. I'll get in touch immediately if anything helpful comes out of it."

"That's good work, Father James. If you need help from our people let me know. In an investigation like this we have to keep an open mind."

Taylor and Orr ordered fresh drinks and waited on Ann's arrival.

After twenty minutes, she arrived, dressed in navy slacks and a wool Norwegian knit sweater. Under her arm was a calf-length navy cashmere coat.

Taylor introduced her to Orr then joked: "You going somewhere, Ann?"

Ann blushed and said: "Oh! I didn't mean to presume. Did you ask the Father?"

"He did and I will be delighted to take you to the Cathedral. If you can let an old man finish his drink, we'll be on our way in a jiffy."

Ann sat down.

"Please," she said. "Take your time."

Even among the eclectic mix of Fifth Avenue passersby, Father Orr and Ann made an odd couple: The tiny, elderly priest and the tall, beautiful woman.

Ann suspected that Father Orr was quietly reveling in the picture they presented and was completely won over by his puckish spirit. As they had left the hotel and walked southward along Madison Avenue he had, like some Victorian gallant, offered his arm. It seemed the most natural thing to do. It reminded her of her grandfather.

New Year's Eve was approaching and the streets were full of new hope and expectation. As they turned west to Fifth Avenue the wind blew throat-tickling smoke from pretzel and chestnut braziers.

She found the priest easy to talk to. His wit was formidable but unthreatening.

They turned left up the steps of the Cathedral and entered through the great bronze doors. Ann knew that her family had been Roman Catholic many generations ago before joining the Episcopal Church.

Now, as she entered the huge Gothic-style Cathedral, she felt somehow she was returning home. After dipping his fingers into a stone fount of Holy water and signing the cross, Father Orr quietly took her through the vestibule to a glittering alcove just to the right. There, he lit a candle for her grandfather and silently prayed. Tears came to her eyes and the candle flames seemed to radiate and become stars. She thanked the little priest.

"Let's have a look at the Cathedral," he said brightly, taking her arm once more.

He gave her a brief and sometimes amusing history of the huge white marble building, shaped in the form of the Latin Cross.

"When the foundation stone was laid, way back in 1858, it was so far north of what was then the center of New York City, smack in the countryside, it was called Hughes' Folly, after Archbishop John Hughes who commissioned it.

"New York's come a long way, literally and figuratively, since then."

They walked along the aisles of the Cathedral, pausing at the many shrines and small chapels. Ann marveled at the beauty of the clustered columns and soaring arches, supporting the great walls of the cleristory and the vaulted roof.

Orr led Ann past the beautiful high altar and Ann noticed a marble stairway leading down to a door below the altar.

"That's the crypt," Father Orr said. "The remains of Archbishop Hughes, along with Cardinals and others who served St. Patrick's are entombed there.

"If you like, we can get the keys and visit. The Crypt is normally open to the public only on All Souls Day and a few sacred anniversaries."

"No, thanks," said Ann, uncertain what she would find down there.

"Fine," said Orr. "Let me show you something most people don't know about."

The priest pointed to the arching roof.

"How's you eyesight, Ann?"

She could just make out something red, high in the ceiling 100 feet above the floor.

"You see it? Yes, it's a hat, with 35-foot long tassels draping down from its flat crown. Look across the ceiling, there are three more. They are ecclesiastical hats called 'galeros' worn only in the College of Cardinals in Rome. They belonged to four famous American Cardinals. There won't be any more hats nailed up there, however. Cardinal Spellman's will be the last to be hung in the Cathedral."

The priest shook his head, smiled, and sighed theatrically.

"We are all slaves to fashion, Ann. In the 1960s, Rome decided on a whole bunch of ceremonial reforms. Among them, the large red tasseled cardinal hats were given the boot. They have a much smaller hat now. Sure, Ann, you wouldn't be able to see it with a telescope if you nailed it up there.

"Such is progress," he sniffed.

Ann glanced at her wristwatch. Orr gently released her arm and said: "Be off with you now. You'll want to rest before regaling me with your fine company at dinner."

She smiled and kissed him on the cheek. Once more it seemed the most natural thing to do — like taking leave of a favorite uncle.

"I'll see you at the restaurant at 8.30," he promised.

As she left the Cathedral, she turned and saw the small slight figure of Orr standing by the altar. Then he walked slowly off toward the Lady Chapel in the far, eastern reach of the Cathedral.

He had left it unsaid, but she knew he was going to pray for her grandfather's soul once more. She loved him for that.

CHAPTER 84
CENTRAL PARK

A fierce wind had swept down from the north, freezing and abrading everything it touched. Even the towering apartment buildings on each side of the park seemed to shiver as it passed.

On the western side of the darkened park, red, blue, green and gold lanterns danced and colored the snow limned branches of a grotto of trees.

Beside them, light blazed from the glass walls and ceiling of the Waterford Room of the Inn on the Park.

Under the chandeliers, Taylor, Ann and Dr. Samuels waited for Father Orr to join them. The restaurant was full, the acoustics jarring.

"The noise level should lower once the late dinner parties finally sit down to eat," said Dr. Samuels anxious to put his hosts at ease.

"I should have picked a quieter place," said Taylor. "Still, I wanted to treat Father Orr. He's been superb to us. I just hope he knows how to find the place."

They waited half an hour then, under the subtle pressure of the hovering maitre d', ordered their first course. Perhaps the old man had dozed off in front of the fireplace. Who could blame him on a night like this?

Ann was intrigued by the unlikely friendship between the ex New York cop and the sophisticated doctor and how it started with a mutual passion for opera. The doctor gently guided her through a menu of operas a beginner might like to hear.

At first, the explosive crash sounded like a huge silver tray of food had been dashed to the ground. There was a sudden icy draft. Taylor turned and saw diners at a window table leap from their chairs.

He instantly remembered a long ago day when he had witnessed a large cankered rat scurry up a man's trouser leg in a crowded football stadium. Far from any amusement it had created the same sudden panic and explosion of movement;—like mullet heaving themselves from the predatory sea.

But the scene in the fairytale, tinkling oasis on the verge of the dark wildwood of Central Park was infinitely more terrible.

The diners had fallen, stumbled, arched backwards and thrown their bodies away from their table — leaving one catatonic woman rooted to her seat in sheer horror. Powdered glass from a broken window sequined her hair and eyebrows. The look on her frozen features made her eyes the focal point of everyone in the hushed room.

Sitting in her lap like some grotesque Christmas Plum Pudding was a partially boiled human head — the head of Father James Orr.

CHAPTER 85

Taylor would never forget the look of agony fixed on the severed head of Father Orr; the teeth whitened and the face burned rouge by the boiling water. The lips were pulled back as if in a snarl, the once bright eyes bulging and clouded.

He had walked quickly through the frozen tableau of terrified diners and ordered a waiter to bring him some table linen from a side cupboard.

He approached the trembling woman, dropped the cloth onto the head in her lap and gently lifted it away.

As the weight of the head was released from her thighs she seemed to fall in upon herself. Her face struck the glass littered table with a smack before she collapsed onto the floor.

Her fall broke the spell of horror and two male companions rushed to help her. There were screams from other parts of the room.

Taylor wrapped the head securely in the linen, identified himself, and pushed his way into the kitchen. He placed the bundled skull into a freezer and ordered a manager and a security man to guard it until police arrived.

He then made his way back to an ashen faced Ann, who was being supported by Dr. Samuels.

For Ann, Orr's murder had shattered the fragile buttress she had erected since Gerry and her grandfather's deaths.

Like a pilot in a dogfight suddenly robbed of spatial sense, she was completely vulnerable to life's blows. She was on the brink of a physical and mental breakdown.

She stared blankly at Taylor, but seemed comforted by the doctor's paternal embrace.

"I think we should take her to my apartment," Dr. Samuels said calmly.

He turned to her and said gently: "It will be quiet there, Ann, You'll be safe there, my dear."

She looked tearfully up at the doctor. To Taylor she had the look of a bewildered child.

"Let's go over there, Ann. Then we'll get you home tomorrow," Taylor reassured her. They walked slowly out of the restaurant and along a broad cobbled path to Central Park West. The first police cruisers were already arriving.

They entered the doctor's apartment and Taylor called the duty men in the New York Field Office of the Agency. A computer-aged photo of Congreve would be circulated to police forces in the area in the unlikely event he was careless enough to allow himself to be seen.

He called Grasso at home. Liddell would be on his way from Washington within the hour.

Then he held Ann closely to him on a fireside sofa. He should never have involved her in the investigation. From now until the final outcome he would keep her safely out of the way in Washington. He had been unprofessional and, as a direct result, her emotions had been scarred, perhaps permanently.

Dr. Samuels built up the fire in the grate then moved off to the kitchen to make hot tea and honey for her. He returned within minutes with the drink and some tranquilizers.

"She can stay here for as long as she wants, John," he said. "She'll be OK with me. You have work to do. I'll give you a key to the apartment. Come and go as you like. I hope you find the bastard who did this quickly."

Taylor hated to leave Ann in that condition, but the doctor was right. She seemed to trust the older man. She was in the best possible hands. Samuels had taken her under his trusty wing. It was as if she had replaced his lost daughter.

Taylor walked onto the street outside the apartment and hailed a cab to the East 51st Street brownstone. He had to review Father Orr's work notes and get there before any police blundered in.

CHAPTER 86

The housekeeper was waiting on the steps of the brownstone with the house keys. She looked annoyed to have been summoned from her apartment two blocks away on a freezing winter's night.

"This isn't good enough," she carped. "I'll be speaking to the Father about this on Monday."

Taylor decided the news of the old priest's death could be broken to her by someone else. It might not be the honorable course, but he had no time to deal with her emotions. He muttered a brief apology, bid her goodnight and entered the house.

He climbed the stairs to the familiar office. Tiny green lights from the computer glinted like emeralds from the gloom. He switched on a wall lamp. The room was tidy. Printouts were stacked in neat piles on polished tables.

There was little left to mark the existence of the old man. A misshapen but comfortable woolen club jacket draped over a chair and scorch marks on the marble mantle piece where he had allowed cigarettes to rest and burn.

A red spectacle case with his spare reading glasses had been placed by the side of one of the computers. Next to it was a notepad with a blue tablet of paper marked MEMO.

On the top sheet Orr had scrawled in his clear script "Genealogy checks. Tell the 2 J's."

Taylor surmised the "2 J's" were Joseph and John — Salemi and himself.

Salemi. Oh God, he would have to call Salemi and tell him the terrible news.

He pulled a small address book from his coat pocket. Salemi had given him the numbers where he or the Bishop could be reached in Rome. He had also given him a personal cell phone number for emergencies.

Taylor double checked the country code for Italy in the information section of a New York Telephone book and dialed.

SICILY

Salemi had awakened in the middle of the night with a sense of foreboding and unease. His mouth was dry; he had a deep thirst.

He had eaten too freely of the salty Pantelleria Capers in vinaigrette just before retiring. The rude local wine hadn't helped either.

He moved to the kitchen refrigerator and pulled out a bottle of mineral water.

He drank deeply, spilling water from the sides of his mouth. He heard the cell phone's shrill, insistent tones.

He stared at it as if it were a malignancy. No good news ever came at this time of night. He had been worried about di Montevecchi's pallor the last time they had met. God, if something happened to the Bishop, all was lost. His enemies would make sure of that.

He picked up the phone and with weary resignation said: "Pronto."

There was a pause, then Taylor's voice, surprisingly clear and loud.

"Is that you Joseph? Joseph, it's John.Taylor. I'm in New York. I've got bad news."

"What's happened, John?"

"I'm afraid it's Father Orr. Congreve got to him."

Salemi's ears burned with anger as he heard the details of the old man's murder and decapitation. The obscene, outrageous action of Orr's killer in hurling that final bloody taunt. He had not only killed that marvelous, saintly man he had deliberately degraded the priest's body, tossed part of it into a crowd of shocked people in calculated contempt. How could he ever reason with a monster like that? But reason, somehow, he must.

"This is truly an evil thing that has been done, John. We must all be careful now. Somehow, he found out Father Orr was hunting him. None of us are safe now. I'll join you in New York as soon as I can. I'll fly from Rome tomorrow. Then we'll try to find out how Congreve found out about our little operation."

He hung up and moved out to the veranda and looked out onto the straits. A long spear of cirrus cloud bisected the waning moon. He knelt and began praying.

CHAPTER 87
NEW YORK
ST. PATRICK'S CATHEDRAL

The first blood stains were discovered at the ornate door which led to the sacred crypt where the Cardinals were entombed deep within the Cathedral. The blood had been thrown at the door in an upward stream as if the actor had tried to reach the heights of the ceiling above and the fading Cardinal hats nailed there.

But the headless body was discovered much farther away, in an underground boiler room, stuffed behind a tool bin. A still dripping steam hose lay in a large china cleaning sink. It was still filled with viscous, bloody water. The head had been par-boiled there.

Liddell thought that Father Orr's body looked like a tiny mannequin. Something discarded by one of the Fifth Avenue stores adjacent to the Cathedral.

He watched the corpse bagged and finally moved out to a green mortuary vehicle parked at a side entrance. He turned and watched Taylor closely. Murder investigations were tough enough. When it was a friend who was lying butchered, it could be impossible. Taylor was aware of the inspection and met the agent's gaze.

"Don't worry, Eugene. I'll handle it," he said tersely.

"That's all I need to hear, John."

They walked up a stone staircase and emerged back into the cleristory of the Cathedral. The police presence had been deliberately down-played. A sign at the end of the South Aisle explained that "annual cleaning" was going on and the public were not allowed to pass that point. The infenestration at the Inn on the park had hit the headlines in the New York tabloids.

There was no identity revealed but the sensational details of a human head being hurled through the windows into a crowded restaurant was being picked up round the world. No amount of deception by police information sources could control that.

Taylor and Liddell turned their backs on the bloody vault and walked out of the Cathedral, down the broad steps and turned left onto Fifth Avenue. The sky was a brilliant blue and the sun dazzled on snow and ice. They decided to walk down to Gramercy Park for an informal look through Father Orr's apartments. They did not expect to find anything there, but it had to be done.

The Avenue was crowded and they turned east to Park Avenue, where the pavements were broader and the foot traffic sparser.

"The medical guys think he was killed late afternoon—early evening" said Liddell.

"Somehow Father Orr was lured down to the boiler room area. It's a deserted part of the Cathedral. His head was severed with one blow. The weapon cut clean through his neck and sliced into a pipe. We are getting a cast of the tool mark from the blade on the pipe. I am sure it will be just like the other murder weapons—a sword or an axe or some combination.

"He then used the steam hose to partially boil the head in the sink. He must have then wrapped it in something. Then at some time during all this he leaves the boiler room, re-enters the main Cathedral with some sort of container of Orr's blood and throws it up the side of the crypt at the high altar. Why would he take the risk of being spotted by someone, particularly security people, doing that.

"Then he takes the head, leaves and a few hours later enters the park and hurls it through the glass exterior of the Waterford Room where he presumably knows you are dining. How does he know this? And how long has he been following us."

"That puzzles me too," said Taylor.

He jumped back onto the curb as a yellow cab blasted its horn and ran a red light.

He shook his head and continued. "If he has been revisiting the scenes of the crimes, he could easily have spotted us, along with other investigators. He must have tailed us to catch onto the priests. We can blame ourselves for Orr's death. We led the bastard right to him.

"But why he is attacking us and the priest in particular, is telling. He must think we are closing in on something he doesn't want us to find.

"But what the hell is that? Did Father Orr stumble upon something?"

They turned left then right and walked down Lexington Avenue. In the 20s, the exotic smells of India reached them from the spice shops and restaurants of the area. Father Orr had told Taylor he loved Indian food and had promised to introduce him to it.

They walked on and turned into Gramercy Park.

Someone had left flowers on the steps leading up to Father Orr's residence.

The white and red flowers, probably cut in Mexico and flown into New York that day looked sad and incongruous. Near them, in the gray packed snow of the gutter, lay the first discarded Christmas trees of the season.

CHAPTER 88
LEONARDO DA VINCI AIRPORT, ROME

Di Montevecchi was waiting for Salemi in the First Class lounge of Alitalia.

They hugged solemnly and then sat at a coffee table in a private corner of the lounge. A uniformed hostess poured coffee and offered croissants.

The Bishop's eyes were moist, fixed in pain. "I loved that old man, Joseph," he said simply. "He died a martyr for his church and for God."

Then he leaned forward and gripped Salemi by the knee. "Perhaps we should end this thing now, Joseph, before you are in any more danger."

Salemi knew he was being offered a way out by an old friend. "God will protect us. Our faith will see us through. I mean to press on." he stated.

Di Montevecchi had known Salemi's answer all along. He had never doubted the young Sicilian's courage and that such fearlessness could lead him to his death.

But, to talk more of personal danger would insult Salemi.

"What are our chances of getting near the Prince and, by extension, the killer in Florida? Will your FBI friends help us?"

The British and Americans are planning a big security meeting in Washington on January 2. The agents are arguing that I be included in their delegation as an expert on the motives of the killer. They are optimistic that I will be allowed to attend," said Salemi.

"Good," said di Montevecchi.

"They still do not know your real quest — to try to talk to the controlling spirit of the killer?

"Oh, they know we believe that Henry's spirit is controlling Congreve," said Salemi.

"And I have told them we want to attempt to contact that spirit, that we have great interest in such an important historical figure.

"But they do not know that we hope to reason with Henry and try to change the course of history."

"Could anyone possibly reason with such a monster? I have grave doubts now, Joseph."

The role of *advocatus diaboli* came easily to the worldly Bishop.

"All we know is that we must try," replied Salemi.

There was a silence and then Salemi broached the question he knew both would rather have left unsaid.

"One thing haunts me. Do you think Father Orr had a chance to speak with the spirit of his killer?"

"I just don't know, Joseph. I am haunted by that, too, I wonder what horror he peered into in the last seconds of his earthly life."

UPSTATE NEW YORK

The grave site was high in a snowy meadow in the Adirondack Mountains on the grounds of a Dominican monastery. It had been a favorite retreat of Father Orr; the Abbott was an old friend and fellow Irishman.

He had loved the serenity of thc mountains, the wild flowers and greenery of the summers the silent stillness of the winters.

A small group of monks had attended the simple graveside ceremony. As the brothers returned to the monastery chantry to offer prayers for Orr's passage, Salemi, Taylor and Liddell thanked the Abbott and drove back down toward the city.

As they navigated the twisting mountain roads, cloud would suddenly blanket them like fog then dissolve into brilliant winter sunshine.

The weather seemed to mockingly reflect the progress of their hunt for the killer; full of shadowy impenetrable mists and sudden fleeting insights.

Two hours later they crawled behind late afternoon traffic into Manhattan and parked in an underground garage near the brownstone on East 51st Street.

They walked to a Second Avenue bar, ordered Scotch and quietly toasted their absent friend.

Taylor pointed to a table near the window and they moved out of earshot of the bar patrons. He turned to Salemi, who was still wearing the black clothes and clerical collar of his faith. It was the first time he had seen Salemi in church "uniform."

"We have to presume that you are in danger too, Joseph. If he was aware of Father Orr's activities in hunting him then he must consider you a threat. From now on, I want you to stick close to us."

"Am I going to be allowed to join you at the Washington security talks?" Salemi asked.

Liddell answered. "Grasso has put your name forward, Joseph. We don't see any problems. You are described, for official purposes, as a psychological behavior expert, a guest of our Quantico behavioral profiling team.

"Good," said Salemi. "I'll stay at the brownstone tonight and travel down to Washington with you tomorrow."

"You'll have company tonight, Father," said Liddell.

"My good self, if you don't mind. And there will be plainclothesmen in the area. We can't take any chances."

Salemi shrugged in acceptance and turned to Taylor. "What about you, John?"

Taylor looked sheepish and felt unprofessional.

"Ann's still here, staying with Dr Samuels. She took Father Orr's murder very badly. I booked us out of the Carlyle. I felt it better to keep an eye on her. Just the thought that monster may have been looking at her as he stalked Father Orr turns my blood cold. I thought I would ..."

Salemi interrupted him: "Of course, my friend. You must be with her. She needs you. You are doing the right thing."

Once more, Taylor was grateful for the priest's innate tact and empathy. He would take Ann back to Washington tomorrow, get her safely home. Then they would prepare the trap in Florida for the killer.

CHAPTER 89
CATOCTIN MOUNTAINS, THE APPALACHIANS, MARYLAND

The Marine detachment in dress blues clicked to attention and the floodlights were switched on full.

Taylor stared out at the blackness. From the mountaintop, the lights caught tracers of sleeting snow in their beams.

Suddenly from below came the clatter and roar of the helicopter. The arcing silver saucer of its rotor blades rose first, then the white fuselage top of the Marine Presidential fleet and the familiar olive green of the body.

The Sikorsky VH-3D Sea King rose 30 feet above them, then dropped to the pad. As usual, a work detail of swabbies had cleared every leaf from its downdraft.

The whine of the engines slowly died and the doors were opened. Out stepped the Vice President of the United States and the Prince.

A brief salute to the officer of the guard and the VIP party were hustled into golf carts and driven along dimly lit bridal paths to their cabins.

It was the first time Taylor had been to Camp David and he was duly impressed.

He, Liddell and Salemi had driven up Route 77 to the little town of Hagerstown. Maryland. There, a U.S. Navy bus waited to take them up the final reaches of the mountain to the Camp. It had been a dark blustery evening when at an elevation of 1,800 feet they had turned up a wooded lane and through the camp gates.

All 30 men on board the bus were security experts with the highest clearances. Yet standing in the bus aisles at every second seat row was an armed Marine sharpshooter. The select group was entering one of the most stringently guarded compounds in the world.

As they passed the gates, Taylor saw the pinkish glow of night lights from the bulletproof glass bubbles of command posts set into the ground throughout the woods.

As they left the bus to walk up to the helicopter landing ground a veteran State Department security man warned Liddell.

"Don't stray off the paths at any cost. You step off to take a piss in these woods and they shoot first and ask questions later. I'm deadly serious," he said.

Taylor looked at his face. He was not smiling.

At night Camp David could be a spooky place to those who patrolled it. Young Marines had often been unnerved by sightings of ghostly glowing balls of ionized air floating through the thick woods, a phenomenon peculiar to the mountain.

After the VIP party arrived, the security group was ferried in golf carts to Rose Lodge. Once inside the long log hall, the doors were locked and armed Marine guards posted outside.

At a raised dais at one end of the hall, a wall had been hung with maps. On a metal desk, individual packages containing maps and code protocols had been stacked. Each had the name of a member of the security party stenciled on it.

The packages differed in weight and content depending on the individual's need- to-know status.

Taylor noted the FBI group's special packages were by no means the heaviest. Politics were in play as usual.

Vice President John Neville relaxed in Aspen Lodge and smiled. The portents for his future were gathering pace around him.

He was seated in the cabin normally reserved for sitting Presidents. It was as if everyone recognized the inevitability of his election next year.

He had laughed when he learned the harried naval work force of Camp David had been laboring to give him the ultimate presidential perk.

A work party had spent the afternoon tweaking the temperamental water system, housed under the tennis courts, to give him the exact pressure he liked for his shower.

Life was good. It would be even better if they got through the year without the disaster of the assassination of the future King of America's best ally.

That would not happen — not on his watch. The Prince was safe here for the next two days.

Every precaution would be taken to safeguard the Royal visitor in Florida. There would be a bonus. The would-be assassin, a serial murderer, would be eliminated by US security forces.

It would send a message around the world about the efficiency and resolve of the United States.

And, like the political star he was, he would be there, victorious on the killing field: the golden boy, as ever.

CHAPTER 90
THE OUTER BANKS,
THE CAROLINAS

The agency jet had been at cruising altitude for an hour. As they flew south from the cold, Taylor saw petals of moisture sailing over the sun-beaded waters of the Gulf Stream far below.

The tiny clouds rose like burgeoning pink blossoms reminding him of the two weeks when the cherry groves turned Washington into a Japanese silk print.

This spring Ann and he would enjoy them together. They would catch this killer and he would be free to spend time with her.

Dr. Samuels had offered to drive her from Manhattan to her house in Virginia. Despite her protestations, he had insisted and Taylor had been glad for that concern and kindness.

The doctor had assured Taylor she was over the worst of the shock. But he would be happy to keep a watchful eye on her.

Taylor realized that the Doctor's new friendship with Ann was a comfort for all of them.

He now felt a certain amount of guilt. The Doctor had been on his own for too long; a recluse since his daughter's death.

Taylor should have done more than simply investigate the murder. He should have been there in New York to support his friend.

The jet began to descend and the waters became a patchwork of turquoise and cobalt shading to purple. The green of the land intensified and became lush, spoiled only by the brown mist of air pollution hovering over the coastal towns.

Six miles from shore they spotted the fleets of small fishing charter boats, then the white sands, rainbow beach cabanas of hotels and the swamp brown waters of the Intra-Coastal Waterway.

The jet banked over the sprawl of West Palm Beach and made its landing at Palm Beach International Airport.

The plane's passenger door opened and the unique dank mixture of over-ripe vegetation and stagnant water that was the essence of Florida flooded into the plane.

On the ground an agent handed over the keys to two rented convertibles. Taylor and Liddell had decided the rentals would fit in with their cover as tourists. Government vehicles would stand out harshly down here.

For Salemi, the bright red soft tops suited his Italian sense of style perfectly.

"They're hardly Ferraris," he teased Liddell, "but for American cars, they're not too bad."

Liddell gave the Italian a hard look, then laughed. “Would you care to drive, Monsignor?" he offered with mock courtesy.

"Tell me where I am going, then try to keep up with me," the priest challenged.

Taylor laughed and motioned Liddell to join Salemi.

"I'll drive ahead of you guys. Just follow me slowly to the hotel and behave like good little boys.”

“The last thing we need is being stopped for speeding by the local cops.

“If you are well behaved, I'll take the scenic route."

They had left the airport exit roads and traveled east on Southern Boulevard. They crossed the Intra-Coastal, then turned at a roundabout into a road canopied by trees.

On either side, white and pink hibiscus and purple bougainvillea danced in the salt breeze. The Ocean arrived spectacularly in front of them and they turned south along Ocean drive.

On the left, a low white wall hid the beach but underlined the intense blue of the ocean. On the right the red tiled Mediterranean style roofs of the Mizner designed mansions were tucked behind mirrored gate posts. Salemi definitely felt at home here. The tiny stretch of road fleetingly reminded him of part of the Low Corniche on the French Riviera.

All too quickly they reached a hairpin bend and drove between rows of ugly high- rise condominiums each one with a name more pretentious than the last.

Just before the Lake Worth Bridge, they turned left into a horseshoe shaped driveway and parked at the hotel entrance.

They were expected and led to three balconied rooms on the top floor of the four-story hotel. Salemi pulled open a glass door leading to the private balcony and stepped out. Immediately the room's air-conditioner shut down, increasing the sound of the waves washing the beach. The sea breeze swept over him like an intoxicating stimulant. Beyond the swimming pool, decorative pods of palm trees stood guard between the thick beach grass edging the sand and the ocean.

Salemi marveled at the corrugation of the Gulf Stream on the horizon as it pushed north against the southern flow of the Atlantic currents. Barely 50 miles out from where he stood, the Bahamas began.

They had arranged to meet in Liddell's suite. When he entered, Salemi was surprised by two new faces.

"Pleased to meet you, Monsignor Salemi," said assistant director Tommy Grasso. "Allow me to introduce special agent Emelina Calderon."

Calderon was tall with short, straight, raven hair and dark eyes set in an oval face. To Salemi her classical features could have graced an ancient Roman coin.

She offered a slim yet strong hand to the visitors.

"Agent Calderon will be helping us down here and coordinating with the local Homeland Security operatives. I don't have to tell you she would not be here if she was not one of the best we have."

The priest was struck by Grasso's effortless ability to command deference from the hard charging agents Taylor and Liddell. He was a man they obviously respected and, more importantly, trusted.

But he also observed a certain indefinable uneasiness between Grasso and himself.

He sensed the Italian-American's conflict over the perceived and accepted pastoral role of a priest reinforced throughout years of Catholic education — and the man from Rome who stood before him.

This was no normal priest. To Grasso, Salemi represented the deepest, most secret reaches of the Church. This was a soldier in some shadowy battle that Grasso didn't fully understand. Grasso would not let his guard down with this man.

But he had decided to accept his men's recommendation to involve and trust the charismatic priest; up to a point.

The balcony door was closed cutting the sound of the waves hitting the beach to a whisper. The air conditioner clicked on and began its hum.

Grasso offered everyone fresh Florida fruit from a bowl on a low glass table in the center of the room. The fruit was picked daily from the chef's own exotic garden in the hotel grounds.

Grasso threw a heavy red file folder onto the table and began.

"That contains the security arrangements, codes, lapel badges, contingency plans and maps for the polo grounds and surroundings. You might want to read it. But in terms of what we are going to do, don't agonize over what's in it."

"We don't believe Congreve has a chance in hell of getting to the Prince at the grounds. Even he must know he'll never get near the target after his near miss in Chicago. If he does try, he's going to be very dead before he gets within a hundred yards. For him to attack he has to have a sporting chance to succeed. He's not afraid of death, he is a risk taker and we don't think he worries about escape if he succeeds in killing the Prince.

"If the security is too tough, we believe he will just wait them out until the next opportunity arises. No one wants that. He's upset too many careers. They want him finished right now. Some of them with extreme prejudice as our CIA brothers euphemistically put it.

"Luckily for us, the British, with their innate love of hammy theatrics, have agreed to help stage a false lure to draw Congreve out.

"The first stages have already begun."

Taylor looked at Grasso, his eyebrows arched questioningly.

Grasso smiled and answered. "We start with the ladies and gentlemen of the press, naturally."

CHAPTER 91

The first rule of creating a successful leak is to swear several journalists to keep the matter secret.

They will do so, but will tell their editors. It's then just a matter of days until it's picked up by the society gossips from loose-tongued friends of the editors and media power-players.

Then mention is made by a television prognosticator and, in turn, noted by the so-called tabloid press. Then the "quality press" feel free to report these rumors.

So it had gone with the carefully crafted leaks about the security worries for the Prince's safety during his visit to the US.

Once the leaks were abroad, the second phase of the operation was instigated by British intelligence. Questions were asked in the House of Commons, assurances for the Prince's safety were given.

Buckingham Palace issued a statement saying that despite the Chicago incident they had confidence in the security precautions but re-stated that the Prince would not be a captive to terrorist threats. Off the record, they admitted they were worried about the Prince's penchant for slipping his protection squad to enjoy his freedom.

In the United States the British Embassy secretly asked top magazine and newspaper publishers to downplay the reports, ensuring even more interest and speculation in the safety aspects of the visit.

In the Palm Beaches, a local television cable news reporter was fed frequent tidbits about how the Prince continually evaded his minders to indulge his need for fun and a private lifestyle.

He would likely slip the leash to go reef diving, it was whispered. He loved to deep-sea fish, someone advised. Look for him to sneak off and turn up on some private yacht with female company, it was darkly suggested.

The leaks were all aimed to tempt one man — Richard Copeland Congreve.

Lt. Ranulf Cuthbert-Jones had appeared in school plays at Eton and was on the entertainment committee for the officers mess annual ball.

If not for a career in the Guards and certain family disapproval, the stage might have beckoned. Now he had been given the role of a lifetime and the chance for military promotion at the same time. With a little make-up and hair dye he would play the Prince. With luck it would not cost him his life.

CHAPTER 92

Salemi fought hard not to show his disdain and disappointment as Grasso explained the plan to lure Congreve into a trap.

To the sophisticated mind of the priest it seemed amateurish and implausible. And worse, if, against all odds it succeeded, there would be little chance of gaining the vital minutes he needed to talk to Congreve and the force that drove him.

Taylor also was unimpressed by the strategy.

"They think they'll lure Congreve out to sea to kill an imposter?"

"That's the plan and the British have the last word on it. It's that or nothing. We're stuck with it," said Grasso.

"Word is being spread at the marinas that a small motor yacht is being sought for the Prince.

"His double will be seen briefly inspecting the boats. If our killer is down here doing his homework that should find its way to him. At least that's the theory."

Taylor could sense Grasso didn't have much faith in the plan either.

Taylor shook his head. "You would expect the Prince to be on some rich friend's private yacht. These fishing charter captains are not fools. Why should we think they'll bite—excuse the pun?"

Calderon answered his question. Her voice had just the faintest trill from her Cuban parents' accented English. Underneath beauty and charm, Taylor detected the strength and focus her parents had brought to the United States and given their children.

"The locals, the fisherman and boat-mates are indeed not stupid," she agreed. "But if we use some of our contacts, they should be able to convince them the Prince is seeking an anonymous vessel to fish in and that the paparazzi will be haunting all the private marinas.

Taylor interrupted her: "Wouldn't they be suspicious if any of our people supplied the information."

"Not at all," she replied smoothly. "Many of the boat captains occasionally supply information to the government. They don't like drug runners or criminals in the Straits of Florida and they keep an eye out for Cuban vessel movements. As a reward, a blind eye might be turned by the Coast Guard and a few helpless refugees will have a chance to reach the U.S.

"Those guys have seen the desperate attempts to reach the mainland. They are not liberal social workers, but they recognize the evils of Communism. They are good old boys at heart. Sometimes it boils down to a simple quid pro quo. We don't ask questions; neither do they."

Taylor still seethed at the overall plan. "It just doesn't make sense," he said. "Every attack so far has been on land. They have been savage assaults with cutting weapons. It would seem Congreve has a need to personally confront the victims.

"How in hell can he do that in the middle of the Ocean on a guarded boat?"

"He uses only weapons from Henry's period," added Liddell.

"What about a bow and arrow or cross-bow shot from another boat or from a diver?" he asked.

Grasso was growing impatient with the defeatist turn the briefing was taking.

"On the other hand he might just launch a missile or a grenade at the fucking boat and leave us a note somewhere saying he had been jerking us off all along," said Grasso sarcastically.

He laughed. "Luckily," he continued, "our behavioral guys think that highly unlikely. The cross-bow quarrel shot is our nightmare for the moment. In the right hands it can deliver a killing shot at 1,000 feet."

"If an attack does occur," said Taylor, "how can we make sure we are in a position to get to Congreve if he is captured?'"

Grasso frowned. "It's going to be pure luck. We will be in one of the interception boats. We just have to pray, if there is an attack and a capture is on our station in the protection area. There's going to be a lot of weaponry out there. Needless to say, they've got several teams of Seals involved. If he does try to attack, he'll most likely be shark bait within minutes.

"We will have a series of chances. The 'bait' is scheduled to go out on a small fishing motor cruiser during the Prince's three-day stay after the official polo tourney.

"All we can do is be ready and hope we get lucky."

Calderon smiled wryly and said: “Perhaps we can help our ‘luck.’

“If we pick the right source, giving the right misinformation, we might even send the killer to the location of our choice, into the area we will be patrolling.”

Taylor and Liddell knew now why Emelina Calderon was on board.

Salemi had turned down the agents' invitation to join them on a tour of the polo grounds. He saw no point. He was sure the killer would not strike there. Besides, he had to talk to Rome. If they were doomed to failure, di Montevecchi would need time to prepare a defense against his enemies.

He changed into sky blue running shorts and a white golf shirt and jogged down the beach in front of the hotel.

Waves from a long Ocean swell broke gently on the sand. The sun, high and to the West, struck the curving arch of the breakers illuminating like shimmering sequins, shoals of tiny fish. .

He jogged southward for a mile and came to the hurricane-blasted remains of a fishing pier — a once-long wooden board walk jutting out into the Atlantic, its furthest concrete supports now naked in the swells.

At a small café at the pier he found a telephone box and called straight through to Rome on a special toll-free line to the Vatican and di Montevecchi.

He repeated the details of the plan to trap Congreve; the Bishop did not interrupt.

He had bad news of his own to impart: "I have heard from our friend Moberley in London," said di Montevecchi.

"He confirms our worst fears. British intelligence and the Americans definitely plan to silence Congreve. There will be no trial. He will be killed on the spot.

"We can only pray for a miracle; that you have the chance to intercede if he is somehow captured."

Salemi gently replaced the salt-stained plastic telephone. Around him children and young mothers played in the sands. Weather-beaten men bought baitfish at a small stand leading to the pier. He suddenly felt shockingly lonely. He envied Liddell his wife and children; Taylor his Ann.

An olive-skinned beauty in a white bikini reminded him of a cat as she slowly patrolled the beach. She also reminded him of the beautiful Cuban agent.

CHAPTER 93
AIR FORCE TWO, THE ATLANTIC

Vice President John Neville was looking forward to the Florida trip.

Quite frankly he was bored with the polo set but they attracted moneyed followers — life blood to his political ambition.

The Prince and his set were pretty boring too, but he too had his uses — primarily photo opportunities that gave the Massachusetts politician added international coverage.

Four hundred miles behind Air Force Two a sleek British Aerospace 146 transport jet bearing the unique red, white and blue livery of Royal Air Force Squadron 32—The Royal Squadron — carried the Prince and his entourage.

All other aircraft were kept clear of the air corridor of the two jets. Along the route down the Eastern Seaboard, rotations of Navy, Air Force and Marine squadrons unobtrusively tracked their progress.

High above, with its 360-degree, 200-mile wide radar "eyes," two AWACS, Air Force Boeing 707s cruised.

Further south two similar watch dogs, Hawkeye aircraft from the carrier Ronald Reagan, joined in—a practical training exercise for the crews.

On board Air Force Two the secret service agents were worried. But the last thing on their minds was the killer stalking the British Prince.

The official part of the trip would be stressful but normal. What they really feared were the four days of private rest and recreation the Vice President had added for his self.

His wife had remained in Washington. The marriage had long ago become one of political convenience.

Now as a uniformed Air Force steward entered the Vice President's day cabin with a scotch on the rocks, they feared the worst. They knew the signs. Neville was slowly building up to one of his secret break-outs.

The Vice President, a handsome 6-foot 2-inch former athlete, had a weakness. He could have had secret liaisons with some of the world's most beautiful women. That, the secret service could have facilitated and protected.

But John Neville's weakness was what, in pornographic circles, is called rough trade.

He liked the danger of sexual dalliance with street hookers, with the floozy in some smoky clip joint; a promiscuous schoolgirl in some country hamlet. He had the destructive obsession of a masochist — a need to be brought down, to roll in the dirt.

CHAPTER 94
BROOKE'S CAY, NORTHERN BAHAMA ISLANDS

For the last year the stranger had come and gone. They would see the 42-foot ketch glide past the head of the mangrove-covered spit that hid his lagoon-side property from public view.

Sometimes Calvin, a local man who was as secretive as his boss, would be seen handling sails or conversing with a powerfully built figure shadowed by the cockpit canopy on deck.

Behind the villa lay dense coppices of mahogany, gum, poisonwood and pigeon plum. Under their cover, pigs had been allowed to breed freely and grow feral.

The estate owner had let it be known that the few local fisherman on the west side of the island were welcome to harvest any pigs that strayed on the edges of his property. In return he asked only that they respect his privacy and discourage unwelcome visitors.

Night had fallen and Congreve sat on a veranda watching the clouds of insects enslaved by the garden lights.

In the bull vines latticing the trees with their bright red blossoms at the forest edge, the Cuban tree frogs gathered to feast on the insects.

Congreve listened to the hoarse squeal of a frog as it was struck by the eight-foot Bahamas boa he had spotted earlier that day.

It promised to be a long and pleasant evening. He would be patient. Tomorrow he would be on the move again.

The yacht slipped silently past the spit and out into the ocean at dawn.

A few hours later they were gliding through the first Sargasso grass weed lines of the Gulf Stream, sailing north with the current.

Congreve could feel the warmth rising from the Stream on his hands and face. As far as he could see were floating green and gold meadows of vegetation with schools of rainbow hued dolphin fish grazing below.

Normally he would have slowed to plunder the iridescent shoals — the best tasting fish in the ocean — but he had a much bigger quarry to hunt.

As the faint wake of the boat trailed away and the ketch disappeared into the horizon the dolphin fish found something new to nibble on.

The fish gathered, darting in and out of the entrails unwinding slowly from the floating corpse of Calvin.

The taciturn islander would be silent forever. He had made his last voyage with Congreve.

In the distances could be heard a faint, whistled melody — one not heard in those historic waters for over 400 years.

CHAPTER 95
FLORIDA

It was a perfect winter day in Palm Beach. The air was dry, stirred by an Ocean breeze; the temperature 78 degrees F.

The spectators and the polo players paraded and competed for attention.

Women, overdressed in studied casualness and chic watched the polo players select their mounts; the sleek ponies gentled and held by colorfully liveried gauchos straight from the Pampas. The best players from Argentina and Uruguay had been hired by the richest teams. Their job: to score goals and make their wealthy teammates look good on the field. They were also discreetly popular with the wives of their benefactors.

A surprise addition to the tournament was the U.S. Military team whose players were drawn from all branches of the armed services. The knowledgeable noticed some unfamiliar faces in the team.

Those riders were secretly briefed to block any on-field attack on the Prince with their own bodies and those of their ponies.

Liddell, Taylor and Calderon sat in a long motor trailer borrowed from the State Police.

A team of State Department, Secret Service and Homeland Security agents manned a command center. Reports constantly crackled in from all quarters of the field.

Far above them in a cloudless blue sky, four helicopters surveilled the grounds. At the west side of the polo grounds, in the open country buffering the swampland, camouflaged SWAT teams held position.

The Prince had played just one chukka before retiring with a "bruised shoulder."

He and Vice President Neville were relaxing with the millionaire panjandrums who ran the polo club. They mixed with their hosts in a glass-enclosed, air-conditioned lounge in a main grandstand.

The chance of a successful attack on the Prince was negligible, yet no one dared relax.

Taylor excused himself and walked out of the trailer. He found a bench shaded by a grove of pine trees and called Ann on his personal cell phone.

Mrs. Green answered at the farmhouse.

"Oh Mr. Taylor, you just missed them. She and the doctor have gone up to the District together. They should be at the Watergate apartment around five."

Taylor thanked her. He was pleased that the Doctor was still with Ann. The two of them seemed to have hit it off. Good for them.

Yet Taylor couldn't help feeling guilty over making the call and a little relieved that she was not there. He was on duty; he shouldn't be making personal calls at a time like this.

Then he laughed to himself. Fuck them. If he couldn't worry over his girl, they could find someone else to do the job.

He saw movement back at the trailer door and returned.

Liddell pulled him aside. "I think we can relax for now, John. They are leaving now.

"The Vice President is going up to his vacation home on Hobe Sound for a few days R&R.

"The Prince will be driven to a bungalow on the polo club grounds for a private reception then will be secretly flown to McDill Air Force base tonight.

"The Royal impostor will emerge tomorrow, move into a seashore property across the Intra-Coastal and start showing up at nightclubs and along the marinas over the next few days."

Taylor watched the black limousines pull away unobtrusively from the grandstand area.

"Let's get back to the hotel," he said.

"I could do with a cool beer and some conch fritters by the swimming pool."

"I'll second that," said Liddell.

They invited Calderon, who declined. "I will stay behind just in case something turns up," she said.

The two agents felt like they had been given a gentle reproof for lack of dedication to the task.

"Do you want us to stay with you?" Liddell asked without enthusiasm.

Calderon laughed. "Go have some fun, boys. I can handle it," she teased.

CHAPTER 96

The request had been made formally to newspaper editors and television directors by the British Embassy press briefers in Florida who had remained behind with the Prince's security detail.

"This part of the trip is private. Please allow HRH to relax and please respect his privacy .We will supply a limited number of film and still photos during the next few days. There will be no pool photographers allowed," a brief statement informed.

The media heads complained but, faced with rock like indifference to their pleas for their own live footage of the Prince, they reluctantly accepted what was offered.

What they did not know was the cinematic pabulum fed to them had been concocted far from the Palm Beaches.

At a remote shore on the Gulf Coast, the real Prince spent several hours of one morning posing in the sea water, sailing a yacht, fixing bait to the outriggers of a fishing boat.

In the afternoon, more video was shot — giving different angles, light and sea conditions.

The photographers were careful not to shoot any cognitive landmarks that could be identified on film.

The story on the East Coast was different. Reports and myriad locations filtered in to the newsrooms. The prince has been in a private VIP room at a tony South Beach nightclub. He had been seen on a yacht exiting the Palm Beach Inlet.

A honeymoon couple had bumped into him walking along the seashore early one morning near Fort Lauderdale. The paparazzi were in a state of arousal.

Two days after the polo match on a breezy, bright morning, Salemi, Taylor, Liddell and Calderon drove up I-95 to Riviera Beach and across the bridge to a marina on Singer Island.

There, waiting on a 51-foot Hatteras sport fisher — was Reinhard Muller, an FBI marksman, and Jules Messier, a Coast Guard officer.

The fishing boat was deceptively fast. To allay suspicion it was skippered and crewed by two locals Captain Fred Dover, a white haired 65-year-old and his mate, Dick Eagle, two weathered Rhode Islanders who came down every winter for the charters.

They looked just like any fishing party. Taylor made a point of buying sandwiches and beers from a quayside bait shop. They wore loud, loose shirts and shorts. Liddell had found a gaudy purple Hawaiian shirt in a dive shop. Calderon disrobed revealing a stunning bikini and sunned herself on the bow—the perfect picture of the rich little Palm Beach princess.

They cast off, turning into a large sheltered inlet. As they moved out into the ocean, the breeze stiffened and the twin engines were ratcheted to three quarters speed. The bow rose and the men automatically took a wide stance and flexed their knees for balance. Calderon retreated sensibly into the spacious cabin. The bright sun lighting the white spray against the blue ocean was intoxicating to the senses.

Salemi watched as flying fish skimmed diagonally away from the slashing bow.

Inside the cabin the Coast Guard officer scanned a small radar console and manned a communications channel.

Other fishing boats dotted the horizon. The killer could be lurking in any of them.

They cruised north and took up a station off the Jupiter lighthouse point.

The "Prince" was due to fish that area on a small a luxury charter most of the day.

Overhead, two single engine planes trailed long canvas steamers advertising a local bar's happy hour and a pitch for suntan lotion.

By the sides of the regular pilots, two government agents combed the ocean below with high-powered lenses.

Five miles out, three Coast Guard choppers hovered on station, ready to assist.

Two crowded dive boats could be seen far from the normal reefs. The divers looked particularly young and fit. They were. As Navy SEALs, they had to be.

It was in the middle of the afternoon when it happened.

The wind had dropped and the waves had subsided into a rolling swell. The dancing light and the gentle rocking and pure, salt air invited sleep. The men struggled to stay alert.

Taylor and Salemi both jumped as they heard the staccato echoes of gunfire. Dover immediately engaged the engine and the mate and Liddell snapped the lines from the outriggers and started furiously reeling in the fishing rods.

Muller dived into the cabin and emerged with a high-powered rifle.

The Coast Guard officer gave the course to Dover who was up on the flying bridge. They were a mile and half away from where the shots had been fired.

They arrived on the scene in time to see the body of a large blond man being hauled over the gunwales of a rubber boat.

Shots from Marine snipers' .338 Lapua Magnum rifles had ripped the blue dive suit diagonally and blood and white vertebrae spilled out from the rubber skin.

Salemi looked on numbly. They had failed. Their chance was irretrievably gone.

CHAPTER 97

When Henrik Wendt failed to return that night, his colleagues held council in the Rum Keg bar of their economy hotel then reluctantly called the Coast Guard.

Wendt, young and aggressive, had ignored the jeers of his fellow paparazzi and rented a skiff for his solo attempt to locate the Prince.

The others had split their resources between canvassing marinas and bribing night club bouncers. Along the southeast coast similar groups of paparazzi planned the next day's search. They had chartered a sports fishing boat just in case they heard of a sighting. But Wendt had decided to try on his own.

A Coast Guard Officer took their report and listed the 26-year-old Swedish photographer as "missing." A search was ordered for the skiff he had rented locally.

It would be officially "found" a day later and Wendt presumed drowned; just one of the unfortunate perils of serving the appetites of the world's cutthroat photo agencies.

For Salemi and Taylor, the realization that a paparazzi had been killed and not Congreve provoked troubling reactions.

They shook their heads at the innocent slaughter of a young but foolish man.

Inwardly they were relieved that they were still in the hunt for Congreve.

They both felt a guilt which was compounded by tolerating the government cover-up of the slaying.

The SEALs rationalized their deadly strike by pointing to the long waterproofed black camera lens — undeniably resembling a weapon the diver had been carrying.

But Taylor and the others knew no warning had been given to the cameraman. He had been taken out coldly and deliberately.

The killing had one chilling effect on their quest. The plan for the double to lure the killer into an ambush was scrapped.

The real Prince would be returning home the next day. The impostor would be rewarded with leave in New York and then sent home, his future promotion assured within his guards regiment and the Royal Court.

CHAPTER 98
FLORIDA

He waited for the others at a weathered wooden table overlooking the tall, blue-green marram grass buffering the hotel from the beach.

The sun was setting, triggering subtle changes of color in the sea before them.

The timeless beauty of the ocean and the end of day always made Salemi inexplicably sad. Perhaps he hated facing the loneliness of his nights, but he would never admit that to himself.

The group slowly assembled, Grasso the last to join them. The senior agent had already booked out of the hotel and was anxious to return to Washington.

"Now we have to go all out to track down Congreve, whereever the hell the bastard is hiding. Somebody, somewhere on this planet must know where he is," he thundered.

He looked disgustedly out to sea. "I knew this whole stupid Brit and State Department plan would backfire in their faces. They are idiots. Sooner or later the truth will come out about that photographer."

He rounded on the group at the table. "Well, it's our own damn fault for sitting on our butts. We should have found him by now. I want everyone back up to Washington and ready to go by next week. That includes you, Emelina."

He turned to Liddell and softened his tone. "Eugene, I know you haven't had much time with your family. There's room on the company plane for you if you want to come back tonight. It will give you the weekend off before we start the hard slog."

He looked at Taylor and Calderon.

"I want you to stay here another day or two. Just to make sure nothing turns up that indicates Congreve was sniffing around."

He shook Salemi's hand in farewell and punched Taylor lightly on the shoulder.

“I'm afraid you fellas will have to catch a commercial jet back. I'll see you two agents next week.”

Taylor watched Grasso and Liddell make their way back past the deserted lounge chairs by the poolside and disappear into the hotel.

He was tired and frustrated, but tried to be animated for Salemi and Calderon.

He turned to the priest. "Well, Joseph. Where shall we begin?"

"I'll check with Rome — the Bishop will be burning the midnight oil — and then I suggest we have dinner," said Salemi.

CHAPTER 99
BAHAMAS

The VIP sat in shadow in a back room listening to the reggae band and the rum-fueled chatter of tourists and sport fishermen crowding Mossy Cook's Neptune Bar.

The local Marlin tournament was just beginning and the tiny island —.eight miles long by eight hundred yards wide — was in party mood.

Inside the bar, the tourists mixed with the locals. Outside, in the dark alleys of Marytown, the slender jet-colored prostitutes from Haiti waited patiently, switching occasionally at the squadrons of no-see-ums biting their bare ankles and calves.

Stars glittered in the hot air above them and the sweet strong odor of ganja wafted from an alleyway across the dusty street.

For Aimee and Penelope, the instinct to flee clutched at them as the two large sun burned white men approached them.

But when they saw the green dollar bills and understood the men's patron wished to use their services they relaxed.

Probably some old rich white man from one of the big yachts. It could be a profitable night after all. That type liked to watch. That would be easy work.

They were directed up an unlit lane to a rocky island point just east of the town to a run down, concrete bungalow rented out by the bar's owner.

They were led inside and told to wait. The bungalow was barely furnished. On the stained, uncarpeted floor was a large palliase; in a corner a small make-shift drinks bar. The room was lit by an oil storm lamp, its smoky flame flickering in the green-yellow light.

The women helped themselves to banana rum, settled on a decrepit, stained couch against a wall, and waited. The large white men left. They could hear the sea washing the jagged concrete foundation under the bungalow.

Back at the Neptune bar, one of the white men looked into the shadowy recess and nodded to the VIP. The VIP acknowledged the man and nodded slowly.

He would stay there, sipping rum and Coca-Cola. Through a sheer curtain in a cut out of the wall he could watch the sensuous local dancers from the anonymity of his darkened lair.

Sometimes he thought anticipation was the sweetest part of sin. He would savor it for as long he could before giving into his urges and going to the bungalow. It was going to be a special night.

Fifteen yards from the ragged concrete drop-off by the bungalow wall, a snorkeled swimmer floated lazily.

In front of him the reef fish darted nervously seeking cover in the hollows and cracks of the submerged point.

At his side, 10 feet away, a lone four-foot barracuda kept silent station. From his scarred head a metal leader line trailed from a hook embedded in his jaw.

Soon it would rust away like all the others had over the years.

A slight current moved the fish and the man slowly back and forth in a strange dance with the sea urchins in the sand below.

They both waited patiently, for their victims.

CHAPTER 100
THE BUNGALOW

The VIP slipped into the bungalow and offered his guests ganja and cocaine.

The drugs would serve to loosen inhibitions and heightened the sense of danger from the social taboos he was about to break. It was almost delicious to think of the shame and disaster if anyone found out. It added to his voluntary degradation.

The women disrobed and he stripped off his own clothes. The tallest prostitute lay down on the palliasse and the VIP poured the white powder onto her taut ebony stomach. He enjoyed the girl's visible anxiety as he ruled the cocaine into four long lines with a safety razor blade. The older woman, Aimee, held the girl's hand in silent support and reassurance. He loved the way the women's eyes met and held at that moment.

The muscles just under the soft black skin of her belly rippled nervously as he snorted the cocaine from a straw. The metallic sting of the cocaine mixed with the earthy smell of her sex.

Then he handed Aimee the black velvet cords and the small leather whip. He lay down beside Penelope, and allowed himself to be tightly tied to her.

To the four bodyguards lounging down the lane, the muffled voices and occasional shrieks triggered no alarm.

They knew the VIP's perversions and had learned to ignore them. Sometimes, though, they felt as used as the harlots who fed his appetite. But it was not for them to judge. Just to protect.

A breeze had come up and it was hard not to succumb to the languor of the ocean and the rustling foliage.

The bungalow became quiet and the agents struggled to stay awake. The VIP had a habit of lingering, even sleeping with his harlots after their exertions, as if reluctant to leave the gutter.

As dawn appeared, one of the guards silently slipped a key into the bungalow door lock and cracked the door ajar.

He peeked in. The room was bathed in orange from the morning sun shining through a window overlooking the sea.

Then he noticed the darker streaks of red on the walls and the crimson pools on the floor.

In a corner of the room one of the nude prostitutes squatted lifeless against a wall. Her throat had been slashed open; the windpipe and larynx bulging onto her chest. Her gray hand still held the leather whip.

On the bloody straw mattress, conjoined in bondage, sex and death, were Penelope and the Vice President of the United States.

Her head had been caved in with terrific force. His spinal cord had been severed. His body was arched back against the cords which bound him to the prostitute, his erection still intact, his penis rigidly trapped within her.

By the side of the grotesque lovers lay a bloody axe. It looked very old.

The Secret Service agent radioed his partner and, still stunned, moved to the window overlooking the ocean.

The bungalow foundations, resting on concrete slabs sloped into the sea just feet from the window. The killer must have entered and escaped this way.

There was no movement in the water save for the orange clownfish and blue-green wrasse. Twenty feet out he could see the dark silver-gray, black-barred shape of a huge barracuda. From its jaw a dark rusty wire dangled.

The reef fish ignored the big predator. It had obviously satisfied its hunger earlier and was no longer a danger to them.

CHAPTER 101
PALM BEACH, FLORIDA

Taylor closed the sliding glass door to the balcony and sealed out the seductive wash of the waves on the white beach.

He picked up yet another incident report from a pile of folders on the bed in his hotel room and flopped into a chair.

He could not resist the illogical thought that he was being punished by Grasso. Damn it! It wasn't his fault that Congreve had not showed up for the Brits' phony welcoming party. If they had learned anything about Congreve it was that he was no fool.

What had they expected? The whole Florida operation had been a shambles. Now here he was stuck in a room combing through useless surveillance and small incident reports from over imaginative local police forces. Calderon, sensing his low spirits, worked in her own room and gave him a wide berth.

Grasso and the others were back home, with their families. Why couldn't he be there, with Ann?

He threw the folder onto an untidy pile on the carpeted floor and reached for the telephone. For the third time that day he would try Ann's Watergate number.

She picked up on the fourth ring.

The welcome in her voice shattered the dark mood that had taken hold of him.

"Much as I love the doctor's company, I am missing YOU," she said brightly. "Tell me you are at the airport ready to come home."

He noted with pleasure and reassurance the word home. Not come back to Washington or the District, but "home."

It was unsaid but they had silently crossed some invisible line and reached an unspoken commitment. It felt the most natural thing in the world to Taylor. After all these years perhaps he had really found a home. It wasn't bricks or mortar but the security of deep friendship and love.

They spoke lightly of the doctor, Ann praising his help and emotional strength. The doctor was taking the opportunity to socialize with old friends in Washington. Ann was glad of his company. The apartment had plenty of space for guests.

Ann was teasing Taylor about the bikini girls on the beach when the cell phone on his bed table buzzed angrily.

"I'll have to go, Ann," said Taylor. "I'll call you back in a few minutes."

It was Grasso.

"Get to the West Palm Field office and a secure line. The fucking crap's hit the fan."

Salemi 's impatience was growing. As he jogged along the beach he decided it was time to leave. Congreve would not be found here. The key to it still lay in Rome, deep in the archives. It had to, he thought desperately.

He had stayed with Taylor in Florida for arguably the most pragmatic of reasons. The Vatican needed to keep a close liaison with the U.S. government investigators.

But on a personal note, he felt strong loyalty to the tall American with his honesty and blunt manners.

But now, it looked as if the hunt might revert back to Britain or wherever the Prince visited next.

He finished his run and washed his feet under a salt stained tap at the beach entrance to the hotel. As he made his way across the pool patio he glanced up and saw Taylor furiously signaling him from his room balcony. He waved back and sprinted across the flagstone patio to a hotel elevator.

WASHINGTON, D.C.

At the White House, communication with the media correspondents abruptly stopped. In the cramped, narrow briefing room that houses the press above a disused swimming pool tempers flared as inquiries were rudely stonewalled.

The entrance from the packed briefing room to the West Wing offices was barred by secret service agents. From noon onwards the powerful from the Senate and the House were ushered in and out of the oval office.

Notably missing was Vice President John Neville. His chief of staff had been seen leaving his official residence, high on Embassy Row, in tears.

Something had happened to Neville, the man considered the runaway favorite to be the next President of the U.S.

At 1 p.m. word came that the president would make an announcement on national television. The news was leaked. Neville was dead.

Ann heard the news of John Neville's death on a taxicab radio as she rode back to her apartment with Dr Samuels. They had lunched with an old Navy friend of the doctor.

The news of the Vice President's sudden death in a boating accident off the Florida coast crushed their high spirits. They entered the apartment and turned on the television.

They saw a picture of the President comforting Neville's widow and daughters. A litany of predictable gestures followed. The stock markets had been closed; flags were at half staff throughout the nation. The big lie was promoted and expanded. The Body had been recovered from the ocean; the family was insisting on a private autopsy and funeral.

It seemed Ann could not escape the ubiquitous march of death. Dr. Samuels saw her distress and put an arm around her shoulder.

She gently moved away from him and picked up the phone.

She called the hotel. She was informed Mr. Taylor was not available, and could not be reached. So too was "Mr" Salemi.

CHAPTER 102
THE BAHAMAS

The single engine Piper began its droning descent over the sparkling indigo waters. Isolated clouds above them cast inkblots on the ocean below.

Taylor remembered a similar flight years before when their pilot had mistaken one of these sharply limned shadows for their intended island. It was only when they had begun their approach that they had realized their folly.

Now he, Calderon and Salemi were being flown by a local FBI agent who was a keen amateur pilot. All official aircraft in the Palm Beaches had been commandeered before them.

They radioed the island tower and throttled back, crossing a few hundred feet above the carcasses of small prop planes partially submerged in the bright green lagoons below—stagnant, watery cemeteries for overloaded drug traffickers risking the unlit, un-policed, night time runway.

The anger and frustration vented by Grasso still rang in Taylor's ears. The FBI was being kept in the dark about the details of Neville's death. Like Mandarins constructing Chinese walls within walls the Secret Service and the Homeland Security chiefs and almost certainly the CIA were blocking out the agency.

The FBI brass knew a massive cover-up of some sort was being manufactured. They knew Neville had died in the stews of Marytown. They strongly suspected he had been murdered. But, until authorization came from the president, they were powerless to investigate.

Agents flown in from Miami and Fort Lauderdale had already been rudely kept away from the death house.

Taylor could only hope that when he reached the tiny island, saner minds would prevail and they would be allowed to investigate.

The manner of death and the weapon might give them a clue to any possible, although unlikely link with Congreve's murderous rampage.

They were driven to Marytown and the decrepit bungalow. There, to their anger, they were denied admittance by a phalanx of Secret Service men and Bahamian police.

That anger grew to numbing rage when they met a Homeland Security liaison agent from Miami whom Calderon knew called Carlos Rivera. He told them grimly: "You are wasting your time here guys. The bastards have sanitized the whole house."

"They have removed everything, every damn piece of evidence. I managed to learn from some unguarded comments by two Secret Service agents that there was a lot of blood. That an axe of some sort was used on Neville."

Even from the dusty lane outside the murder house they could smell the choking fumes of strong disinfectant. The waves of harsh chemicals hung in the air forming an invisible barrier between the faded white washed house walls and the clouds of flying insects.

"They washed the whole damn room sometime this morning. The orders must have come right from the top," said the exasperated agent.

"Do we know where they took any weapons?" asked Calderon.

"I can only guess they were spirited off the island with the bodies," said Rivera.

"Bodies? What fucking bodies?" asked Taylor.

Rivera silently motioned them to follow him back down the lane, away from the other agents and police. As they walked back down the dusty road, he glanced pointedly at the Neptune Inn.

"One of our guys, who is a keen fisherman, tells me he has heard rumors that Neville was here a few years ago. And that the word was that he liked perverse threesomes with the local young ladies of the night."

"Christ almighty," gasped Taylor. "Surely the bastard wasn't stupid enough to pull some hookers and risk everything."

Then Taylor remembered the dark whispers that had occasionally surfaced about the Vice President and his sexual inclinations. No one, including himself had ever given them credence. Taylor knew instinctively that whoever had been with Neville would be dead.

Rivera confirmed his dark thoughts.

"Whoever the hooker or hookers were, they no longer exist. The prostitutes on this island are dirt poor, mostly young and from Haiti.

No one will miss the poor souls. I'll bet they died with Neville."

He squinted and looked out to the sun-burnished ocean.

"Their corpses are probably floating out there somewhere right now dropped far out in the ocean by the CIA. If their bodies are ever found, it will just be a few more poor Haitians who perished at sea. Anyone who did know them is scared for their lives. Every pimp has left the island already."

Taylor and Salemi both knew it would be pointless to stay in Marytown any longer.

As far as the Bahamian and U.S. authorities were concerned, nothing had happened here.

Those few who did know would never speak. The innkeeper would be silent. He had his livelihood and his life to protect.

Within weeks the crumbling concrete bungalow would be leveled.

CHAPTER 103

Far below, Coastguard cutters left boiling, white wakes—fatuous post-mortem patrols ordered by panicked officials.

Cutting across the Gulf Stream, the giant cruise ships plowed their carefree way south-east to the Caribbean.

The security chiefs and the White House, though never admitting it publicly, would condemn their hapless subordinates for being so wrong. All were asking the same question. Why Neville?

The dispirited group, Taylor, Calderon and Salemi arrived back at the Palm Beach hotel and arranged to meet in the late afternoon at the beach-side patio. Taylor went to his room and found two messages from Ann.

She would have to wait. First he must call Washington. Grasso had been fighting his own frustrating battle in the treacherous, roiling atmosphere of intrigue and uncertainty Neville's death had caused.

Grasso was terse. "Stay down there with Calderon, John. Give it another day in case we need you there. Then both of you come up to D.C. We still have a hell of a job in front of us."

"Are you still taking a lot of incoming, boss?" asked Taylor.

"Nothing I haven't faced before."

Grasso was touched by Taylor's concern but his toughness ruled.

"You let me worry about that. You and Calderon get out of any fucking funk you're feeling.

"You are both in for a long, hard slog up here. I want you bright and enthusiastic. Tell Calderon she has a day to pack, and organize what little social life she might have."

Grasso hung up. Taylor decided he would wait until evening to call Ann. He was in no mood for pleasantries. He had a lot of thinking to do.

A tiny kitten played in the sandy soil under the grove of broad leafed sea grape that edged the patio from the grasses and yellow and violet wild flowers which stretched down to the beach. Six feet away, its mother watched sphinx-like, ready to intervene if danger approached.

The kitten, part of a friendly tribe of white feral cats that lived on the hotel grounds had caught a small green lizard. The lizard was teased, released, re-captured and juggled by the slim short-haired kitten. Tiring of his game the kitten began to eat the reptile.

Salemi did not miss the irony in both their situations. Congreve had played with them just like the cat had with the lizard.

He sat alone at the weathered, wooden table in the patio area. The lunch guests had long gone. Most of the cats had been fed their table scraps and retired to sleep.

The disaster in the Bahamas had challenged every concept they had relied on. How had they been so completely wrong? The priest glanced back across the deserted pool and caught the flash of brief white shorts and the long, bronze legs of Calderon. She was tipped back in a chair on the balcony of her room, her slim ankles resting on the rail. The sea breeze swept through her dark hair.

He quickly turned his gaze back to the ocean.

Feelings he had long ago presumed mastered were insidiously returning; lustful memories of the vivacious girls of his Sicilian youth, long since sublimated, fought their way back from his subconscious.

They had begun with his proximity with Ann in London and caught fire in the company of the beautiful Cuban agent.

It was yet another reason to leave Florida, close down their New York operation and resume the hunt in Europe, if the Vatican powers could be persuaded.

Calderon looked down from her balcony at the ocean. Despite all her years in Florida she continued to take succor from the shifting seas and the sunlight. In an hour she was due to meet the others down on the patio.

She allowed the sea breeze and the sound of the waves to relax her. She followed the flight of an echelon of Louisiana Brown Pelicans as they swooped upon a shoal of blue fish that had been herded into the shallows by larger predators.

The birds disappeared behind the sea grape trees sheltering the patio area. She spotted the two white cats and followed their path to the feet of Salemi.

Her natural instinct to flirt with the handsome, athletic Sicilian had been stifled when Grasso had explained his real identity. Her first thought had been "What a waste."

Perversely it was a pleasant change to meet a man who did not feel obliged to hit on her. She also felt like a hypocrite. A part of her wanted to turn his head. Her conscience ruled that would be cruel.

She was aware of the effect she had on men. She was pragmatic. She had used her looks to gain attention but prided herself on her perfectionism and discipline to earn her way through any career doors that opened for her.

The other agents had quickly learned she was a professional who kept a cool head in any emergency.

Taylor and Calderon joined the priest at the table. A waiter from the poolside bar brought them beer, salsa and taco chips. The patio area was still, the beach deserted save for a few locals strolling and taking in the changing sea colors as the sun set.

Calderon sensed the priest was deeply troubled. Taylor noticed that the fire, like the sinking sun, seemed to have disappeared from Salemi's eyes.

The agents knew that Neville's murder had dealt the priest's mission a massive setback if not a finishing blow. They wished they could give Salemi some solace but they would not insult him with spurious optimism.

The priest saw their sympathetic looks and shook himself from the melancholy that had briefly cloaked him.

"Life and the quest go on, my friends," he said with a faint smile.

"You must go forward with the hunt for your vice president's killer. I must continue on my mission. It has been a great honor to work with you. I am sure we will always remain friends. I will still keep you informed of any developments. It has been a pleasure."

Taylor reached over and grasped the priest's shoulder.

"The pleasure has been ours, Joseph. We have no intention of forgetting you in the hunt for Congreve. Even if he was misdirecting us all along, your work was still invaluable in alerting us to him and his murders. This thing isn't finished, my friend."

Calderon nodded her approval and asked: "Will you be coming up to Washington with us?"

Salemi smiled again, this time more genuinely.

"I think the American part of my journey is over. I will go up to New York and close up our operation there, what's left of it, in the brownstone. I will pay my respects to Father Orr by settling any business he left unfinished. I came to love the old man."

"I think we all did," said Taylor. "We'll keep in touch."

Salemi raised his glass.

"Salute."

Salemi looked at his new friends and saw their concern for him. He decided to fully reveal his and his church's motives in the pursuit of the killer. What was the point of continued concealment. His mission had failed, the dream of contact with Henry's spirit just that—a dream.

A brown, dessicated sea grape leaf, blown by the ocean breeze clattered onto the table surface, breaking the silence.

He began: "I know that you all must have been suspicious of the true intent of the Church's intense interest in this whole affair. I told you we were intrigued by the possibility that the troubled spirit of Henry VIII had somehow entered the body of the serial killer and was controlling his actions. This was true. We wanted to communicate with the killer.

He looked directly at Taylor.

"I told you and Eugene that we wanted to talk to the killer simply to find out if he was influenced by the spirit of Henry and if anything of historical importance could be gleaned from this encounter.

"That part if true but our burning quest was to speak directly to Henry, to see, in fact, if we could influence him, influence him before his return to his own time."

Calderon, who was hearing the time travel story for the first time could not mask her astonishment.

"I don't believe what I'm hearing," she said with bewilderment. "You guys really believe a spirit was controlling Congreve—and you could talk to it."

Taylor was annoyed at Calderon's undiplomatic outburst. He could not openly admit in front of Salemi that he had gone along with the premise simply to use the intelligence efforts of the world wide dragnet the Vatican had authorized.

Salemi thought he saw signs of embarrassment on Taylor's face and jumped in.

He met Calderon's stare and explained: "I and my small group in the Church believed that. I can assure that John and Eugene were, at least, skeptical but I believe they always kept open minds.

"As for our motive in wanting to influence the spirit of Henry it was and is brutally simple, to try and change the course of history. We wanted to prevent the success of the English Reformation and for England to remain under the Catholic faith.

"If somehow we could convince Henry to not break with the Church it would have had great moment for the world. In hind sight it now looks like it was a forlorn hope, bordering on the ridiculous."

Calderon was stunned to realize this highly intelligent priest was deadly serious but she asked:" tell me why this Reformation was so important.

Salemi frowned and said; "A very crude and simple answer is that during Henry's reign Europe was in the throes of a general reform movement among different religious factions who broke from the absolute rule and obedience to the laws of the Catholic Church in Rome.

"Ironically in England Henry and his ministers had prosecuted, executed or forced into exile many of these same protestant activists.

"But for the scandal of the divorce from Katherine of Aragon which offended the most powerful ruler in Europe, her nephew, the English king would have remained true to his title as Defender of the Catholic faith.

"England would have remained Catholic for centuries to come. No doubt the Catholic Church would have adjusted to the times but the faith would have remained strong in England."

Salemi smiled wryly. "I know it sounds fantastic, Emmi. Perhaps it is. But for many of us, if there was the slightest chance that this was the true spirit of Henry bending through time to speak to this killer, it was chance worth taking."

Then as if his expiation of the quest had suddenly cleared his mind of failure and renewed his faith Salemi promised: "Even now I cannot give up. Somewhere, somehow we will pick up the trail again. There are too many unanswered questions. For you it is over and I understand that and wish you all well."

Far out on the horizon, a water spout roiled down to the sea surface like a heavy drop of water descending from an ink blot. The spout quickly dissipated into a dark purple veil draped from the anvil cloud, racing toward shore. The wind, pushed ahead of the squall, shook the sea grapes above them. There was nothing more to say. Quickly and silently they stood, then walked back to the sanctuary of the hotel.

CHAPTER 104
LONDON

The news of the Vice President's "accidental" death rocked the London news media as it swept around the world.

Sir Moberley Johns was in no mood for the mundane, daily business of the College of Arms. On terms of strictest secrecy, he had been informed of the true cause of Neville's death. He understood that the political turmoil from the murder would eventually extend into the corridors of the Vatican and could topple Bishop di Montevecchi. Inevitably, his enemies would learn the truth and seize on Neville's murder to sabotage their quest.

After lunch at his club, he walked toward the Thames and Westminster. The grey river and the threatening sky matched his mood. In moments of crisis his faith supplied an anchor and he yielded to the pull of the massive gothic entrance to Westminster Abbey.

A walk among the tombs and walled coffins of Britain's, kings, queens, poets and politicians would put the transient problems of the day back into perspective

For all their power and pomp, none of those glorious figures had out-witted death.

He passed by the Lady Chapel where Henry VIII's Plantagenet mother was entombed and paused by a series of wall plaques commemorating lesser scions of the star-crossed Royal House of York, whose reign had ended when Henry's father had defeated and killed Richard III on bloody Bosworth Field on a hot August day in 1485.

On the wall opposite were plaques and inset statues, coats of arms; momenti mori of the once powerful Plantagenet nobles, the Greys, the Courtneys, the Poles, the Nevilles. One seemed to beckon him more than the others. A relief carving of a 15th Century woman—an English queen who was married to the last Plantaganet king — Richard III.

Her family name suddenly seared flared into his thoughts—Neville … Good grief- The house of Neville!

Moberley walked quickly out of the Abbey toward Parliament Square and hailed a taxi. Suddenly the College of Arms and its fount of genealogical history had become attractive once more. There was work to be done. Perhaps all was not lost.

Johns' long-suffering office assistant was surprised to see her suddenly invigorated leader bound into the room and nonchalantly throw his coat and jacket onto the cracked leather of a battered sofa.

She had just placed a pile of calf- skin bound books on Johns' cluttered desk.

"What the devil are these?" Johns challenged. "Clear 'em out, my dear. There's work to be done."

The assistant was used to Johns' eccentric management style. She sternly reminded him.

"THESE are the collections of Henry VIII letters you have been agitating for all week. I can always send them back."

Johns' attitude changed.

"My sincere apologies, Maude. They stay, of course. They stay, and thank you. Now, out with you, my dear. I must not be disturbed.

She left and warned the security staff that Sir Moberley looked to be in for the night. Strategically warned, they would not challenge the light coming from the door of the old herald's office.

At 8 p.m. Johns called Rome and asked di Montevecchi to unleash his Vatican research team to table the genealogy of the Nevilles and the old Plantagenet families up to the last direct survivors. He had his own computer program running, but it was no match for the enormous task.

ROME

After thanking Johns, Luca di Montevecchi launched the special team of *scrittori* and researchers on the new effort. He checked the time. Salemi was not due to arrive in New York from Florida until late evening. He would let

Salemi have some rest. He would call him at 11 a.m. the next day—5 a.m. New York time — and get him to check Father Orr's research and tell him of the Neville theory. The news had resurrected his lost appetite. He would have a leisurely supper at his favorite restaurant.

But first he would visit his private chapel and offer prayers. There was still hope, thanks be to God and a tireless old British aristocrat.

NEW YORK

Salemi had caught a late-night flight up to New York and, despite weather delays, reached the crowds at JFK airport. From there, a diocesan driver had ferried him to a small boutique hotel on Lexington Avenue in midtown Manhattan near the Cathedral.

He had said his farewells to the FBI team with mixed feelings. They had become a close part of his life. That would not do. He must put aside any emotions. He must discipline himself. Back to the ascetic life he had chosen, back to his life's work.

Salemi was surprised by the energy and sanguinity in the Bishop's voice when the telephone woke him up.

"There is still hope, Joseph. Stay in New York for the moment. Check all of Father Orr's research work and documents. Concentrate on any genealogical avenues he pursued." Di Montevecchi explained Johns' chilling insight and

Salemi felt a surge of energy and purpose return.

"I'll get over to the East Side brownstone and the Gramercy Park apartment as soon as I can. They are both church owned and nothing has been touched. They have been effectively sealed," said Salemi.

"Make sure your cell phone is charged, Joseph. We must move quickly on this. I must be kept informed."

Salemi laughed to himself. The Bishop, he who hated cell phones, had finally ventured reluctantly into the electronic age.

CHAPTER 105
NEW YORK

The 51st Street brownstone had lost the quaint charm it once held for Salemi. The warmth that emanated from the wood fire and the persona of Father Orr was gone. The rooms as empty as the fire grate.

He crossed to the mantelpiece and saw the brown scores made in the marble by Orr's secretive cigarette lapses. Salemi had always taken the old man's claims to have given up his tobacco habit lightly. Somehow the burn stains conjured Orr more than any photograph. He could see the tiny priest warming himself beside the crackling fire, absent mindedly letting the cigarettes smolder and burn out as some idea occupied his thoughts.

The office still bore the marks of the perfunctory examination by the special FBI and police squad which had searched the rooms immediately after the murder. Their focus had been limited to clues to Orr's murder. No obvious pointers to that crime had been found in the brownstone.

Orr's neatly organized computer disks and notes had been stored in a desk drawer. Salemi opened it and gleaned the list; nothing surprising there. He put them into a briefcase and left the brownstone for the last time.

He walked to Second Avenue and flagged a cab to Gramercy Park just over a mile to the south. An elderly priest from the diocese was waiting and let him into Orr's apartment.

A small cardboard box containing a faded black-and-white picture of Orr's parents, a worn rosary, a cheap wristwatch and a Bible awaited shipment to a surviving niece in Armagh — all that was left of the old priest's presence on Earth. Any clothes and shoes he had possessed had already gone to the homeless.

Near a large window, overlooking the private park below, an oak bookcase stood against a wall. A polished wooden desk supported his computer equipment.

Salemi began to review Orr's files. He scrolled until he came to the relevant title, genealogy. He opened these files, they were the most recent. Had the old man been ahead of the experts in London and Rome?

Orr had utilized international genealogical sites and employed the vast resources of the Mormon Church. Like many people he was dimly aware of the Mormon Church's interest in genealogy. Bishop di Montevecchi had once explained to him the Mormon Church's underlying interest in the dead of the past.

On an almost daily basis in Mormon Temples throughout the world, thousands of the Mormon faithful are vicariously baptized for the dead. Teams of young Mormons volunteer their help and assist genealogical centers throughout the world, compiling birth and death records which will eventually be available to the church's vast library.

The church believes that those who have died and were not baptized Mormons while alive can, by proxy, be made Mormons after their death and released from their "spiritual prison."

It was into this immense depository of records that Father Orr had begun to delve. He had been checking the family histories of all of the murder victims believed slaughtered by Congreve. Obviously, he had died before Neville's murder and could not have foreseen that death. Still his instinct had been right.

Salemi looked out and watched a light snow fall begin to coat the park and the windward aspects of the tree trunks and bare limbs.

Rome was working on the genealogical trails as was Sir Moberley in London. It would take time. He mused for a few minutes then slapped his palm sharply on the waxed desktop. What was he thinking? There was a better way. Did he not have friends in one of the most powerful security forces in the world? A vast organization with entry to the most powerful computer search engines in the world.

He made a call to di Montevecchi, and received his imprimatur. The monsignor then spent an hour trying to track down his FBI friends. If they could convince the powers to grant mainframe computer time the answer would come quickly.

Taylor and Calderon, he was informed, had checked out of the Palm Beach hotel and were not expected back. Their cell phones did not answer. In the agency's Washington office, Liddell was not expected back until Monday. Grasso was unavailable but a message could be left with an assistant.

Salemi decided the message would be better presented in person. Taylor and Calderon would be in the capital in the morning.

Salemi called the concierge at his hotel and asked for the scheduled time of the first morning flight to Washington, D.C.

CHAPTER 106
WASHINGTON, D.C.

Dr. Samuels could see the frustration slowly grow in his beautiful hostess and smiled.

It had been a long time ago, but he recalled the ache, impatience and uncertainty of newly discovered love.

He was delighted for his friend Taylor and amused by Ann's sudden irritation when John's name was mentioned. At first, as they followed the tourist trails round the Washington landmarks, she had been reticent about discussing him. But at their dinners she betrayed her burning curiosity over the tall, enigmatic Taylor.

The doctor had indulged her, telling her about his friend and in the retelling of old anecdotes and observations began to understand Taylor more acutely himself.

He had enjoyed the company of this vivacious, intelligent beauty and hoped everything would go well with her and Taylor. Taylor had been a loner for too long. Samuels had sensed something of the same in Ann.

The winter storm had briefly paused, leaving banks of snow throughout the city. It was still pristine and beautiful. She should be enjoying it with Taylor not some old doctor from New York.

He hoped Taylor would be here soon. It was time for him to go home to the old life, and time for Ann and John to start the new.

CHAPTER 107
LONDON

Sir Moberley Johns had launched the search engine synapses issuing from London and Rome and sat back flushed with adrenaline in his office at the College of Arms.

In the College's library the unique collections and records dating back to the 15th Century were searched by archivists promised healthy extra payments funded personally by Moberley.

Three men scoured the vast records for clues to any living Plantagenet descendants. Every minor cadet family was exhaustively tracked. Inevitably the searchers would find that line had become extinct centuries ago. Some who claimed direct descent were ruled out on ruthless inspection of their claims.

One man carefully viewed the thousands of armorial bearings, scrutinizing the myriad quarterings of heraldic shields, searching for the emblems which would signify a Plantagenet ancestor. It was a painstaking task. Many shields had as many as 30 or more tiny quarterings, each denoting a family tie.

Moberley had asked the Vatican to scour similar records throughout Europe by whatever computer sources they could muster. The common task was clear: Find a direct Plantagenet descendant.

Moberley had also instructed the Vatican researchers to go further than just the official records. He wanted to investigate the rumors and innuendo which haunt history; the bastard sons and daughters of the famous who did not necessarily bear their father's noble name. For a vengeful Henry not even the illegitimate would be spared.

He had done all he could for the moment.

He thought once more about Henry's implacable rage against his Plantagenet relatives. He picked up a volume of Henry's published letters and flipped idly through the collection. His assistant had studiously ear-marked those letters that might be germane to his research.

There it was. A scorching example of Henry's welling poison against them. A letter written to Sir Thomas Wyatt, the English ambassador in Madrid at the court of the Holy Roman Emperor Charles V. Wyatt was commanded to urge the Emperor to give no sanctuary to Reginald de la Pole, the Plantagenet cousin who had fled to Europe; a man Henry now described as "that cankerous traitor Pole."

Pole had once fled Henry's palace in terror and tears after the furious King had punched his face for his obstinacy to the proposed divorce.

There were at least a dozen other references describing Henry's vituperative attacks on his once-favored cousin.

Henry had learned that Rome had sent Pole to Spain to try to persuade the most powerful ruler in Europe, the emperor Charles V, to invade England and restore the Catholic faith there. The Hapsburg emperor controlled a huge part of Europe; the low-countries Netherlands, Austro-Hungary, the riches of Spain. He was the man who had sacked Rome and made the Pope his puppet. He was also the nephew of Catherine of Aragon, the devout Catholic wife Henry was trying to shed.

Henry's fury had stretched to Pole's Neville relatives. How many others in the various Yorkist families Johns wondered?

Yes. They should concentrate on all septs of the Plantagenet family descendants. Perhaps there were others who had been murdered, who had links to that ill-fated family.

He entered the new, wider search suggestions into the computer and copied them to the Vatican.

CHAPTER 108

A Nor'easter was pumping moisture up the coast which turned into swirling snow just north of the Carolinas.

The 25-year-old Citation jet Taylor and Calderon had hitched a ride on bounced and chattered to itself in the turbulence 20 miles off the coastline. After two jarring hours, the pilot, a retired special agent who ran his own jet-leasing company, left his co-pilot in control and wandered back to the cabin.

"The storm's dropping buckets of snow in the D.C. area, John. It's a major blizzard. It hasn't reached Philadelphia yet—we can just squeeze in there if our luck holds. They are arranging a car for you at the airport."

Taylor thanked the pilot and gazed down at the muddy grey blanket below. He smiled at Calderon.

"Hope you packed your snow shoes."

Calderon laughed nervously. She was not looking forward to "squeezing" into an airport ahead of a massive snow storm.

The dark mass of clouds below and the uncertainty of the flight matched their spirits.

Their release from Florida had come in the late afternoon, by which time commercial flights north were already being cancelled due to the storm.

Taylor had tried to reach Ann, but, as usual, she was not answering her cell phone. She had either switched it of or left it at home.

On approach to Philadelphia the pilots lost altitude as expediently as possible and landed before the first snow flurries hit the airport. As they braked on the runway there was an almost palpable release of tension. No one would admit it but they were all thanking their private Gods they were safely on the ground.

As they drove south, the sky darkened into a huge menacing ink blot and the first snow flakes flicked through the car's headlights like moths clustering around a lamp.

Soon he had to slow as the black tarmac turned grey-white and luminous.

The almost horizontally driven snow began to choke traffic.

Somewhere ahead, the inevitable jackknifed tractor-trailer had closed two lanes and the back-up began.

Taylor looked at Calderon and saw her exhaustion and traces of anxiety. He pulled off an exit ramp and stopped at a motel. It was not fair to keep going and risk her life because he was anxious to see Ann. They would have dinner, get some sleep and arrive fresh in the morning.

CHAPTER 109

After freshening up in their rooms, Calderon and Taylor met in the motel's spacious lounge-restaurant area, ordered beer and burgers and sat in a booth. At the other end of the lounge a trio played, ignored by most of the patrons.

On the flight north, both agents had pondered the false trails laid by Neville's killer.

Taylor produced a notebook and pen. Calderon was amused by Taylor's stubborn refusal to use modern, pocket computer aids, which he dismissed as unreliable toys.

Over sips of beer they detailed what they now knew, attempting to catalogue the latent clues they had missed, indicators which would have pointed them towards Neville as the target, not the Prince.

Taylor neatly listed the murder sites, at least those they knew of.

"Let's start with Chicago," he said.

"In hindsight that was obvious enough. The vice president was there with the Prince. My friend's daughter and her love interest were just in the wrong place, smack in his murderous path."

"Or," Calderon added, "The killer, frustrated at not getting to Neville, slaughtered them in anger, then placed the bloody, severed arm in the Prince's tent to throw us way off the true target."

Taylor had been told Calderon was noted for her analytical powers. Now she was showing it.

"Yes," said Taylor. "I think what threw us off was that arm and the swath of blood streaked across the Prince's arms or flag or whatever the hell the Brits call it.

"What the priests called the 'talismans' that he collected were nothing but a trail of red herrings, stinking up the investigation, leading us to the Prince and away from Neville.

"The break-in murder and theft in Wilchester, Mass., at that arms museum; the stolen axe that was used in the Central Park attack — pure misdirection."

Calderon gently raised her wrist and elegant hand in a slight stop sign. "I don't think so, John."

Taylor raised his eyebrows quizzically. "Why?"

"Because the Neville family estate, where he grew up and often retreats to, is 33 miles away from Wilchester. And if we check, we'll probably find he was due to visit there."

"Well done, but how do we know he visits the place?"

"Down in Florida I killed some time with his Secret Service detail. It didn't seem relevant at the time. They were bitching about what a pain it was protecting him because of his habit of giving them the slip for his mystery assignations. As a matter of routine the murder in that area had attracted their attention.

"It's my fault. I should have brought it to your attention. I screwed up, I guess."

"Nonsense, Emmi. None of us would have linked it to Neville, even if you had raised it. We were all convinced it was about the Prince. We all fell for the killer's smoke and mirrors and the priests' theories like a bunch of fucking amateurs."

Calderon's insight struck like a bell in Taylor's mind.

"My God! How stupid could we have been. The British Embassy garden murders — more fucking misdirection. What do the garden walls of the British Embassy border?"

"Jeez!" Calderon caught her breath. "The official residence of the Vice President."

"Exactly," said Taylor. He remembered a visit years before to the naval station which served as the Vice President's estate off Embassy Row, in the heart of Washington. He recalled the grassy acres, the small bungalow-like residence at the top of a gentle hill approached by a winding road.

"Neville had been known to wander alone with his two Labrador dogs around the estate. It would have been unlikely the killer could not have entered over the wall undetected. But if he was fast enough, lucky enough, and did not care about surviving after an attack on the Vice President, he just might have succeeded."

They both knew there was no defense against fanatics.

"The bastard wasn't targeting the Embassy at all. He was trying to slip through the Embassy gardens and get to the adjoining wall. These poor bastards simply got in his way."

"So the other Washington murder, that young actor, and the theft from the Croft library was just another calculated misdirection," said Calderon.

"Must be," said Taylor.

"He wants the book to fit in with the talisman idea, and amuses himself torturing and slaughtering that poor friend of Ann's just to make us believe we are dealing with a ritualistic murder. What a sick bastard."

Calderon could sense Taylor's rising emotional levels. He was becoming stressed out. She had never heard him swear so often in her presence. An out-of-control Taylor would not do. She touched his arm lightly. A subtle admonition to calm down.

Taylor felt ashamed at his outburst. He had to separate any emotions from his analysis of the case. He appreciated Calderon's gentle reproof.

They sipped their beer in silence, then continued.

"What about New York," she asked.

"The Metropolitan museum murder was that damned talisman thing again. The slaughter of the English arms expert and the attack on the gay guys in 'The Rambles' was meant to throw us off the trail again; make it look like a lunatic was behind the thefts and killings. He was playing with us again. The bastard's true target that time was Father Orr, possibly Monsignor Salemi, or even me. He knew we were on the trail. I'll never forgive him for what he did to that gentle old priest. He didn't have the balls to come after me, or Liddell or Salemi."

He felt his emotions roiling again and checked himself.

"We'll have to check whether the Vice President had any engagements, official or otherwise in New York, during that period,' said Calderon, steering him back from his anger.

Once again Taylor appreciated her skill and clinical attitude in deflating his anger.

She went on: "In fact we will have to re-think all incidents in relation to Neville's movements over the past year."

"I agree, Emmi. Grasso and thc team are probably onto it but we will emphasize it tomorrow anyway."

They pushed their half-eaten burgers and cardboard French fries away.

"Let's get a night cap at the bar." The crowd had thinned and the trio played some medley of mush. The tawdry atmosphere did nothing for their spirits.

CHAPTER 110
WASHINGTON, D.C.

It was early Saturday morning, when Taylor and Calderon entered Grasso's office at the agency headquarters.

Taylor had not tried to contact Ann. He would wait until he was certain he was free to see her and had some spare time.

On the drive south to D.C., Calderon had been silent, distracted. Her thoughts were racing back to the past. Long forgotten landmarks charged her memory of an intense summer romance while she had taken a refresher course at Quantico, the FBI facility in Virginia.

At first the young army major had seemed a charming, harmless diversion, someone to enjoy restaurants and the limited nightlife of Washington. At weekends they would speed on his Harley Davidson to his small cottage on the Maryland seashore. Days sailing on the Chesapeake, quiet evenings at the cottage with wine and freshly caught seafood. In their hearts they both knew it would have to end. Both were career people. Neither one was prepared for commitment or subordination to the other's goals. But the parting had still hurt deeply. They had corresponded for a month or two, then a new posting for him cut what cords were left.

Taylor rapped sharply on the closed office door and entered. Grasso was sitting at his desk smiling at Taylor and Calderon's surprised facial expressions.

"The Vatican fire you, Joseph?" asked Taylor, grinning.

"Not yet, John," laughed Salemi.

Grasso interrupted the joviality.

"The good father has some new leads which we will be following up. But his presence here is strictly unofficial. We have a lot of work ahead of us and I know you guys want some time off. You have till Monday."

Gee! A whole day and a half, thought Taylor but decided to keep his thoughts to himself.

"We have booked agent Calderon into a hotel," said Grasso.

Taylor had offered Calderon the spare room in his canal side apartment. With luck he would be spending his time in Ann's Watergate bedroom. But the agent had politely declined. It would not have been the first time that an innocent act of friendship had been distorted into something darker by office gossips.

Grasso motioned to the telephone console on his desk.

"Greetings, brothers and sister," came Liddell's disembodied voice.

"I didn't have the heart to drag him from his family," said Grasso. "But that will all change on Monday," he warned.

Salemi told them of the latest turn in their research — the Neville-Plantagenet link.

Salemi could not help feeling they were all politely listening to him in a well-meaning but patronizing way. He could not blame them. Even he could sniff the whiff of desperation in his latest theory.

At least they all seemed to agree to explore it. A slim hope, but still hope.

CHAPTER 111
THE VATICAN

The ancient walls of the Vatican seemed to be closing in on Bishop Luca di Montevecchi. His solace was the gentle winter rain which kept the gardens deserted and allowed him solitude on his daily walks. Now he had left the self-imposed confines for a tried and trusted respite; a lunch with his old friend Sir Moberley Johns at the Vivendo restaurant at Le Grand.Hotel.

Johns had flown in that morning. Both men had decided their mission would be better served by the English genealogical expert supervising the computer programs running in the secret Vatican "war-room."

"We have more information coming in than we know what to do with," said the Bishop. "It is better you are here. We need your insight to cut through the mass of information."

Johns didn't have the heart to formulate the odds of tracking down any direct descendants of the protagonists in a Tudor intrigue, but he would do his best. The most he could do would be to skim the lists of names and hope for divine inspiration. At least there wasn't a better place to hope for that, he thought wryly.

After a lunch of fresh grilled bass and an excellent wine they drove back to the Vatican under pewter skies and Johns began his work.

He scrolled through the lists of those who, however remotely, could trace a relative back to one of the Plantagenets. The connections were remote, almost absurd. He advised the *scrittori* to concentrate on only those who might prove a direct line.

It seemed an impossible task. His eyes, losing their fight against weariness and age, were on the point of rebellion when a young *scrittore* excitedly pulled a hard copy from a computer and placed it in front of him. A jackpot of sorts. A direct descendant of Henry's hated cousin, Reginald de La Pole, from his exile in the Netherlands.

God help us, thought Johns.

It was the late afternoon the clouds had scattered and the pale Roman light was now streaming and slanting through the windows. Johns excitedly called di Montevecchi in his apartments. They immediately began to place desperate calls to Washington and Salemi.

CHAPTER 112

The group left the FBI offices. As usual, much to Taylor's frustration, Ann had her cell phone switched off. The apartment telephone flipped into the message-mode, and he told her he would be at the Watergate Hotel with Salemi and Calderon for a late lunch.

He felt it would be ungentlemanly to abandon Calderon to her agency-selected room at the Holiday Inn. Calderon would have loved nothing better. She would have preferred shopping for some winter clothes, but went along with his plan, not wanting to offend him. Salemi, as usual, was booked into the Watergate.

They dropped Calderon's luggage off at her hotel, retaining the distinctive silvered metal cases containing their official briefs, travel equipment and their service pistols. The daily accessories they never allowed out of their possession. After she registered, they drove down past Foggy Bottom to the concrete dreadnaught of the Watergate complex.

Brightly colored foreign flags snapped in the wind over the metal canopy at the hotel entrance. Taylor gave the keys of the agency car to a valet for the underground car park. Before entering the hotel Taylor instinctively glanced across the driveway up to Ann's apartment.

Snow had drifted on the balcony, crisp and shining in the sunshine.

Where the iron balcony bars of the apartments met the concrete, rust stains winnowed like tributaries into the pebbled surface.

The brilliant light caught white sails of fabric billowing from one of the balconies — Ann's. Despite the cold, the window was open, the breeze pulling and playing with the curtains, wildly flagging her apartment from the others.

There the rust stains seemed to be much more extensive, as if magnified. He had not observed that before.

A sudden searing release of acid in his stomach; a surge of warning adrenaline brought a metallic sick taste to his mouth.

A Spanish tourist was waiting at the entrance for a taxi cab. Around his neck was an expensive professional camera with a large 300mm zoom lens. Taylor asked he if could use it. The man misunderstood and shied away. Calderon stepped in, speaking to the man in Spanish. He looked anxious but re-assured and surrendered the camera to her. Salemi saw Taylor's agitation but still did not understand what it was that had alarmed his friend.

Taylor looked through the lens and focused on the balcony.

The sparkling rectangle of snow was drenched with large opaque swaths of blood spreading in different hues of red from the open glass door of the living room to the balcony edge, pooling and puddling the powdery surface.

Taylor thrust the camera back into the hands of the startled tourist and sprinted across the driveway, down a set of steps to the small shopping plaza between the hotel and the apartment complex.

The duty doorman, alone because of an emergency call for his partner would not leave the desk to let Taylor into Ann's apartment and refused to surrender the pass key.

Seconds before Taylor was about to assault him, Calderon arrived with Salemi. She showed him her FBI ID and demanded the keys. Together they commandeered the service elevator and ascended to Ann's floor As soon as they stepped into her hallway, they sensed a breeze coming from her unclosed door.

Taylor kicked it open ready for the fight of his life. On the rich, cream-and-gold carpet a bloody hacked body lay. Dr Samuels had met the same fate as his daughter.

Taylor felt horror then a sense of guilty relief as shock turned to hope that Ann might still be alive. He sprinted up the circular wooden staircase leading to the upper rooms of the duplex. They were strangely neat and divorced from the carnage below.

He returned downstairs and looked at the shocked faces of Calderon and Salemi. Both had their cell phones to their ears. Calderon was speaking to Grasso. Salemi was speaking in Italian.

Bishop Luca di Montevecchi was excitedly warning Salemi who the last direct descendant of Cardinal Reginald de la Pole was.

Salemi switched to English. “We already know your grace. We are in her apartment.”

Floating on a puddle of arterial blood was a crumpled note on Ann’s navy bordered, monogrammed note paper.

Taylor picked it up—to hell with forensic procedure.

Written in Ann’s distinctive script was a message to Samuels.

“Doc, I should be back from Foxlair at 8 p.m. by the latest. With luck, our wandering agent friend will get in touch and we will celebrate his return with a fancy dinner. Love, Ann.”

CHAPTER 113
MANASSAS, NORTHERN VIRGINIA

He could sense the lost souls wandering the old battlegrounds, the frantic spirits of the killing fields. This had been a festival of death, brave men dying in furious combat. Their restless ghosts gave him succor. He was at home here among them, in the haunted countryside which looked so much like England. Everything seemed perfect for his triumphant, vengeful return.

Hardened to the unusually cold winters of his reign, the air temperature above the gently rolling meadows of snow felt almost like spring. He sniffed the keen, rich air like a hound and smelled wood smoke from the house on the hill. He clambered over a dry stone wall bordering the estate.

He saw wisps of grey-brown smoke trail from the chimney signaling life. Fresh wheel tracks led up the cindered drive to the garage. He moved easily, quietly through the powdered snow of the hillside, anticipating, savoring, the coming kill. The heavy 500-year old axe glittered in the afternoon sunlight. Other weapons were strapped to a backpack on his broad shoulders.

CHAPTER 114
NORTH VIRGINIA

This time the hunt would be solely the responsibility of Grasso and his team. The director was not going to allow the other agencies to interfere. Their own small team would handle it — back-up could arrive later, to hell with the consequences.

Liddell, whose North Virginia home was nearest Ann's estate was the first to be alerted. His wife pulled him off snow-shoveling duties to answer Grasso's call.

He pushed the run-down, complaining family SUV to its limits, racing along roads treacherous with melting snow.

Ten minutes behind him, Taylor with Calderon driving, hurtled through suburban traffic before reaching slippery stretches of countryside road.

Taylor turned round in his seat and told Salemi: "We should never have doubted you, Joseph. He has been going for the descendents of those he hated. He was after Ann all the time. The murder in the theatre. Ann's friend Gerry had the bad luck to be in her dressing room. Father Orr was with Ann just before his death in the

Cathedral. Her grandfather was tracked down in Bermuda and killed; his body slashed and hacked then dumped at sea so we would think the mutilation was the result of boat propellers. I've been such a dumb-ass."

Salemi tried to console Taylor. "We could not possibly have known that, John. It took Neville's death to realize the spirit's true motives."

Taylor's face darkened with anger. Calderon, an expert chase driver, deftly controlled the skidding car.

Salemi sat quietly in the back of the vehicle, not wanting to invite procedural concerns over his presence. It was unspoken that he would let them deal with the police action ahead.

Taylor and Calderon also became quiet, already in professional mode. Years of training and field experience flooded their minds and prepared their bodies for action. Their silence was only interrupted by the curt exchange of progress between Taylor and Grasso by cell phone.

For the priest there was an ebb and flow of emotions. He prayed that Ann would be safe and understood the agents' focus to stop Congreve with whatever violence was required.

He accepted that any chances for intercession they had been prepared to grant him in his mission to reach Henry's spirit had unspokenly been cancelled.

If only a miracle occurred and he had a chance to talk to Congreve and his tortured spirit before he was blasted to hell by the furious agents.

They reached the outskirts of Ann's estate and Taylor saw the familiar shape of Liddell's rusty family car. The blue SUV was parked on the edge of the road and the snow-banked shoulder next to the estate's stone wall. The door was ajar. There was no sign of Liddell, but boot tracks led to the wall. He was inside the estate, hunting Congreve.

Taylor and Calderon drew their hand guns from their cases and scrambled over the dry-stone. Taylor should have cautiously surveyed the house, taking cover among the copse of birch trees and bushes between the wall and the half-timbered main house. He should have waited for the back-up team scrambled from the field office.

But he burst from the forest cover and ran for the house, the snow carpet sucking and pulling at his feet and ankles.

He turned a corner of the house and saw Liddell, lying in agony, his blood spurting and sprinkling the snow from a huge leg gash and a severed tendon. The tough ex-football player was in the early stages of shock from trauma and loss of blood.

He recognized Taylor and focused his eyes angrily toward the open main door of the house. He grimaced and ordered Taylor: "Go John. Go!'

His anguished look urged Taylor to press on, through the doorway, across a hallway and into the large day room-library of the house. Taylor looked toward the blazing log fire and his heart sank. Ann lay in front of the fireplace a black cast-iron poker she had tried to defend herself with by her hand. She lay immobile, her pale face frozen in horror, her once white cashmere sweater now crimson with blood, her skirt a vivid patchwork of bloody stains. She was either unconscious or dead.

He forced himself to look around the room. The sun, setting low on the crest of a hill, coruscated along the packed snow, flaring into his retinae, half blinding him.

A rush of sound alerted him, followed by an explosion of pain which took him down like a hunted deer. A quarrel from a cross-bow had smashed through flesh and shattered his kneecap. He looked to the window and saw the large silhouette of Congreve, his blond hair blood red in the sinking sun.

Instinctively, Taylor fired a gut shot, but the round flew high. He heard a gasp from Congreve. The figure lurched backwards, whirled around, shattered and shouldered his way through the large library window and disappeared.

Taylor tried to stand and nearly passed out from the pain. He shouted to the icy, still air for help.

Calderon had followed Taylor's wild attack on the house more cautiously. She had checked on Liddell, tearing open his already ripped trouser leg and applying an emergency compress to the gaping leg wound. She strapped it with his trouser belt. He assured her he could handle the wound from there. She covered him with her coat and heard Taylor's cries. She stepped into the house, her weapon at the ready. She saw the gory body of Ann. Taylor was propped against a library case on the verge of passing out with pain from his shattered knee. A fine spray of his blood was spattering over a row of cream colored calf skinned volumes next to his leg. He pointed to the jagged remains of the window. She looked out. There was no sign of Congreve.

CHAPTER 115

The prone body lay at the crest of the hill. The light, dying in concert with the killer, streaked one side of his face vermillion, casting a huge grotesque shadow of him down the hillside.

Salemi approached, praying that there was conscious life left in Congreve, a fleeting chance to contact Henry's spirit before he fled back through the centuries. He knelt by the gasping figure. A round from Taylor had entered Congreve's chest and exploded upwards, exiting through his neck. Blood spurted from his nose and mouth.

The priest spoke softly to Congreve in the English and Latin he and Henry were fluent in: "Come back, come back to the Holy Mother Church. Rome needs you. For the sake of your eternal soul, change. Come back to us."

The wild eyes seemed to calm and clear, then a focused, chilling glare fixed them. The lips moved. The terrible figure was trying to talk to him. Salemi lowered his head and placed his ear near the dying man's mouth.

He heard words, phrases, like echoes trapped in Congreve's great body. A look of horror and defeat struck Salemi's face. A gout of blood from the killer's mouth exploded over the priest's face and chest.

Congreve's head rolled back, the face slipped into a smile. The eye pupils narrowed to small points and Salemi was staring at a corpse.

He remained kneeling in the snow, praying silently, his hands clutching his bloody head.

In the forest, the birds and small animals began moving again. A flock of crows screeched their return to the woods.

CHAPTER 116
GREENWICH PALACE, 1536

On a rough oak table in a saddle room, just yards from the tiltyard, Henry VIII lay still, his pulse barely detectable.

It had been three hours now since the dramatic fall. Couriers had already ridden out to the powerful elite with the dramatic news: the King was dead. Anne Boleyn, out of favor, and the subject of the King's anger, uttered a prayer of relief when the news reached her at her country refuge. The King was dead. She would be saved from his anger. There was hope of power for herself and the crown for her daughter, Elizabeth.

Factions began to form and strengthen, desperate deadly bets on who would gain power and the throne.

Around the body were the churchmen and the fatalistic court physicians. The King's jester sat weeping on the floor beneath his feet, like a favored hound.

Suddenly there was a gasp from a physician. The King's eyelids began to flutter. A faint flush of color tinged the chalk-white face.

The hooded eyes flew open, their pale blue irises clouded, puzzled. Then they slowly cleared. There was a new coldness, a penetrating, cruel aspect to them. The King glared at those assembled. In an instant he took in the shocked expressions of his courtiers, instantly deciding who, if any, looked glad to see his return; who he imagined fearful, disappointed.

The courtiers shouted their joy and prayers, trying to mask the sudden, indelible terror that now chilled their souls.

Historical Note:

Within three months of Henry's traumatic fall, Anne Boleyn was executed.

His Plantaganet aunt, Cardinal Pole's mother, was also beheaded in the Tower.

She was followed by his uncles, cousins and any other relatives and friends of the Plantagenet camp.

And so it continued…